A
Political
Man

Jim McDermott

Abbreviations and acronyms used in the text

BND – *Bundesnachrichtendienst*: Federal Intelligence Service of West Germany (from 1956; formerly the Gehlen Organization (or 'Org')

CDU – *Christlich Demokratische Union Deutschlands*: Christian Democratic Party, Germany

Cheka - *Vserossíyskaya chrezvycháynaya komíssiya*: All Russian Extraordinary Commission, Soviet secret police service 1918 - 1923, forerunner of **OGPU**

CIA – *Central Intelligence Agency*: US foreign intelligence service

DSP - *Deutschsoziale Partei*: Far-right, antisemitic political party, active in Germany from the 1880s until the end of the First World War

GRU - *Glavnoye Razvedyvatel'noye Upravleniye*: Soviet military intelligence directorate

GSOVG - *Gruppa sovetskikh okkupatsionnykh voysk v Germanii*: Group of Soviet occupation forces in Germany

KGB - *Komitet Gosudarstvennoy Bezopasnosti*: state security agency of the Soviet Union, formed in 1954 by the amalgamation of former domestic (**MVD**) and foreign (**MGB**) security agencies

Komsomol — *Kommunisticheskiy Soyuz Molodyozh*: Soviet political youth organization

MfS - *Ministerium für Staatssicherheit*: East German Ministry for State Security; also *Stasi*

MGB - *Ministerstvo Gosudarstvennoy Bezopasnosti* SSSR: Ministry for State Security, foreign intelligence successor organization (from March 1946) to the former **NKGB**, and part-forerunner of **KGB**

MVD – *Ministerstvo Vnutrennikh Del SSSR*: Ministry of Internal Security, domestic intelligence successor organization (from March 1946) to **NKVD**, and part-forerunner of **KGB**

OGPU - *Obyedinyonnoye gosudarstvennoye politicheskoye upravleniye pri SNK SSSR*: Joint State Political Directorate: secret police of the USSR from 1923 – 1934; absorbed into **NKVD** thereafter

SB - *Ministerstwo Bezpieczeństwa Publicznego*: Polish Ministry of Public Security

SDECE - *Service de Documentation Extérieure et de Contre-Espionnage*: French State counter-intelligence service, 1944 - 1982

SED - *Sozialistische Einheitspartei Deutschlands*: German Socialist Unity Party, which governed the **DDR** throughout its existence.

SIS – *Secret Intelligence Service*: British foreign intelligence service; known also as MI6

SPD - *Sozialdemokratische Partei Deutschlands*: German Social Democratic Party

StB - *Státní Bezpečnost*: Communist Czechoslovakia's state security agency

Tver, 3 April 1940

They had been told to expect the orders, so he arranged to be in the building when they arrived. He had read them already, almost a month earlier, before the six signatures making them official were dry on the page. The document had sat on Beria's desk ever since, suspended in the curious space that the Soviet system often placed between the formal process and the unspeakable things it authorized. He often wondered what it was about their thinking, that required a further accumulation of will to take the final step.

He had driven up from Moscow that morning, wanting to talk it through with Blokhin. The man was utterly reliable, but this was a business that had to proceed as if controlled by a jewelled movement – an extremely quiet, precise mechanism that drew absolutely no attention to itself. He would explain what was required as he always did, by asking the questions that needed to be considered. If answers were forthcoming he could reassure himself that matters were in hand; if not, it wasn't too late to take direct control himself. It would mean that his fingerprints would be on it, but that couldn't be helped. If it went as it should – and it *would*, under his direction – nothing could ever see the light.

He found Blokhin at a desk in a borrowed office, surrounded by his people, poring over the mass of paperwork that Moscow had sent three days earlier. He was pleased to see that it hadn't been shoved into a corner, to be consulted after the event (if at all). He'd known too many operations fail because everyone assumed they'd mastered the detail and understood their error only when the nuzzle pressed against the back of their heads. That sort of attitude was alright for the Army (who could always make up their losses), but it wouldn't do for NKVD.

When his presence was noticed they scattered like sheep from a dog. He tossed his head and the office was evacuated, leaving Blokhin rigidly to text-book attention. When the door closed he relaxed and took his seat once more without first offering a salute.

'Good afternoon, Comrade. Did you have a pleasant journey?'

The question was obtuse, but he let it pass. As Deputy Commissar of the NKVD his official car was lent the wings of angels. Anything that threatened to impede his passage – herds of bison, old ladies, the ghosts of long-dead Tsars – was swept off the roads by an advance guard of heavily-armed motorcyclists. *All* his official journeys were pleasant, or at least uncomplicated. He nodded at the pile of documents.

'Are you ready, Vasily Mikhailovich?'

'Entirely so, Comrade.'

'The other sites?'

'Reported in this morning. All are waiting for the word.'

'What total do you have?'

Blokhin consulted his notes 'Twenty one thousand, eight hundred and sixty.'

The order was for more than twenty five thousands, but it was deliberately overstated to allow for miscounts. His own, more accurate estimate was within twenty of Blokhin's number, a difference that could easily be accounted for by roundings. The man looked too smug, though, so he pressed the point.

'There's a discrepancy.'

'Yes, I calculate eighteen. Most are suicides; three were attempted escapes.' Blokhin looked up. 'From Kozelsk, two days ago.'

'Very good. The cells?'

'All ready. They've been sandbagged and felted – nothing can be heard beyond twenty metres. There are two here, two at Kharkov and three at Smolensk.'

'The transportation?'

'Assembled. All NKVD, obviously.'

'What's the timetable?'

Blokhin pursed his lips. 'That depends on the rate we can achieve – which we can't know until we begin, of course. I'm trying for three hundred per night here; the other sites will report on what they've achieved after the first two days. I anticipate completion in twenty-one days at best, perhaps seven more if the goal proves unfeasible.'

'That's acceptable. The Boss said it had to be done within the month, from start to finish - *finish* being the onset of collective amnesia.'

The other man nodded. 'A month from now, it will never have happened. And there'll be precisely nothing to prove it.'

'In that case ...' He removed the orders from his tunic and held them out. Blokhin's arm extended, paused for a moment and then completed its passage. He opened the document, scanned the signatures appended and looked up.

'Not Beria?'

'He isn't Politburo.'

'No, but this was his idea.'

'Have you ever known Lavrenty Pavlovich to shine a light upon his work? Let the others take credit for this.'

Blokhin looked at the paper again and smiled. 'Kalinin's on it, as upon everything else that's ever signed. It's strange - I don't what he *does*, exactly.'

'No-one knows - the *Boss* doesn't know. The man's made himself safe by assuming the precise colour of whatever he's standing in front of. And look how it's turned out - he's even had a city renamed in his honour. This one, in fact.'

'It's why I noticed him, and the irony. He wants to be invisible, but his name's attached to something that will stain him forever if posterity gets wind of it.'

'Yet you've just assured me that it couldn't possibly get wind of it.'

.

Deputy Kommissar I. A. Serov was smiling as he said it, and Blokhin took this as seriously as he always did. He waited, and said nothing. Eventually, the smile went away. Serov leaned forward and tapped the orders with a finger.

'Don't worry. Events are how the victors choose to write them, and one thing's for certain - the Poles won't be holding the pen.'

1

'Please, call me Otto.'

'Then you must call me Herbert. Do you drink?'

The generality of the question was sharpened by the accompanying manoeuvre, which brought half a bottle of Scotch whisky from a drawer. The honest answer was God, yes; but the hour – a little after 9.30am – tapped Fischer's shoulder to remind him that first impressions were important.

'Later, perhaps?'

Disappointed, Herbert Lamm replaced the bottle. 'Forgive me. We keep such odd hours here that the proprieties loosen considerably.' Surprised by his indiscretion, he looked up quickly. 'Regarding drinking, I mean.'

'It must be difficult, the long sittings.'

'My wife makes me wear a name badge, to remind her.'

Lamm smiled regretfully as he said it, and reached out to touch a framed photograph on his desk. On the strength of several minutes' acquaintance, Fischer decided that he quite liked the man. He had been braced for an ordeal, a new boy's testing, but had been made to feel as welcome as anyone pushed into a diary at a moment's notice had the right to expect.

Being unfamiliar with the way things worked here, he had feared that he might be starting his new career under a cloud.

Lamm himself (and a majority of his colleagues) were obliged to put themselves at the mercy of their constituencies every five years – to press hands, kiss unpleasant children and pretend an earnest interest in every inconsequential gripe that was thrust rudely at them. Fischer, in contrast, was a List man, making up the second-vote numbers at the direct appointment of the Party (assuming it won a greater share of the vote next time, which was almost inevitable), and would soon take his seat with no greater inconvenience to himself than the wording of the letter of thanks he'd deliver to the Appointments Committee. It would be unfortunate if he arrived at the *Abgeordnetenhaus* with a reputation as a favourite son, or arse-kisser.

Lamm didn't seem to be holding it against him, though. Rules were rules, and Fischer hadn't bent, twisted or slid between any of them. He had worked unspectacularly for his local SPD Branch for more than two years now and been recommended, rather than put himself forward, for one of the List vacancies for House Representative. That the recommendation was the result of considerable manipulation of local Party officials by men who didn't believe in democratic values, much less the fine work of the SPD, wasn't something he intended to mention much.

He was at Rathaus Schöneberg to be introduced to some of his future colleagues, and to the building itself. In fact, he had been here once before, some five years earlier, but under circumstances that wouldn't look better for being dragged out of their dark closet. So, he intended to give a strong first-day-at-school impression, and ask every question at least twice. It would make him seem slightly dull-witted - a useful, secondary goal.

Lamm had been consulting a piece of paper. He looked up, his eyebrows raised to give an impression of engagement.

'You're a clockmaker by trade?'

'I was a *repairer*, of timepieces and gramophones. My premises burned down.'

'Oh, dear! You had insurance, I hope?'

'I did, thank you.'

'So, this will be your main employment now?'

'And writing. I'm preparing a history, of the war.'

Lamm swallowed visibly. 'Is that … wise?'

'It's nothing controversial - a purely military survey, of the campaigns of the *Fallschirmjäger* from the Outbreak to Crete.' Fischer waved a hand at his face. 'I was there throughout, but earned this a little later, near Moscow.'

'Ah! Well, I suppose our heroes deserve their proper recognition.'

He said this with all the enthusiasm of a volunteering latrine-digger. Since embarking upon his project, Fischer had received much free advice, all of which had attempted to head him off. Thirteen years after the Surrender, the market for any reminders of the conflict was winter-fallow, at least in Germany. It was as well that he wasn't doing it for the money, or reputation - or even publication, if it came to that. He wrote as an exercise, to keep his head busy enough not to dwell too much upon his recent losses and impeding political career.

The piece of paper was being scanned again, and it offered Lamm a way out of the dangerous corner into which he'd dragged them.

'You're a Lichterfelder, yes?'

'Not a native. I've lived there for several years. It's where my business was located.'

'It won't be a savage commute, then. Some of us see most of West Berlin on the way to and from the Chamber.'

It was an exaggeration (the Rathaus was fairly centrally located), but understandable from a long-term inmate, and Lamm had represented his Wedding constituency since 1950, before the city government was reorganized and the *Abgeordnetenhaus* replaced the old *Stadtverordnetenversammlung*.

'No - about forty minutes, if the traffic's helpful.'

'It's a lovely part of the city, Lichterfelde. My wife's from Steglitz, originally.'

The small-talk eased Fischer's nerves (and Lamm's, he suspected). He had awoken today with the heavy realization that his long-deferred career as a traitor was upon him, at least to the extent of the pressed uniform being laid out and his body invited to fill it. The alarm had sounded two days earlier, of course, as it had for everyone else. His fond hopes of oblivion, of the men in Moscow accidentally dropping a card as they shuffled their pack, had all fallen to shit during the course of one short radio bulletin. The world had heard it and shivered; Berlin had heard it and convulsed; Fischer had heard it, sighed and made a cup of coffee (into which he'd poured a stupid measure of schnapps), knowing that nothing more could be done, other than to watch the avalanche approach.

The news of the hour had been surprising, but his call to arms was already in the diary. Four weeks earlier, a quiet knock on the door of the late Ferdinand Grabner's home (now the property of Fischer's landlord, Jonas Kleiber) had politely removed any plans he might have entertained for a future not entirely tied to the whims of the Kremlin. The messenger - whom Fischer had very much wanted to shoot, if not disembowel - was a man named Paul Globnow, a genial Pomeranian Jew who had survived the Reich by pawning his soul to Lenin and then (more or less by default) to Stalin. As a harbinger of darkness he was by no means unfamiliar. For more than two years he had been an occasional, discomfiting visitor, bringing no great news and staying no longer than necessary to remind the victim that he was soon to be such. Fischer had gradually come to believe that the man had a faculty for sensing when anxiety subsided below a certain level, at which point he would hasten to Lichterfelde to sustain it before it dissipated entirely. The Americans would call him a *handler*; what Fischer would call him wasn't fit to inflict upon polite society.

'The General sends his very best, and asks if you wouldn't mind stepping forward,' Globnow had told him, seasoning the news with a slightly apologetic smile. 'He actually posed it as a question, though I don't know if he meant it as it sounds.'

'He didn't.'

'Well, the elections are in five weeks' time, so you must have been expecting this. I've arranged for you to visit the *Abgeordnetenhaus*, to speak to a man named Lamm. He'll introduce you to how things work there.'

'Is he one of yours?'

'Ours, Fischer – *ours*. No, he's just someone who sits to the left of the Party and doesn't much like the way things are moving.'

Things in this case almost certainly meant one thing – Willy Brandt, their glorious leader, the American Pensioner (as some Party members had daubed him, only half-scurrilously). For several years he had headed the Party in Berlin while keeping a warm seat in Bonn as one of the city's delegates to the Federal Republic. Latterly, he'd served as President of the *Bundesrat*, and, since Otto Suhr's death the previous year, Governing Mayor of Berlin also – an accretion of power that made his position within the SDP seem very much like the Führer's within National Socialism. Had he been remotely pink-tinged, this might not have mattered to the Party's rank-and-file, but his youthful socialist leanings had given way to a virulent anti-communism that often seemed indistinguishable from Adenauer's. The more traditional membership, cleaving to their historic working-class loyalties, were beginning to wonder where their Moses was leading them.

Fischer didn't give two hearty proverbials about any of it, but he could hardly say so. He hadn't yet formed an opinion as to which wing of the Party he would incline towards, because to date Globnow hadn't provided instructions. Logically, shoring up the anti-Brandt wing would be in Moscow's best interests, but logic seemed to have very little place in the physics of espionage. Equally, the Kremlin might want the man to rise until, like Icarus, he could be burned at an altitude that precluded any chance of survival – in which case the tongue of Otto Fischer, rather than defame and vilify, might be required to explore the Brandt fundament to some depth. He had wondered for some time now whether being employed in the honest, reputable role of assassin might not have been the merciful option.

His head struggled back to the moment. His colleague-to-be Lamm was watching him - assuming, probably, that the new man was slightly overwhelmed by the prospect of the job. He waved a hand around the room.

'You'll be sharing an office with at least three other representatives, as we all do. We occupy our two desks on alternate days, though we barter time occasionally when one of us is busier than the rest.'

'Hm? Oh, right.' With difficulty, Fischer found a topic that might interest a new man. 'I assume there's a cafe in the building? A restaurant?'

'Both, though not very good. You'll get a list of the local facilities on your first official day in the job, but here ...' Lamm dipped into the drawer once more; '... take mine. It was updated three months ago. If you enjoy Spanish cuisine, I can recommend *Casa Borja*, on Innsbruckerstrasse. It's cheap, and the owner's very pleasant - for a fascist.'

'Thank you.' Belatedly, Fischer thought to ask something pertinent. 'How do you find the work?'

'What we do?' Lamm seemed slightly surprised by the question. 'Legislating for a large city is an important job, anywhere else. Here, whatever we *decide* has to be ratified by the Allies before it becomes law, so we take care beforehand to know what they do and don't want us to do. Our most important function is agreeing the budget - and keeping the CDU out of power, naturally.'

'But they're in coalition with us.'

'How better to neuter them? We hardly needed to invite them in – we have an absolute majority in the Chamber - but Otto

Suhr always thought it best to put a leash on the enemy.' Lamm smirked. 'In any case, it makes us look collegial, and them needy.'

'Ah.' Naively, Fischer had imagined that the coalition was an exercise in pulling together for the common good, but Lamm's revelation was depressingly convincing. It reminded him once more of why so much sleep had gone wanting at the prospect of his coming career.

Lamm was checking his watch. Gratefully, his guest took the hint. 'You're very busy ...'

'No, it's that there's to be a briefing on the, ah, situation. It isn't restricted, as far as I know. Would you like to come?'

'Very much, yes.' This wasn't a lie. Given that Fischer's presence at the Rathaus at that moment was in large part a result of the *situation*, he was interested to hear what his distinguished colleagues and soon-to-be adversaries were being told. No doubt Globnow - had he known about it - would have insisted that he attend, and make notes.

He tried and failed to memorize the route from Lamm's office to the Chamber, a trek through several storeys and at least eight corridors. When they arrived, a small throng of men in suits was remonstrating with an elderly gentleman, dressed in a frock-coat of the style that had once been *de rigeur* at armistice-signings. He was holding keys, which, apparently, serviced the large, closed doors immediately behind him.

Quietly, Lamm consulted a rotund, red-faced fellow standing at the periphery of the clench and then returned to Fischer's side.

'Brandt was going to present the briefing, but he's been summoned to Bonn. Adenauer thinks it's an ultimatum dressed up as a nudge, so he wants to consult, apparently.'

'But it's aimed at the Americans and British, not Bonn.'

Lamm smiled brightly. 'Have you read the full speech?'

'Of course not.'

'Apart from ripping up the Potsdam Agreement, Khrushchev accuses the Federal Republic of staffing its new Army with a Nazi General Staff, which isn't entirely slanderous. He also implies that if the West twitches the wrong way he might unleash a one-day war on that part of Germany he's not fond of – which probably means atomic bombs, rather than a good natured brawl followed by tea.'

'You think it'll come to that?'

'I have no idea. But expecting the worst is one thing we Germans do better than almost anyone else. And if Adenauer's right, the worst is right around the corner, pulling on its mailed gloves.'

2

'Did you know that he was going to do it?'

Surprised, General Zarubin looked up from a briefing paper. 'That's a *remarkably* impertinent question, Levin.'

His secretary half-shrugged. 'I know. I couldn't think of a better way to put it.'

Zarubin considered this for a few moments. 'You might have asked if the present situation was one that I had foreseen in its precise particulars or anticipated only broadly.'

'Yes, but then I would have forgotten what it was that I was asking.'

Zarubin had often wondered whether he was the only official within the Kremlin Palace more prepared to employ Boris Levin than have him shot. The man was hugely industrious, entirely loyal and could chase an elusive secret down a dark drain better than a small dog would a rat; but he was also disrespectful, iconoclastic (strangely, not a desirable trait in Soviet politics), wantonly provocative and incapable of giving the slightest nod to the Way Things Were Done. His survival – prior to being taken on in his present role - seemed to have been predicated upon whatever sympathy his all-too visible scars of childhood polio could excite (though God knew, plenty of similarly afflicted wretches hadn't been spared). He was far too valuable to waste on an unmarked grave, but the temptation was always there, pressing to a degree.

'In that case, no, I didn't.'

'He offered no hints?'

That was a good question, and Zarubin considered it. One had to separate the public and private pronouncements, obviously. What, on the podium, came over as spontaneous and ill-thought-out was often rehearsed carefully, while a seemingly sincere, unguarded remark, offered after a drink or two, might be intended only to drag out a betraying reaction. Even those who knew him well didn't know precisely where they stood, and it was Zarubin's firm opinion that this, too, was something he'd worked on, not least as a defensive mechanism. When you climbed to the top of the Soviet cliff-face, it was wise not to leave too many crampons in place behind you.

Yes, he *had* hinted; but at nothing that a purpose could be tied to. He had asked Zarubin's opinion on several matters that might have impacted a decision, but not in words that gave away more than a necessary need to understand the situation as it *had* been. Looking back, Zarubin couldn't say that he had missed anything, because nothing had been offered.

'Not that I picked up.'

'Hm.' Levin frowned as if it were a matter within a thousand kilometres of his right to consider. 'Of course, it's well known that he considered Malenkov's *measured* strategy a depreciating asset, so I assume – in the absence of further information – that he's decided to sidestep our weaknesses and play to the power of dislocation.'

'I'm sure the Central Committee will be grateful to hear your invaluable insights. What are your thoughts on the present

Five-Year Plan? The long-range bomber gap? The price of vodka?'

'They aren't my business, Comrade General.'

'And yet the mind of the General Secretary *is*.'

'Isn't it everyone's business? Sticking a finger up the Americans' noses is likely to get it snotted.'

'I'm sure the potential exposures were considered.'

Levin mumbled something under his breath.

'What?'

'I said that if it wasn't a thing to be considered by the likes of me, perhaps he shouldn't have made a public speech about it.'

This was vastly more verbose than the brief, *sotto voce* utterance, and Zarubin assumed that the sentiment had been sterilized for his benefit.

'Are you worried about your mother, Boris Petrovich?'

Levin's surviving parent lived in a small village outside Leningrad - a primary target for the B-52s, should any missteps occur.

'I'm worried about the end of the world.'

'Then any initiative to discourage American adventurism should be applauded, not questioned.'

'Of course, Comrade General. Have you any word from Berlin about how the speech was received there?'

Zarubin stared at his secretary, suspecting the man of outright insolence. He knew perfectly well what the situation was regarding Berlin. Ten years earlier, a fly couldn't have traversed the city without a timely report on its progress landing on young Major Zarubin's desk; these days, he got better (and more easily-accessed) information from the *London Times'* foreign news section.

'Had I done so, you would have noticed it among my pending correspondence.'

Levin shook his head and sighed. 'You need a man at Karlshorst.'

With difficulty, Zarubin held his temper and spoke evenly. 'I very much need a man at Karlshorst. Unfortunately, I'm not greatly loved there.'

Levin sighed again. 'They *do* bear a grudge, don't they?'

A few years earlier, Zarubin had defected to the Americans (a necessary, if hasty, choice to avoid disembowelment or worse at the hands of a rogue Soviet quartermaster-general). He had taken no deep secrets with him, betrayed no Soviet agent and eventually returned with (seemingly) good intelligence on what the CIA knew of Politburo in-fighting; yet none of that – nor his donation of every fingernail of one hand by way of apology – had eased the hurt of his betrayal in the minds of his former KGB colleagues. To the contrary, he had rubbed in quantities of salt by backing the right man in the post-Stalin power struggle, rising swiftly thereafter and getting an office that overlooked the Palace Gardens rather than Dzerzhinsky Square. His skin was thick enough to bear their ill-will, but its consequences for the flow of information were tiresome. These days, KGB Chairman Serov took particular care to ensure that the traitor had access to nothing that wasn't dragged forcibly from his hands by Zarubin's allies in the Council of Ministers.

He had a few friends in Berlin still, most of them former (German) employees of MGB or KGB; but none had access to classified data. Their opinion of the situation was that of citizens caught in a potential crossfire, not of professional spies. Several had tried to respond to his urgent queries as best they could, but their efforts had only emphasized how adrift he was from the mainstream of current intelligence.

He had raised the matter with the Boss of course, but the man owed as much to Serov as he did to Zarubin himself (and in any case, it wasn't wise to press any point too persistently upon someone whose attention span was notoriously brief), so any resolution of the situation that wasn't aided by some sort of shove was likely to move at the same pace that the Himalayas marched northwards.

This *thing* had come upon them too suddenly. Levin impertinent question hadn't quite got to the worst of it – that Zarubin had indeed anticipated a confrontation, but not yet. He had thought that Khrushchev would have at least attempted to address some of the Soviet Union's more glaring strategic weaknesses before moving so decisively. He had hoped for 1960, and more so for 1962; but the Terminal Case was coughing ever more loudly in its bed, and couldn't be ignored. It was horribly inconvenient, but if they didn't do something to resolve the matter of the German Democratic Republic there soon wouldn't be one. Every year, its larger western twin drew further ahead, opening a gulf across which hundreds of thousands of East Germans fled to a better, fatter life, handily providing the additional workforce to feed a vastly expanding economy and manifestly prove the transcendental pull of greed over altruism. What was the point of settling for a car, a holiday, a decent job, if you could have more of each? How could the quality of one's life be measured, if not in specie? It was remarkable (though Zarubin wouldn't ever say so, not even to his secretary), that the Communist model was failing in Germany because it tried – however unconsciously – to honour the values that had earned Christ a crucifixion, while the superficially pious West succeeded most obviously by paying less than a single lip's service to them.

The contradiction exercised the Praesidium constantly, not least with respect to the Soviet Union itself. Malenkov had tried to rebalance the economy to make fewer tanks and more of what the people thought they needed. Khrushchev had followed the same path for a while, but command consumerism didn't seem to work and their economists couldn't tell them why. So, he had defaulted to Stalin's solution – if you couldn't achieve world revolution, and defeating capitalism by example didn't work (at least, not yet), try to scare it into taking a step back.

Levin had a familiar look on his face – a hesitant, lilting cast, as if he wanted say something too contentious even for his stunted sense of self-preservation. Zarubin might have helped it along, but his patience had worn thinly by now. He went back to his briefing paper, the frown intending to discourage whatever the man had in mind.

Naturally, it didn't work. Levin cleared his throat.

'I've been doing some research.'

'Ah. Good.'

'Into personnel. At Karlshorst.'

This time, the briefing paper slipped both from Zarubin's attention and fingers. Anything concerning KGB was a matter for KGB, the Council or Praesidium. It was not remotely within the purview of Zarubin himself, much less that of a mere personal secretary. If the slightest trace of his *research* left a mark in passing, both of them might be facing a rigorous, ninety-second enquiry.

Not trusting himself to speak, Zarubin waited. Levin had pulled several sheets of paper from his notepad, thus confirming that he had been wandering around the Kremlin with a loaded pistol. At any point on that perambulation, one of Serov's people might have intercepted and searched him (Palace security often conduct spot-checks on clerical staff), and then all of Zarubin's niggling concerns would have resolved themselves, neatly and finally.

'I heard a small piece of gossip several weeks ago, regarding an officer in the Third Directorate at Karlshorst. I didn't want to bother you with it at the time, because it seemed unlikely to have any meat on it; but it's gradually become interesting. In fact, it could be considered quite fascinating.'

Dear God. 'You've been conducting an intelligence operation – against KGB?'

Levin seemed offended. 'Of course not, Comrade General. I went after historic information, little of which appears to have been caught by whoever recruited this person.'

'What do you have?'

'Well ...' without asking permission, Levin drew up a chair and sat down next to Zarubin; '... to begin with, I have a birth certificate.'

'How wondrous.'

'You might well conclude that. It was issued by a civil registrar in the city of Thorn, on 12 June, 1904.'

'German? Polish?'

'Polish. Which is worthy of remark.'

'Why?'

'Because in 1940, the town's new masters – or returned old masters, if you like – ordered all census records relating to the town's citizens of Polish descent to be destroyed. It was another little step in the process of removing that part of Poland from history.'

'So you think this is a forgery.'

'Almost certainly.' Levin looked up at the ceiling. 'It would have to be a very *good* one, mind, to fool KGB – and, by the same token, for this person to have the confidence to present it *to* them in the first place'.

Zarubin thought about that for a few moments. 'A Pole, wanting to join KGB badly enough to take risks. It's interesting, but ...'

'Please, Comrade General. Thorn – or Toruń, as we should say now – interested me.'

'I hear it's a pretty place.'

'Not for that reason, though I've heard the same. My old doctor is a native of the town.'

'Doctor?'

Levin gestured to a point somewhere beneath the desk. 'The one who got these to work. He used to be a specialist, in polio rehabilitation.'

'It's a small world.'

'He went home, after the First War, to help build the new Poland. Later, he somehow survived the Nazis – which is surprising in itself, as they targeted the intelligentsia. He sought me out after the Surrender, to ask my help to find what remained of his family. I was with NKGB by then, of course ...'

'So you had access to displacement files.'

'I did, yes. I found a sister, but she died a few weeks after they were reunited. Still, he was very grateful, and writes to me occasionally. It occurred to me that he might know someone who knew people in his birthplace.'

'Did he?'

'Several, but one in particular - a man known in Toruń as the Archivist.'

'Of what?'

'Of *Umsiedlungslager Thorn*, a transit camp set up to process Poles expelled from the city after 1939. He was a trustee there, and secretly took details from those who passed through – of their families, homes and other property, in case things turned for the better and they returned one day. He recorded everything on cigarette papers, and had them smuggled out to friends in Warsaw.'

'How did he survive?'

'I don't know. He was a publisher by trade, and therefore one of the same intelligentsia that Hermann and Forster were keen to expunge. Perhaps he managed to convince them of some innate quality of idiocy.'

'What information did he have?'

'We tried the name I'd been given – Wolinski – but it was a common one was in the Toruń district before the war. The gentleman then asked if there might be any distinguishing features. I didn't know, so I poked a friend in the Lubyanka, to get me a photograph.'

Jesus.

'Don't worry, he won't say anything - he made a copy, so he's as guilty as I am. It turned out that there *were* distinguishing features, and having seen them the archivist himself was able immediately to make an identification.'

Levin pulled a photograph from his file and passed it to Zarubin, who gave it a cursory glance but then picked it up and stared intently.

Levin smiled. 'I know. Remarkable, isn't it? What's more so is that this pretender has every reason to despise rather than love KGB – or at least, its predecessor.'

'You have a history?'

'A broad one, of the family. It wasn't difficult, once I had the real surname.'

Zarubin sat back and took a deep breath as another piece of paper was pushed in front of him. Levin's forefinger directed his attention to the second paragraph. 'And a little more burrowing allowed me to put our friend *here* on *this* date. Not necessarily in the same room, but ...'

'Fuck your Mother!' Zarubin's hand dropped and pinned the paper to the table, as if he feared it might blow away. 'Bring me everything you've got – *everything*. I want to know that it's all sound, and not just wishful thinking. Have you made any copies?'

'Of course not, Comrade General.'

'Don't. And thank you, Boris Petrovich – this is *most* useful.'

'It will help?'

For the first time that morning – in fact, in as long as he could recall – Zarubin put his heart as well as his teeth into a smile.

'If it's all as you say, we're back.'

'Back?'

'In Berlin.'

'It's *that* important?'

'Right now, it's the centre of the world.'

3

For about the tenth time, Fischer pushed his finger through the damn things and peered out self-consciously. He hated lace curtains - they reminded him of the grey past, of bereavements, old ladies and moth-chewed secrets for which no-one gave a damn anyway. For two years he had been promising himself that he would rip down every pair in the house, yet the chore had been pushed aside and then allowed to mature in its corner. A few months earlier he'd even had his housekeeper Frau Benner take them down, wash and then rehang them, so that his ordeal might be endured in a slightly lighter shade of gloom. His prevarication was on a point of them having been put up originally by someone who was now out of the world. Though not of a superstitious temperament, Fischer didn't like to disturb the dead unnecessarily.

His previous squints out on to Lipaerstrasse had revealed nothing, which both relieved and made him more anxious. In the darkened room the curtains hid him effectively, but their twitching also flagged his curiosity to anyone passing by, so he was relieved that no-one had as yet passed by. His anxiety was on a point of anticipation – of an arrival, unwelcome but as inevitable as death itself. He wanted to get it over with yet have it not happen at all, a discordance that removed any pretence of peace of mind. He had woken much too early that morning, pushed away breakfast without tasting it and then shaved as badly as if he'd just commenced puberty. Even Frau Benner (who, usually, was oblivious as a houseplant to her surroundings) had noticed his face, frowned and was tapping her cheek whenever the damage threatened to drip onto one of the carpets. Distracted, he hardly noticed the gesture – nor, for that matter, the small messes he was making.

He told himself that he was being ridiculous, and he was; but he hadn't rehearsed a convincing story and suspected that nothing he improvised would be believed. He was going to be interrogated by an expert, someone who smelled fiction before he heard it, so whatever was said had to be as close to the truth as a lie could be. It had struck him as more than a little ironic, to be attempting to deceive a great deceiver, yet he failed to be entertained by his predicament.

By ten o'clock he was ready to have a go at the north face of his sitting room, so he dragged himself into the study to work on his monograph. It was little more than a framework still, his personal reminiscences awaiting much of the technical detail he had yet to research to confirm or contradict his memory. He had started to wonder how other writers managed to overcome the overwhelming intimacy of war – how massive clashes could be portrayed as such, rather than the gruesomely personal encounters that a man experienced even in the company of a hundred thousand comrades. Detachment was a thing to be learned, it seemed, not put on like a hat, and he wasn't sure he had the faculty for it.

On paper, his younger self was presently in retraining following the Norway campaign, during which his regiment had both covered itself in glory and stumbled up against the disadvantages of deploying airborne troops. When it all went well, enemy formations could be broken up, a prepared front line dissolved and collective panic induced among their commanders; get it slightly wrong and it took only a few cool heads, refusing to run away, to turn a potential breakthrough into a field-sport in which even indifferent marksmen could bag a heavy haul. He had lost dozens of friends at Sola air station to a single Norwegian machine-gunner who hadn't considered retreating. Eventually, they'd managed to kill him, but the victory hadn't felt anything like such.

Too late, he realized that he shouldn't have returned to the work on this of all mornings. He didn't want to think about the world as it currently was, much less the past. Reminiscing tended to bring out the scales, in which he was likely to weigh the worst he knew about himself and the best he could hope for. His war record didn't worry him; he'd done alright (though no-one could accuse him of having earned his Knight's Cross) and then paid as heavy a price for it as a man could and still draw breath. His life before the war had been another reality altogether, and not worth considering. It was the space between Otto Fischer's personal surrender (several weeks before the official one) and the present day that he feared the most for what it would say about his mark upon the world.

What had he done in that time? Met, married and buried a wonderful woman, enjoyed the hospitality of NKVD for three years and thereafter devoted his days to the bowels of ailing timepieces and gramophones, an occupation cut short by a ruptured gas main and the small print in his insurance policy. If any of that constituted a mark, it was the sort left by a warm, bare foot upon cold concrete, and likely to endure as long.

Usually, it was self-pity that brought him to this, but today it seemed to be something more – an audit, to mark the end of one thing and beginning of another. Until now he could blame his personal potholes upon filthy luck, or bad judgement, or the clashing of celestial spheres too close to the Fischer orbit; but he was about to embark upon a deliberate course, one that was likely to put him on to rocks. That he had little choice in the matter gave him only slight comfort. He'd had more than two years' warning of what was coming - time in which he might have hidden or run away, perhaps made a new life somewhere other than in one of the two Germanies. But the weight of the familiar had been that of a drenched blanket, holding him close despite every sensible objection and the clear view he'd had of the approaching storm.

'There's someone at the door.'

How, dragging more mass than a harbour chain, Frau Benner could move silently was a mystery Fischer had yet to fathom, but suddenly she was at his shoulder, peering disapprovingly over it at his summary of *Fallschirmjäger* dispositions, post-Norway. He put down the pen he hadn't begun to use and sighed. If it had been a tradesman she could have dealt with the interruption; had she any idea of what it was the gentleman wanted she would have said so, or at least guessed at it; and had an acquaintance or SPD colleague announced himself at anything like a normal volume Fischer would have heard it and been halfway to the door already. The sum of his deductions was that the unwelcome moment was upon him.

He was surprised, therefore, to confront a stranger at the front door, dressed for manual work but with a leather apron covering the rest. The young man smiled cheerfully and held out a board and pencil.

'A signature, please, if you're the householder.'

'For …?'

He turned and nodded at the front gate, where his mate leaned upon an upright box, roughly the size and shape of a traveller's trunk. Fischer couldn't recollect ordering it, or anything it might contain.

'Are you sure it's for me?'

'You're Lipaerstrasse 87?'

Fischer nodded. He was indubitably that, so he took the pencil and signed. They brought it up to the house on a hand trolley, negotiated the door-jamb and retreated immediately without waiting for a tip. With Frau Benner, Fischer stared at the object dumbly for a few moments before deciding to close the door. Of all days in which to receive surprise gifts or mistaken deliveries, he would have spared himself this one. It looked heavy – too heavy to move as it stood – so it had to be unpacked quickly or his imminent, unwelcome guest would need to negotiate the blockage. There was a catch on the roof of the box that allowed it to be opened end-on; he flipped it, and lifted the lid.

An angry face peered up at him. It was attached to a large body, wedged uncomfortably into that confined space. One arm was wrapped around a below-the-knee artificial leg, detached to allow its human host a little more squirming room.

Fischer opened his mouth to speak, but the consignment beat him to it.

'Otto! What the Sweet Holy Fuck is going on?'

4

On 25 November, the Chief of Third Directorate at Karlshorst's KGB Rezidentura, a man named Bolkov, received disturbing intelligence. It came to his desk via a well-used internal mail envelope, bearing enough previous addressees to make its most recent recipient a matter of wild guesswork. He read through the information twice, and then, because this *was* KGB, immediately picked up the telephone receiver and referred the matter to his Director in Moscow, rather than to the Karlshorst Resident, A. M. Korotkov. Despite the best reforming efforts of intelligence committees, this empire was stacked vertically still.

He got his instructions within two hours. The accused was to be removed from all duties pending an investigation. Korotkov was to be informed as if the matter had just come to light, but told that the information had come directly from Moscow. Bolkov was to insist – with all due respect – that he took charge of the investigation personally, rather than allow it to be handed to the Investigative Department. Obviously, any and all findings, both provisional and definitive, were to be presented first to Moscow rather than Korotkov, who would see and hear what was thought prudent.

Bolkov had been a close friend of Karlshorst's previous Resident, Y.P. Pitovranov, a quiet, thoughtful man. He resented the fact of his displacement, and more so his successor's noisy, confrontational manner, so these instructions gave him no problem. Clearly, this was a matter that needed to be dealt with delicately, and Korotkov seemed incapable of delicacy. No doubt he would attempt to control the investigation, but Bolkov would dig in his heels, endure the spit-flecked tirade, and, if necessary, refer him directly to the Lubyanka.

He sent for his deputy and told him to relieve Captain-Lieutenant Wolinski of all present duties. He asked also for Wolinski's personnel file, including Internal Security's data on all known acquaintances both at Karlshorst and Wünsdorf Camp. The Captain-Lieutenant was to be detained but not placed under formal arrest (which would require paperwork), and held for interrogation somewhere other than at either location. His deputy made the obvious suggestion – Leistikowstrasse Prison in Potsdam, where KGB usually put their counter-intelligence catches. It had the advantage of being administered by GSOVG rather than KGB, yet would stand scrutiny as being the logical place to squeeze a traitor - if that's what Wolinski was. Bolkov agreed, and ordered the transfer to take place within the next half-hour.

Bolkov was well aware that he could be hurt badly by his subordinate's treacheries, so everything had to be done correctly. Naturally, Korotkov regarded him as one of Pitovranov's clique, to be flushed away if at all possible. The moment he received the news he would be on the 'phone to Moscow, not-so-subtly suggesting to KGB Chairman Serov that a rotten wound should be cleaned thoroughly if the infection wasn't to spread. Bolkov counted Serov as an ally, but he knew how little relationships mattered in such situations. The Chairman moved slowly and carefully, but he wouldn't have hesitated to have his own mother dug up and shot if a weight of evidence pointed her way.

It had been alleged that Wolinski was passing information to the Americans. It wasn't yet clear if this meant CIA or CIC; nor did Third Directorate's responsibilities – preserving the political integrity of the Soviet Union's armed forces – offer any easy clues as to how and why one of its agents had come to be speaking to the Americans in the first place. However, given the latters' penetration of Karlshorst in the past (usually through German nationals working in the compound), the vagueness of the accusation took away nothing of its potency. Wolinski's defence - if there was a defence to be made - would be that any American contact was a potential agent, and gaining their trust (even at the expense of offering a little harmless intelligence) was therefore part of the job. In any case, 'passing secrets to the enemy' was the first allegation thrown at every rival in their community, and as difficult to disprove as a divine revelation. If Wolinski had made enemies in KGB, this was just the sort of weapon that *would* be deployed. On the other hand, why hadn't Wolinski done the right thing by handing over this contact to First Directorate immediately? And on the other, other hand, Wolinski was Polish.

Poles could make good communists, of course, and even Soviet patriots (the Moscow square in which KGB Headquarters sat was named after one); but in situations like this the old racial enmity could be pointed like a finger. Even if no more concrete evidence came to light, it might well be asked *can - should - we really trust this one?* At which point, Bolkov would need to make a decision about his own career. He didn't want it to come to that. He would much prefer complete exoneration or enough damning testimony for him to act quickly, and decisively.

It was a pity, either way. Wolinski was one of Bolkov's better operatives, a bloodhound who had exposed a great deal of wrong thinking (black marketeering, illegal fraternization and gambling) among the men at Wünsdorf Camp. Still, ability was no proof of loyalty, as KGB's star prize George Blake proved only too graphically (being lionized in London at present, even as he continued his sterling work for the Soviet Union). It would be more than unfortunate if Bolkov's Section at Karlshorst was hosting a similar Judas.

It might have come at a better time. The Allies' military intelligence networks in Berlin and the Federal Republic had been buzzing since Khrushchev's speech, so Karlshorst needed no fratricidal distractions. Bolkov couldn't help but wonder if the attack on Wolinski was directed at himself, rather than intending merely to wound him collaterally. He knew who his enemies were; it was more difficult to judge how far they'd go, and when. Perhaps this was the moment, the thrust intended to be camouflaged within the broader tumult.

He returned to his other correspondence, to which he gave half his attention at most. He told himself that he'd acted quickly, and now it was in the hands of the men at Potsdam – men he could trust to push every word they prised from Wolinski through his office. Nevertheless, he decided it would be prudent to draft a quick note to Serov himself, emphasising his concern to see the business dealt with swiftly and effectively. It would read like what it was, a preemptive *mea non culpa*, but a man needed a paper trail ready for when the finger swivelled to point in his direction.

In another office in the Section, Bolkov's deputy dialled a secure prefix and then completed a Moscow number. When the receiver was lifted at the other end he spoke without preamble.

'It's done.'

'Where?'

'Leistikowstrasse.'

'Ah, yes. Thank you.'

'Please don't call again. Ever.'

'Of course not.'

Sixteen hundred kilometres east of Karlshorst (his old posting, still much missed), General Zarubin put his hand on the telephone cradle, lifted it and dialled his secretary's extension. Less than ten seconds later, Levin was in the room. He seemed slightly irritated, as he always did when interrupted. Zarubin smiled, as if he hadn't noticed.

'It seems that someone's been arrested. For talking to the Enemy.'

'Dear me. Do you have a name?'

'I believe that it might be Wolinski. I'm guessing, mind.'

Levin smiled. 'Let's see now if you can extract the prisoner.'

'Don't take too much as read. First, I have to stop the bullet.'

5

'But ... a *politician*?'

Put like that – for the fourth time – Fischer couldn't think of a way to improve upon his past three replies.

'Yes, Freddie, a politician. In the *Abgeordnetenhaus*.'

'Well, fuck me up, down and sideways.'

Not being used to front-line language, Frau Benner winced once more. She had offered their visitor a tea or coffee, but Holleman hadn't yet applied his mind to the question, so she was obliged to remain within earshot of much more than a yes or no, thank you.

'I told you five days ago, when I telephoned.'

'Yes, but ...' Holleman scratched his head. '... you can't have thought I'd believe it? You don't *like* politicians, or politics, or what politicians *do* to politics. I've heard you call them names even *I* wouldn't use.'

'I'll only be a representative. We ensure the city runs as it should, that's all. I'm not aiming for the *Bundestag*.'

'*Why*, though?'

It was the much-dreaded question, the one for which Fischer needed a well-rehearsed answer; but if the wanting-to-make-a-contribution argument had barely managed to convince Jonas

Kleiber (who loved and trusted him), it stood no chance with Freddie Holleman (who loved and knew him). He couldn't tell him the truth, obviously, and wasn't sure that he could borrow someone else's truth, because it eluded him still. Why did men (and, occasionally, women) want to become politicians? Was a driving compulsion to order other people's lives? An altruistic urge to better the lot of strangers? Or were his cynical instincts correct – that it was all self-justifying nonsense, a love of the sound of one's own voice, amplified endlessly? A way to deal with a lack of talent for doing something worthwhile with one's days? It hardly mattered what he settled upon; Holleman *knew* him, and would no more believe that it was about empty vanity than he would selflessness.

The problem was given only a few more fruitless moments' thought before Fischer seized the offered distraction.

'Freddie, why did you arrive in a box?'

'I didn't want to be seen.'

'Wouldn't a hat have done the job?'

'Not for the leg, it wouldn't. I've been out of Berlin for more than five years, and I doubt that I'm on any active *Stasi* kill-list; but would they pass up an easy chance if it was offered?'

Having been one of *VolksPolizei*'s most senior officers in Berlin, Holleman owned a legacy that didn't extend to a generous pension. The DDR had lost a million more defectors since he jumped the fence, but his personal betrayal must have continued to rankle. Police had longer memories than ordinary people; it was why he had fled as far west as a German could and not call himself a foreigner.

'How long were you in it? The box?'

Holleman regarded his friend as though he were a dolt. 'Four days.'

'Eh?'

'About fifteen minutes, you cock! An old *OrPo* comrade from before the war, he has a removals business in Steglitz these days. He put me in it himself, so his lads had no idea what they were delivering.'

'That was good thinking.'

'Wasn't it? I took an arse-about taxi-ride from Zoo Bahnhof to his shop, so if I was made anywhere on the way from Trier to Berlin, they can't say where I *went*.'

Fischer was impressed that Holleman had acquired a layer of subtlety in his life's late-afternoon. There was a time when his preferred method of throwing off a pursuer would have been a vigorous beating in an alleyway.

Frau Benner coughed. For a moment, Holleman regarded her with faint suspicion, and then smiled broadly.

'Coffee, if you don't mind.'

When she had shuffled into the kitchen he turned to Fischer. 'Is she ...'

'As quiet as a grave. You risked a lot, coming to Berlin.'

'But I *had* to - even Kristin said so. She said 'that's not Otto, is it?' when I told her what you were doing.'

'Christ, it isn't as though I'm joining the Freemasons. What's so unbelievable about wanting to go into politics? *You* were a politician.'

'That was different. I was a good communist because I *had* to be.' Holleman looked pointedly at his friend. 'Given who I was, allegedly.'

In 1943, Fischer had unearthed a wonderfully convenient identity with which Holleman and his family had fled the Third Reich (at least, as far as the Spreewald). It had come with baggage, though, as they discovered much too late. After the Surrender, their Soviets occupiers had rummaged through it and raised the *ersatz* Kurt Beckendorp from lucky obscurity to unfortunate prominence. After that, he'd needed to live up to a street-fighting revolutionary's past that wasn't his own.

It was a reminder, not an admonishment - in any case, Fischer had exhausted the many ways of apologizing for that particular error of judgement, so he didn't make the further attempt. He reminded himself that he didn't need to *prove* that he wanted to enter the *Abgeordnetenhaus* - the fact that he was about to do so gave a certain weight to his claimed ambition – but even games had rules, and he feared that Holleman was determined to check the deck thoroughly. He wasn't sure that he could keep the facts from a sustained assault.

He took his own coffee from Frau Benner and tried to sound casual.

'Look, it's for five years, then I'll probably step down - five years of budget debates and cobbling together covering laws to make it seem like we're part of the Federal Republic will probably kill any enthusiasm I can muster. In the meantime, I get paid and add to my tiny pension fund. What's wrong with that?'

Holleman lifted his cup to his mouth, lowered it, repeated the manoeuvre and still hadn't taken a first sip. He had a familiar expression on his face - someone who didn't know him might have mistaken it for dull incomprehension, tinged with the sort of irritation that *mittelschule* dunces devote to examination papers; but Fischer knew that the man was shuffling around a puzzle with the intention of grappling it to the ground.

The scowl on his large, unlovely face deepened. 'Didn't you get a big cheque? From the insurance company?'

'Big? How could it have been *big*? They pointed out that the entire block was ripe for renovation or demolition anyway, so the bricks and roof were worth little. As for stock, what value would they put on a set of repaired gramophones and time-pieces? I was paid more for the melted music, and *that* was hardly generous. When I mentioned the goodwill I'd built up they just laughed at me. With what they offered I couldn't have afforded to restart the business even if I'd wanted to. Jonas lets me live here for a pretend rent so I don't starve.'

'The boy?'

'He isn't a boy any more. The gentleman who bequeathed this house to him gave him the newspaper business too. That's gone of course, but there was a fat bank account. It's encouraged him to grow up quickly.'

Holleman glanced around incuriously. 'Where is he?'

'London, for some months now. He writes foreign news stories for German newspapers. He's actually syndicated.'

'That's good?'

'Sweeter than tits, he says. How's my godson, by the way?'

'Don't change the subject.'

'You already did. Let's have a late breakfast.'

Fischer wasn't hungry, but full mouths couldn't interrogate. Frau Benner knew how to treat even unexpected guests, and since dispensing beverages had been busily cooking the next two days' meat supply. With bread and English marmalade (courtesy of a recent food parcel from London) Holleman was kept busy for the next twenty minutes, though this didn't stop him pinning his friend with a disbelieving stare that broke off only momentarily whenever a *bregenwurst* needed attention.

Fischer's stunted appetite was shrivelled further by the prospect of orange-peel jelly being loaded on to sausage, and he picked at his own, small portion while trying to conceive new distractions that wouldn't look like such. Freddie Holleman compensated for his lack of high intellect by single-mindedly using what he had (to Fischer's former artilleryman's mind, he laid his single gun very carefully, and rarely missed), so a clumsy attempt to further divert his attention from *why* would only focus it.

The post arrived before their second coffee was finished. By now, Fischer knew what was and wasn't SPD business before he opened an envelope, so he left the small pile untouched. He had managed to wash his hands - in every sense - of the local Party's drains oversight portfolio only a few months earlier (passing the job to a former sanitation engineer who had thrown himself enthusiastically into what saner men would have recoiled from). It had been replaced by a watching-brief over the Borough's near non-existent absorption of refugees, a business so weighty that its most debated issue seemed to be whether they *should* be called refugees or something else. The

Federal Republic had decided the point already, but of course the local SPD regarded this as not nearly conclusive. They grudgingly accepted that *ossies* fleeing political persecution should be labelled *Sowjetzonenflüchtlinge* because a Federal law that said they should; but what about the illegals – that is, those who fled for other reasons? 'Border-crossers' was the general, lazy term employed, but it referred also to native Berliners who worked on one side of the Line but lived on the other. The local Party despised such lack of precision. Legal illegals (economic refugees seeking to make a new life in the West) needed to be distinguished from illegal illegals (black-marketeers, pimps and those seeking to steal a new life in the West); otherwise, how could Steglitz-Lichterfelde's persistent refusal to accept them be debated effectively?

Fischer's scream-reflex had developed dangerously during meetings devoted to the matter. To his mind, it ranked with angels and pinheads as a consummate inconsequence, but the ghostly presence of Herr Globnow and his KGB bosses had restrained him from saying so. His anguish was tweaked by the suspicion that, once he was in his seat at the *Abgeordnetenhaus*, his recent experiences would incline someone to offer him a particularly short and soiled straw. The three-man tribunals that considered asylum requests from refugees (whatever they were called) were appointed by a commission of the House, and comprised some of the least-loved people in Berlin. In the Federal Republic, such tribunals' decisions could be appealed; those of Berlin's were final. So, the decent tribunalists had gradually been outvoted by their colleagues - and, disheartened, resigned to make way for the sort of people who enjoyed dispensing disappointment. Fischer could see his name on one of the commission seats already, the paint newly-applied and damp still. It was another little anticipation to add to the rest, and if he mentioned it to Holleman it would be even more difficult to convince him that he was descending into political life willingly.

He must have been staring at his unopened mail for too long, because his friend picked it up and dropped it onto the floor.

'If any of it moves, stamp hard. The rest, just ignore.'

'I wish I could, Freddie. How long are you staying?'

'Until you can tell me something convincing enough to fool a cat. Or until *Stasi* find out that I've crept home and cack me.'

Fischer had noticed the carpet-bag sitting beneath the box's principal contents. An optimist might have parsed it as an overnight bag, but he knew how lightly Holleman packed. The man considered a change of underwear as mildly effete, so this looked worryingly like a campaign – and, if the remorseless Kristin had sent him with her blessing, it was one with serious second-echelon support.

The other man slapped the table with both hands, sat back and beamed.

'Just sniff out a murder for us, and it'll be the best of times again! Holleman and his dull mate Fischer against everybody else!'

6

'He's been murdered.'

'No, he was just ... old. And ill.'

Paul tried to sound convincing for his daughter's sake, but minutes earlier he'd found the evidence on the floor, beneath the armchair. It was conclusive – someone had wanted him dead, and they'd showed no mercy.

He knew who the killer was, of course. There had been a clear opportunity, and a bad heart was motive enough. It would have taken a moment only - a clean, easy shot and no witnesses. It wasn't as if the victim could have dodged it, even if he'd seen it coming.

His daughter held the corpse, willing it to move, but the eyes were closed and a drop of blood fell from the beak. Willi had been old, hatched when Paul's father was still alive, and had been part of the man's thin inheritance to his son. Traudl was the third generation to call the little fellow her best friend, but now he was gone, removed at the whim of a boy with an air-rifle, half the brain and a quarter of the character of his victim.

Willi had been tame enough to spend most of every day out of his cage. He had never spoken (though parrotlets were known for it), but his games had kept the family entertained for almost thirty otherwise-foul years. He had survived the Depression, Hitler, the Allied air-forces, Soviet artillery and a parlous shortage of bird-seed in the years following the Surrender, only to be be expunged by a BB pellet because a young lout hadn't been able to find anything better to do with a wet Tuesday morning. The boy's bedroom was directly across the street; the assistance of Sherlock Holmes was not required.

'Can I use that old cigar box full of photographs?'

'Of course, sweetheart. I'll empty it for you.'

He was glad that she had turned already to the practicalities, but as her mother's daughter it didn't surprise him. He wished, desperately, that Emma could be here to tell her daughter that things were fine in the way that one woman did to another, but cancer didn't hold fire for the sake of smaller family emergencies. It was his job now to be both parts of that universe, and the manual that explained how he might do it had yet to be written.

He wanted, very much, to walk across the road and beat an inconsequence to death, but that wasn't reasonable. He would appeal, then, to what some people might consider decency. It would be time and breath wasted, but it was what a father should do, he felt.

The Macke family had moved into their street six months ago. Refugees from Leipzig, they had expressed their gratitude to their new neighbours by going on to the offensive. In their first week here the father, Luther, had beaten up a local grocer, who, allegedly, had called him *ossie* scum. Paul knew the victim – a slight, timid gentleman, a refugee himself, who in eight years in the district hadn't once been anything other than polite to anyone who wandered into his shop. Paul suspected that the assault had rather been upon a point of credit, refused.

Another month into the Mackes' tenure in Körnerstrasse, and the general opinion was that the family had not fled the East but been herded to the border and shoved across it. Petty theft and vandalism, formerly a tiny problem locally, became a daily topic of conversation, and while most people tried to avoid the lazy, ugly conclusion that this must be the fault of *ausländers*, it was difficult to exclude Mother Macke, Father Macke and little Stefan Macke from any list of suspects. Loud, self-aware and brazen, they could be caught with unpaid-for items in hand and still manage to shame the accuser with taunts of prejudice and intolerance; their outraged denials, supported by no evidence or credibility, acquired strength simply by being repeated, without variation, until the victims of their felonies raised their hands in surrender and walked away.

Until now, Paul's personal experience of this onslaught had been limited to a broken kitchen window, the culprit fled unseen when noises from within had warned that the house was occupied. He would have cast no stone, but blood on the jagged edge of the break was very much the same shade of red as that seeping from a bandage he noticed on Stefan's hand barely an hour later. He told himself that the coincidence alone couldn't have convinced a jury (unless one or more of their number lived on Körnerstrasse), but from that moment he had tried to keep at least one eye trained on the enemy redoubt. Now, he wished that he had tried a little harder.

He waited until Traudl's Grandmother came for her afternoon visit then went across the street and knocked on the Mackes' front door. It was opened by the father - a large specimen with no apparent disabilities, who nevertheless had not only avoided military service during the war but now claimed social assistance in lieu of the wages he didn't earn.

The disinterested sneer failed to deter Paul, but he reminded himself once more to keep his temper.

'Your boy fired his rifle at my house.'

'No, he didn't.'

'He killed my daughter's bird.'

'No, he didn't.'

'What are you going to do about it?'

'Fuck off.'

The door closed. Paul knocked again, slowly but harder this time, and when no-one seemed to notice the commotion he carried on. After about two minutes he heard the latch once more and stepped back slightly. The punch missed him, but its momentum carried Luther Macke forward and Paul's fist had very little work to do to break the nose it met. The householder went down like coal into a cellar, and as messily.

Paul was in his own house once more before Frau Macke began to scream. He was ashamed of himself, angry because the culprit remained unpunished (unless the injured party took revenge for his new nose upon the cause of it) and worried that the police would hear a wholly unfair version of events. It was a tremendous seizure of the low ground against all odds, and he could almost see the disappointment on his dead wife's face, her tired acceptance of his impulsive nature.

I'm sorry, darling. I'll be better, I promise.

She hadn't lived to see him keep it, so each relapse was a slap to her memory. He wondered if she'd be amused that he now had a job that required him above all to be a reconciler of angry temperaments; that just about everyone who worked with him thought he couldn't be ruffled by any day's minor disasters. *Steady Paul*, they called him – even his bosses, the so-called Enemy.

Paul was a union convener, representing the roughly forty-percent of workers on West Berlin's S-Bahn network who didn't cross the Line at the end of every shift. Though the entire city's overground rail system was run by the DDR's *Deutsche Reichsbahn*, it was obliged to employ thousands of *wessies* (not least because the East German state had been leaking employees for years as they and their families defected). They were an odd constituency, politically of the west yet in many other ways a colony - entitled to East German healthcare but not that of their own city-state, permanently suspected of at least potential disloyalties by both sides of the divide, and, of course, paid much less than what an equivalent, western employer would have been offered for the same job. Since western trades unions weren't recognized officially in the East, Paul himself was an anomaly, acknowledged principally because *Deutsche Reichsbahn* needed a head to talk to, one that could speak for the body as a whole. And speak he did, often. Besides the usual terms and conditions of employment, he had to deal with complaints of harassment (from the DDR's BahnPolizei, who were authorized to patrol all stations and S-Bahn sidings in both halves of the city), anti-capitalist propaganda (the company insisted on putting up 'Americans go home' posters in all its western stations, and anyone caught tearing them down was liable to dismissal) and not-infrequent attempts to turn workers to the cause of International Socialism (not that some of them needed encouragement). With all of that, Steady Paul's skills as an oil-pourer were as in demand as any diplomat's.

Still, he enjoyed his work. The official hours weren't too crushing, no two days brought the same problems and only recently he had achieved his greatest professional success to date. For months over the summer he had been commuting to East Berlin to negotiate concessions for his workers after *Deutsche Reichsbahn* completed the Berlin Outer Circle rail extension, which allowed all express services from the DDR to be diverted around West Berlin directly into the eastern city. Since then, DR's West Berliner employees entering any part of the DDR other than East Berlin had required a special permit, and workers who commuted from Staaken to their jobs (previously a quick s-bahn journey), were obliged to suffer long diversions. Paul's persistence eventually convinced his masters of the injustice of this, and he had persuaded them to issue permanent waiver-permits to their affected staff. He even managed to secure a (very small) allowance to compensate them for their inconvenience.

And now this well-respected, professional negotiator had smashed his fist into a neighbour's face. He tried to tell himself that it had been self-defence, but the truth was that he'd more than half-hoped for the assault. Luther Macke had a set to his face that invited punishment, and Steady Paul had obliged him – not least because he couldn't do the same to his brat of a son. He knew that the Mackes wouldn't be quiet about this - like all parasites, their sense of persecution was fully developed, and no doubt the story would be embellished at each noisy public re-telling. Paul had lived here for twelve years and knew almost everyone on Körnerstrasse. He doubted that many of them would take the word of a Macke against his, but he would still need to speak of it - if only to redress the false accusations - and if word spread too far he might lose his job. *Deutsche Reichsbahn* were sensitive about their western employees, and held them to higher standards than their eastern counterparts (the DDR's employment legislation rendered the latter almost immune to dismissal). He couldn't afford to be unemployed, not with a young daughter to raise and an ageing mother-in-law to keep above ground.

He could recross the road, knock on the door and apologize - or, far more effectively, offer money by way of compensation. He would be humiliated, but that was better than the alternative. He would probably be marked as a source of further donations, but that, too, was better than unemployment. Looking at it sensibly, he had no choice.

But he *couldn't* look at it that way. A crime – small enough, but a crime still - had been committed against his own, he'd been mocked and then resisted an assault, and now he was thinking of placating the guilty parties. How far did a man need to sink, to consider surrender a solution? He needed something else – something that would calm things yet let him look in the mirror still. *Think*, he told himself, *as if it was work, and you were being asked to make honey from a turd.*

He tried that for a while, but though he was agile when diagnosing other men's problems, his own sat like a damp sheet, smothering any spark of cleverness. It didn't help that he needed to think quickly - that the Mackes would lose little time broadcasting his alleged crime to the world. *No I didn't*, or *he deserved it*, weren't strong defences in the court of public opinion.

His only good idea came late, as his mother-in-law was about to leave. He begged her to stay to keep her eye on Traudl for a further half-hour, put on his jacket and almost ran to an address in Martinstrasse. He had been here before only once, about nine months earlier, at the invitation of a retiring rail worker who wanted to know if his East German pension rights might be transferable to some future employment. At the time, Paul had been more than pleased to give what advice he could and then leave. He'd quickly discovered that the man – his name was Hahn Siebert – was like a sweet liqueur, in that a very little amount of him was enough and more than that was definitely too much. He was an agitator, an inciter, a hellion – and all of it to one end, which was to squeeze every little due and right that accrued to him in his elbow-thrusting passage through life. He regarded everyone as a potential or actual adversary until the moment – as had fallen to Paul – that he could be of some use. Their conversation (or rather monologue) had been a personal Iliad, the epic tale of Herr Siebert's war against *Them* (a vague conglomerate, comprising elements of officialdom, the military and several specimens of the Man in the Street), all of whom, eventually, had felt the jackboot of bitter defeat pressing on their throats.

Though Paul's smile had became a matter of effort during this oration, he'd gained a strong impression that Siebert was a man who knew his way around things – tiresomely, but probably effectively. He hadn't intended ever to test this theory, but that was before the Mackes marched into his world. If anyone knew how to deal with people who understood every last one of their rights, it was someone who fully understood his own.

Herr Siebert lived alone. He invited in his unexpected visitor, offered coffee and cake and seemed a little disappointed when both were declined. With very little preamble, Paul explained the purpose of his call, and as he did so Siebert's mood rose, settling at a curious point between outrage and grim satisfaction. He tutted disapprovingly as the nose-breaking episode was recounted (as if Paul had spoiled an otherwise promising canvas with a garish splash of red), but his head hardly stopped nodding as the catalogue of Macke misdemeanors unfolded.

After the story was told, Siebert pursed his lips, cast his eyes around his sitting room, hummed something quietly and scratched his cheek. Eventually, Paul cracked.

'Should I go to the police?'

Siebert snorted. 'Why? They'll make a careful note of events and lose it.'

'Won't they speak to the Mackes?'

'Possibly. But his ruined nose will speak more loudly than an alleged parrot-slaying.'

'Parrotlet.'

'In any case, the fact that they're refugees is unhelpful. Brandt wants as many of them over here as possible, so the police go easy on them, even the bad ones. Unless you filmed the assassination, they won't do a thing.'

'So, I should forget it? Or wait until they bring a complaint against me?'

'Of course not. It's outrageous!'

'So what can I do?'

'Get them evicted.' Siebert said it slowly, tasting the words. 'There'll be enough of your neighbours willing to give their own testimony. There are rules, and these people don't believe in them. They'll be rehoused somewhere, of course, but it won't be *your* problem then.'

'I should go to the Council?'

'If you want to be told there's nothing to be done, yes. Or speak to someone with a stick, who likes to prod the silvered arses.'

'Do you know anyone like that?'

'I know a man who nagged Steglitz into flushing the entire main section of the Borough's sewage system.'

'I thought the rain did that.'

'It's suppose to, but have you ever noticed the smell?'

'Who hasn't?'

'Yet eighteen months ago we had weeks of sweetness, thanks to this fellow.'

'Who is he?'

Siebert glanced around his sitting room (as if he feared that the walls were leaning in to eavesdrop), and leaned forward.

'A man hungry to get on in local politics. You can't miss him – he has half a face. Fischer, he's called – Otto Fischer. The best part is, he's now the local SPD's man on the refugee problem.'

7

Section Chief Bolkov received the week's second unpleasant surprise as he towelled himself dry and tried to forget the previous ninety minutes. The game had been a gross mismatch between desk-soldiers and a young, fit and talented Red Army XI (the scoreline fully reflected it), but like every other opportunity to emphasize his peasant roots - however counterfeited – he had seized it gratefully. No doubt the post-match enquiry would focus upon how a man of his girth could fill a goalmouth so inadequately, overlooking the fact that his lack of skills - and his willingness to expose them gamely to ridicule – had been the whole point of the exercise.

Team Rezidentura's left-back, who had shone dimly by comparison, was examining the fungus between his toes on the bench next to Bolkov when a thought appeared to occur to him. He looked up.

'I hear you have a cuckoo in the nest.'

Bolkov's gullet filled with acid, and he almost belched. *Fucking Korotkov.* It was just like the man to broadcast the news – with such damaging ammunition he couldn't have kept his mouth closed if his lips ha been sewed together with piano wire. Clearly, this was his counter-thrust for having had the matter taken from him, and a damn shrewd one. He had lit up Bolkov's yet-to-commence investigation, ensuring that whatever conclusions he drew would be nailed to a bulletin board and pored over; worse, Third Directorate's Chief in Moscow would feel the heat on his own arse, and cast all the blame at his subordinate for it.

How could this have come as a surprise? How could be not have anticipated an obvious, economical gesture that both embarrassed him and virtually sealed Wolinski's fate? Now, anything other than the most cursory investigation followed by a head-shot would be regarded by Bolkov's best friends as evidence that he, too, was on an American payroll. And even with his subordinate safely dead, who wouldn't suspect that the one had been sacrificed to preserve the other? It was how the collective KGB mind – hell, the Soviet mind – worked.

He swallowed twice, so as not to squeak a response.

'It's an allegation. I'm looking into it.'

The left-back, a second-deputy in Twelfth Department (Wire-tapping and Surveillance, Enclosed Spaces), picked at a chunk of rotting foot-skin, shook his head and sighed.

'It's Berlin - like a tart's muff to a seminary student. They know it means damnation, but ...'

There it was - the guilty verdict, or as good as. Unfortunately, it was a shrewd judgement. Both sides had seen too many defectors from this front-line posting – the Americans and British because they'd been caught with their cocks out (and just a few, like Blake, who Believed); the Russians and their allies because the enemy could offer cash by the kilo and the promise of a new life somewhere else. Berlin was both the prize and the snare, the jewel and the nasty rash, and at that moment Bolkov fervently wished himself in some other, less important posting. An accusation of sedition at a listening station on Novaya Zemlya might be argued away on a point of credibility; here, why *wouldn't* someone believe it?

He had no choice. He would need to demand that his own record be examined rigorously - that his entire Section be re-vetted, and preferably by men who had most to gain by his removal. In effect, he would invite destruction as the only means of avoiding it. Of course, the disadvantage of any courageous strategy was that it was ... courageous. Those who wanted him gone might well push to see that he went, and with Korotkov's enthusiastic support it was hard to see how they might fail.

It was shit - a single, uncorroborated denunciation of a good operative, and the door had been lifted off its hinges. He dressed himself without recalling the process and walked back to the main building, his still-damp hair helping a cutting early December breeze to do its business. He rehearsed his near-suicide note in his head, trying and failing to find a form of words that might allow his Directorate Chief V.A. Yudkin to spare him the worst of what he was going to demand.

By the time he reached his office, stress and the cold had tightened a band around his head. It was given a further twist by his deputy, who was waiting for him wearing one of his bad news faces.

'Comrade Yudkin called. He says you're to get back to him the moment you come in.'

Little time was being wasted, then. In the same way that Bolkov was preparing to throw Wolinski to the wolves, Yudkin was doing the same favour for his man in Berlin. It was already too late, apparently, for any sort of half-cooked survival strategy.

Not trusting himself to speak, he dismissed his deputy with a nod and lit a cigarette. When it was half-finished he stubbed it out, picked up the telephone receiver and asked for a number in the Lubyanka. The other party answered almost instantly.

'Andrei! Good. Listen, about this traitor, Wolinski ...'

'I was about to call you, Comrade ...'

'*Listen*, I said. I've been speaking to members of the Council of Ministers, and this is something bigger than a solitary fence-jumper. There's a sub-committee for special causes, they're looking at the day-to day running of our most prized assets in Germany. Obviously, this proceeds from dissatisfaction with security at Karlshorst, given the recent defections. Anyway, when they heard about Wolinski they became interested, and set themselves to digging. They issued preliminary orders this morning. The committee will assume sole responsibility for the case. The prisoner will remain physically at Leistikowstrasse, but they're going to supervise the interrogation procedure from Moscow. No-one at Karlshorst is to interfere.'

Fuck. If it was this big, any hopes that Bolkov had entertained for his future could be shoved out of his office window. At the least, there'd be a special investigation, with all suspected parties shot first and then asked the necessary questions.

His silence must have spoken loudly. At the other end of the line, Yudkin snorted.

'Don't worry, Andrei – this is better than we thought. There'll be no blame attached to your Section for what's happened.'

'How is that possible, Comrade Director?'

'Your Wolinski has a brother – *he's* the American contact. A former Polish national, of course, but he now works for the US Military. To be precise, he works on a scientific programme so secret it that doesn't have an official designation, apparently. If this intervention succeeds, our task will be to find a way to take our share of the credit when the bouquets start falling. If it doesn't, we'll hold up our hands, shake our heads and say if only the thing hadn't been snatched away from us before we could deal decisively with it ...'

8

The provisional election results were released before midnight on voting day. Fischer had hoped, hopelessly, that the newspapers, political pundits, tea-leaves, poultry giblets and his native common sense were all wide of the mark, but everything fell out much as expected. Both the SPD and CDU did very well, picking up seats at the expense of the only other Party in the *Abgeordnetenhaus*, the Free Democrats, who, moving from nineteen representatives to zero, were set free to be as democratic (or otherwise) as they cared to be.

The SPD gained fourteen seats, and one of them had Otto Fischer's name on it. He took a 'phone call after midnight from the Chairman of the Appointments Committee (who Fischer suspected of having spoken to every other new man before himself) and was congratulated on his success, given a verbal timetable of his commitments over the next few days – a welcoming speech from Governing Mayor Brandt, a plenary session of all SPD House Representatives, the drafting of an anodyne speech on his ambitions as one of their number over the next five years (to be vetted before release to the public, obviously) and his attendance at a group photograph session for the newspapers – and told to watch out for the postal confirmation of everything he'd just heard. It was only after he replaced the receiver that the question occurred to him.

Who and what will I represent?

The Borough of Steglitz had its full quota of Representatives already, so as a List man he'd be assuming responsibilities that weren't based on territoriality. But what, exactly? Logic told him that it would be something that everyone else had dodged like a flung turd, but perhaps it didn't work that way. Perhaps there was a spare, unwanted seat on a parklands commission, or a fresh pair of eyes needed to examine the troubled issue of sourcing fine wines for the metropolitan area. He went to sleep with these and similarly pleasing possibilities drifting in his head, and awoke to the certainty that none were remotely likely to fall his way.

When he went down to breakfast, Holleman was already at the table, picking at an omelette with the reticence of a starving wolf. He paused, fork halfway to his mouth, and looked up.

'What was the commotion last night?'

'A telephone call. I was being congratulated on winning a seat in the House.'

'It's done, then?'

'It is.'

'What was the score?'

'All seats were taken either by the SPD or CDU. It was more or less as predicted.'

'And the two are going to be in coalition still?'

'That's what Willy Brandt promised.'

Holleman sniggered and continued his breakfast.

'What?'

There was a brief pause while too much omelette forced its way southwards. 'I remember hearing a lot of crap from you about the SED's stranglehold in the East, and how Democracy did it differently.'

'But this is choice, not coercion.'

'Whose choice? A bunch of fat politicos, dividing the spoils and then waiting for the Allies to tell them what they should vote for? I don't see much difference. Germans get the stick shoved up their arses whichever side of the Line they're on.'

Fischer wanted to argue, but he wasn't sure he had the ammunition. He thanked Frau Benner when his own omelette and coffee appeared, ate without any pleasure and thought about going up to Rathaus Schöneberg that morning, if only to show his new boy's face. To his shame, however, he realised that he hadn't even bothered to check what was happening there today. Were old names being peeled from office doors at that moment? Was there some sort of ritual cleansing taking place, to wash out the congealed layers of hypocrisy and prepare for the new? He imagined that other newly-elected representatives – the ones who actually *wanted* their jobs – had a deep understanding of every stage of the transition from one administration to its successor; but all that he knew about it was whatever had wormed its way subliminally into his memory from old, half-read newspaper stories. An entirely disinterested, unpolitical novice was about to take his place in the city's engine room – and, indulging that metaphor, he wondered if his most likely appointment would be as coal-shoveller, third class.

'You're *very* quiet, Otto. Are the bowels beginning to move in anticipation?'

'Something like that.'

Holleman sat back and picked his teeth. 'It's the same for everyone. When they first voted me in as a councillor I wandered around the Neues Stadthaus, mouth agape like a country boy in a Ku'damm homo bar. If someone had asked me where the light came from I wouldn't have thought to point at a window.'

'It's just … I have no idea what I'm going to be doing.'

'Ha! You don't need to. You'll be given strict instructions when to blink, breathe and fart. As with any new conscript, someone's already got plans for your every move. They'll probably tie all you first - day'ers together with string, so you don't wander off.'

Strangely, prior assumptions of his uselessness made Fischer feel slightly better (he could hardly fail to meet expectations if there weren't any). In any case, there would be a certain pleasing symmetry to being pointed in a direction and told what to do by Willy Brandt while getting exactly the same treatment from Moscow.

Frau Brenner came into the dining room and tossed her head.

'There's a man at the door.'

Christ! Don't let it be Globnow. He told himself that KGB wouldn't be so eager or stupid as to send him his traitor's portfolio on the morning following his election. Even so, every step of the journey from table to front door was paced by the painful thud in his chest, and when he saw the young stranger on the doorstep he almost needed to sit down.

The visitor seemed equally unmanned. His hands moved awkwardly by his sides for want of something to clutch, and his feet shuffled uncertainly as if, too far out onto ice, he had suddenly thought better of it. However, he didn't react to his first sight of Fischer's mutilated face other than to nod and clear his throat.

'Herr Fischer?'

'Yes?'

'I have a problem with neighbours. A friend said that you might be able to advise me.'

Fischer liked the sound of *advise*. It didn't suggest that the supplicant imagined he was going to *do* anything.

'I don't know if I can. Come in.'

The breakfast plates had been cleared away. Holleman, nursing his third coffee, stared at the newcomer with unabashed curiosity.

'Who're you?

The young man cleared his throat once more. 'Paul Heinkel.'

'No relation?'

That raised a thin, tired smile. 'No.'

Fischer gestured to one of the stand chairs. 'What's the problem?'

'We have new people across the road – it's Körnerstrasse, in Steglitz. They arrived a few months ago, and they're trouble. A few people have complained, but not too loudly. The son, he has an air-rifle, and he killed my daughter's pet bird with it.'

'Little bastard.'

'Hush, Freddie. Please, go on ...'

'I went 'round to complain, but I was laughed off by the father. He took a swing at me, and I punched him in the face. I think I broke his nose. Anyway, the police came the next day and told me to behave myself – said they'd noted me down as a troublemaker. I doubt that I'd get a fair hearing from the Council, but something should be done, and I don't know what.'

Fischer shook his head. 'Hitting him was a mistake, even if he deserved it.'

'No, it was a *half* mistake.'

'What do you mean, Freddie?'

Holleman leaned forward in his chair, and for the first time Paul noticed the artificial leg.

'After you punched him you should have put a blade to his eye and told him that if he or his brood ever squeaked again you'd blind him.'

Fischer frowned. 'That's not helpful ...'

'Or threatened to stuff his severed cock into his wife's mouth. That usually works - if he has a wife, I mean.'

Confused, Paul said nothing. The man whose advice he'd come to ask stared at his friend for a few moments and then turned.

'I should say that this gentleman is a policeman. Though not in Berlin, thankfully.'

Holleman snorted. 'I *was* a policeman. Now, I move paper between trays. You wouldn't believe it, but I once ...'

'I think Herr Heinkel might consider making a formal complaint. It isn't necessarily going to move anyone, but it's good to have the record of what happened.'

Paul nodded. 'I was going to do that. But this family, they're refugees, so it probably won't help.'

'What kind of refugees?'

'Political - *Sowjetzonenflüchtlinge.*'

'That's ... unhelpful.'

Holleman looked from one man to the other. 'Why?'

'The city makes a great deal of taking in those who flee political persecution. It's part of our image – the island of freedom in a sea of oppression. We don't want to be seen providing accommodation for that sort and then evicting them. The other side could make a lot of it - *see, they ran to the West, but they were treated better here.*'

'I swear, Otto, this country – both parts of it - is going fucking mad. When hooligans can be raised up as martyrs, what's the point in anyone trying to be better?'

Fischer shrugged. 'It's the times. Everyone's *for* this and *against* that. There are two teams fighting for the cup, and Berlin's the field they're playing on.'

Paul (who was beginning to feel that the conversation was slipping away) coughed quietly. 'Is there anything else I can do?'

'In other circumstances, I'd say the best chance you have is to get them re-housed. Unfortunately, there's a shortage of family accommodation. That's why, against the local Party's strenuous objections, they were put here in Steglitz - it wasn't too damaged in the war, unlike the working-class areas. Brandt keeps talking about building for the masses, but so far it's been the prestige projects, like *Interbau* and areas to the south of Tiergarten, that have got the money. Until they redevelop the large sites in Neukölln and Wittenau, there won't be spare capacity.'

Aware that he was crushing expectations, Fischer tried to find the glint of light. 'Look, the fact that you stood up to the man means they'll probably try to avoid giving further cause for complaint. Talk to your neighbours – get them to give you their experiences. Make a diary of what's happened on Körnerstrasse since the refugees arrived. If it looks bad enough, the local Housing people will have to do something about it, even if it's only to issue a stern warning.'

Paul brightened slightly. 'Do you know any of them?'

'Only distantly. I wasn't involved with policy. Look ...'

It was Fischer's first day as a Representative, so some sort of effort seemed appropriate. He'd wanted to give the business of refugees a wide berth, but here it was, sucking him in. He hoped earnestly that none of his new colleagues would mistake it for an area of interest, much less a vocation.

'... I'll speak with someone at the Rathaus and see if there's a process for problems like this. It must have happened before.'

'Really? I didn't expect ...'

Holleman laughed and slapped the breakfast table. 'It's Herr Fischer's job to sort things! Tell your friends that from now on he's the man to speak to in Steglitz.'

Fischer managed a thin smile but said nothing more. He had never thought to observe the process by which Holleman attached and removed his metal leg. He wished now that he had, because he wanted very much to flick a handy release, snatch away the thing and beat his friend senseless with it. Assuming that was possible, of course.

9

By the time that Zarubin landed at Schönefeld his rear end was as numb as upon a previous occasion, more than five years earlier, when an American C54 had carried him from RAF Lakenheath to Tempelhof. That device, too, had eschewed the merest degree of padding for its passengers' most tender parts. It made him wonder if aviation designers as a breed colluded with the colonic surgery business.

He had flown out of Khodynka Aerodrome two hours earlier, not wishing to be noticed. These days the field was used only to receive newly-built Ilyushin aircraft from their factory, so the chances of being spotted by KGB personnel were minimal. His pilot and co-pilot were Red Army regulars, requested by name from a list of known good men kept by the indefatigable Levin. Both their silence and loyalty had been bought with Purveyance Board vodka and a hamper of smoked meats, courtesy of the Kremlin Palace kitchens (whose principal housekeeper was on the same list).

Given the unfortunate, immoveable fact of West Berlin, the round-about car journey from Schönefeld to Potsdam stole another hour. Fortunately, the GAZ M21 that transported him had excellent seats (giving no impression whatsoever of a rubble-pile), and he was able to clear a little of his normal day's paperwork.

His driver had his instructions already, and when they reached Am Neuen Garten he parked the car at the main south entrance. Usually, he would have stepped out smartly, opened his passenger's door and saluted smartly, but on this point, too, he had been briefed. He sat to attention in his seat while Zarubin helped himself out, as if to compensate for this gross breach of protocol.

The Gardens were usefully massive, and Zarubin didn't bother to try to be smaller, less conspicuous or anything else that usually gave away a cautious man. It was very likely that staff from Leistikowstrasse 1 took the air here during their off-duty hours, but the prison was almost two kilometres to the north, and he had no intention of straying in that direction. He stepped off the path at its closest point to the Helliger See and waited at the water's edge, pretending an interest in the local duck cohort.

After a few minutes he sensed someone standing at his left side, and he turned. It pleased him that Gaev was of the same mind as himself, and had chosen to wear civilian clothes. Usually, he was to be seen in army trousers, boots and a bloodied shirt, braces off the shoulders and sleeves rolled up, the better to swing his fists at a face. Today, he was in a sober suit and slightly loud tie, of the sort definitely not affected by off-duty KGB interrogators. The contrast between the Germanic dress-sense and a Volgograd quarryman's face was quite striking; Zarubin hadn't seen the man for some years, but like many ugly types he hadn't aged nearly so badly as the pretty ones.

Gaev nodded slightly, his head turned towards the over-surveilled poultry. 'Comrade General.'

'Hello, Yuri. How is the knee?'

'No worse, thank you. They still can't get at the shrapnel.'

'Pity. Have you a report for me?'

'I assume you want only a verbal account?'

'Yes.'

'And ... the other thing?'

'Your mother was transferred yesterday, to Moscow University Clinic. She'll have the same treatment as any Politburo member, I promise you.'

'Thank you. Wolinski ...'

'The *prisoner*, please.'

'Of course. The prisoner expresses considerable surprise at the accusation, and claims that there has been no contact with the brother since before the Victory.'

'That's very likely to be true. He died in Paris, in 1946, from a pulmonary embolism.'

Gaev seemed surprised. 'I was told he worked for the Americans, on very secret matters.'

'A fiction, to lend credibility. I wanted Third Directorate not to mind us taking the problem out of their hands.'

'Us?'

'Myself and the General Secretary.'

Gaev's mouth dropped open. 'Really? I ...'

'A slight exaggeration. His office authorizes me to use Wol ... the prisoner independently of the Lubyanka for a limited period and purpose. A full account of the business will be submitted to the sub-committee for special causes once it's done. The need for secrecy is why you and I are presently watching wildlife, rather than sipping tea at Leistikowstrasse.'

Apart from that last statement, everything Zarubin had said was a lie, but it did its job. The other man stiffened. 'I'll do everything I can to assist this project, General.'

'I know, Yuri – it's why I chose you. What else did the prisoner say?'

'Not much. The threat of pain doesn't seem to be very effective. I haven't yet applied much, as you asked.'

'You put the specific question I gave you?'

'Yes. I received confirmation that the prisoner was present on that date, that's all. No further details were sought or offered.'

'There might not *be* further details.'

'I don't understand.'

'I mean there might not have been a crime. Only the suggestion that the prisoner had been present made me think that it was at least a possibility. Our current understanding of the events of that day is that there were no suspicious circumstances.'

Gaev nodded. He looked uncomfortable. His job was not a complicated one, requiring only that he extract truths from people who wanted them not to be known. It sometimes happened that there were no truths to be extracted, but that didn't detract from the necessity of what he did. Once a determination had been made that an interrogation was necessary his part in it was fully validated, whatever the outcome. He was only made uneasy when the process itself was unsound, or even questionable.

Zarubin didn't need to parse the expression on the other man's face. 'I said our *current* understanding. It's becoming increasingly clear that we may have been misled. Certainly, this interrogation is most necessary.'

'I understand, Comrade General.'

'Now, I need you to put a further question to the prisoner. It's an offer, so no violence please. Explain that certain high-ranking parties in Moscow require a source of local intelligence that, in the short-term, won't flow through recognized KGB channels. A contact will be provided outside Karlshorst who will provide adequate proof that this is not some enemy operation or other form of bear-trap. The same person will be the sole conduit for all requested information. If the prisoner accepts the offer, the current investigation will end promptly, and provide complete exoneration.'

'May I ask why you won't be putting the offer in person? Wouldn't that remove any need for verification?'

'Because I'm not in Berlin, Yuri, nor ever likely to be.'

'And the Prison Administration?'

'Will receive their instructions from the General Secretary's Office immediately after I get word from you that our prisoner is compliant.'

Gaev addressed more of his attention to the ducks, and rubbed his chin. 'I've never done anything like this.'

Zarubin followed his gaze. By now he had decided that the little Pomeranian taking on all the other drakes in turn was his personal favourite – brave, industrious and stupid, the perfect soldier.

'No. It rarely falls to someone of your rank to have a hand in matters of State.'

The other man swallowed audibly. 'It's *that*, is it?'

The General snorted, startling the Pomeranian into breaking off its latest mugging. 'Would anything else bring me *here*, of all places?'

10

'Well?'

Herbert Lamm's smile was too slight to be read easily, but Fischer would have guessed at *supercilious*.

'Well, what?'

'Was their a surge of electricity? A sense of manifest destiny, faintly imparted? A hint of righteous revulsion for the Red barbarism that hangs fire a mere three kilometres to our East?'

'Herbert, what are you talking about?'

'The *handshake*, man! You had his benediction – you were benedicted!'

'It was firm but not crushing, a little moist, and it lasted about a half-second. Despite my face's best efforts, I don't think he noticed me.'

Lamm laughed. 'You have no feel for History, Otto. How can you do justice to the moment, when you tell your grandchildren?'

'That isn't likely to be a problem.'

'Your biographer, then? When you search the dusty corners of your memory for the good bits, what if there aren't any?'

'I assume you've shaken his hand at some point. What did you get from it?'

'Disapproval! I think he got a ripe whiff of Lamm the barricade-builder. You're looking at a man whose career-path in the Party has since dipped its nose towards the water.'

They were sitting in Lamm's office once more, each nursing a small glass of whisky to mark the new boy's grand entrance into Berlin Politics. The House wasn't sitting yet, and it seemed that Lamm had come down from Wedding solely for the occasion, which Fischer took kindly. He felt a little lost and a little more preposterous, so some genial company that took itself no less frivolously was very welcome.

'I'm still wondering what it is I'll be doing here.'

Lamm beamed. 'As a List man, you were raised to greatness on the softest of pillows - no campaigning, no need to rinse your mouth with false promises, no earache from never-gruntled constituents. You're about to pay the penalty for all that sweetness.'

'Penalty?'

'You. Have. No. Constituency. That means two things. Firstly, you won't be able to stand up in the House and say that the people who sent you here want this or that, because you were *sent* by a committee. Secondly – and this is the gruesome bit – you can't claim pressure of constituents' business when attempting to turn down committee work. In fact, List men are seen very much as committee fodder, and chosen accordingly. They have the time to sit – and sit, and sit; more importantly, they're valued on the committees because they do want they're told to do. As someone who owes his seat entirely to the Party's grace and favour you'll be expected to speak, vote and defecate exactly as the Party wishes – which means as our Governing Mayor wishes. Otto, my friend, you're a cipher. *I* can disappoint Willy Brandt until my voters tire of me, but you're not allowed that privilege.'

'Oh, God.'

Why hadn't he seen it? When Globnow ordered him to put his name forward, he'd expected the local Party to dismiss him as a pushy *arriviste*. Their enthusiasm had been surprising, and (if he was honest about it) a little flattering. Had he been so distracted by the horror of his impending career that he'd been blinded to just *how* horrific it might be?

Not much of his life had been spent preparing for committee work. Taking testimonies, pretending an interest in matters arcane or impenetrable (and probably both), a toil of endless hours, poring over gordian clauses with a pedant's eye, hoping to make what was already obscure into something beyond the wit of God or man to parse - it all demanded a degree of soulless intellectualism, salted with a flagellant's taste for the lash, and he feared he'd be unable to bear it long enough to memorize his colleagues' names.

Lamm was enjoying himself hugely. 'You'll almost certainly get Housing. It's Willy's flagship policy – that, and giving the finger to the Ivans. He's promised massive new building programmes, and there are at least four working groups devoted to analyzing why they haven't happened yet.'

'*Why* haven't they?'

'Lots of reasons, but always money. Building in Berlin is expensive.'

'I've heard that, but it puzzles me. Everything's flattened already where they're most likely to put new houses.'

'There are several reasons. Because we have to import the materials from the Federal Republic; because, stupidly, we mocked the Reds' obsession with tower blocks and promised individual homes for the common man, and finding a way out of that pit is proving difficult; because an immutable law of municipal physics states that the rate at which the city purse expands is matched precisely by increasing calls upon it, mainly from the *ossies* who pour in each year – who also, incidentally, add to the housing shortage crisis.'

The last stirred an unpleasant, nagging priority. The previous morning, when Paul Heinkel had finished his account of difficult neighbours and departed, a brief examination of minutes of previous meetings had confirmed why the name Macke had rung a bell in Fischer's head. About seven months earlier, he had taken on the rest of the Borough's Housing Committee in a near-stand-up fight, on a matter of providing accommodation for refugees – specifically, for a family of three. The arguments against had been spurious, obvious attempts to shovel responsibility somewhere else, and they had lit up his temper. Nevertheless, he had been able to argue cogently and with enough force to shame a majority of downward-pointing thumbs into thinking again. The achievement – and he'd thought it such - had now soured somewhat. Single-handedly, he'd been responsible for unleashing the Mackes upon Steglitz.

He had no intention of telling Heinkel about it. He wished very much that he hadn't confessed himself to Freddie Holleman, who'd laughed so hard he'd almost puked up his breakfast omelette. It made a vague promise into something of a commitment, obviously; he just didn't know how he might make good the terrible, unthinking wrong he'd done. Perhaps being sentenced to time on Berlin's housing issues would be both a suitable punishment and offer a necessary education on the ways and means of shifting undesirable tenants.

'Of course, you could always anticipate things by volunteering for Sewage and Drains. No-one would fight you for *that* one.'

Fischer shuddered. In contrast to his vagueness on eviction law, he had a deep and noisome understanding of What went Where after the event. If he chose to admit to it he had no doubt he'd be invited to join the doomed attempt to keep the city fragrant, so he intended not to say a single word on the matter, either as a volunteer or oracle to those more willing to seize the shitted baton.

'Is there no cakes and pastries standards committee?'

Lamm laughed. 'If there was, you'd have to fight naked at knife-point for it. Even *I'd* put myself forward, and I'm an instinctive retreater. No, of the *real* committees, the one to aim for is Convergence.'

'What's that?'

'A sweet, sweet nothingness. A group of our representatives liaise with the Federal Interior Ministry to prepare for the longed-for absorption of West Berlin into 'free' Germany. It's a conceptual thing, naturally, so there's very little work to be done. Best of all, you'd need to be in Bonn more or less permanently.'

'And how does one get on to this committee?'

'By the intervention of God, principally. Failing that, a photograph of the Mayor in bed with at least four teenage Romanian prostitutes would be useful.'

The only man with a camera known to Fischer was ace journalist Jonas Kleiber. He was in London these days, so it couldn't be borrowed even if the golden moment presented itself. As for God, infrequent applications to that party had yet to be answered in any discernible manner. There was a third possibility of course, unknown to Lamm, but even Globnow probably didn't have enough dirt on enough Berlin politicians to get them to help a new man into such a golden chariot. And thoughts of Globnow made an appointment to a soul-draining committee seem less that the worst prospect. If he pointed himself in a direction before a decision was made on his behalf (a decision involving something worse than Sewage and Drains, even), what could Zarubin do about it? Demote him?

He sighed. 'How do I put myself forward for one of the Housing committees?'

11

Ostensibly, Karlshorst's KGB Station Resident had every right to summon to his presence any of the separate Directorate Heads; but even Korotkov, otherwise keenly sensitive to his status, preferred to apply a gentler touch. Each of the Directors had his own guardian angel in Moscow, after all, and no man knew when a needlessly vindictive gesture might come back to bite his tender parts.

Bolkov wasn't surprised, therefore, when he received an invitation to a cup of tea with the Resident. What *did* surprise him was the silver samovar from which it was poured, an old-fashioned, hospitable gesture (Karlshorst's catering was very much a western-style, convenience model, intended to discourage lingering or enjoyment). The blend was premium Sochi, rather than the teeth-scouring *chifir* variety that everyone from the top floor of the Lubyanka to their victims in the gulags seemed to prefer, poured into glasses rather than cups, and it kept company with a large plate of lemon cakes. Bolkov began to wonder if he was going to be tapped for the use of his wife.

She was one of the topics of a series of polite enquiries that Korotkov made as he poured for them both, which in sum exceeded all the pleasantries he'd had from the man since his arrival at Karlshorst the previous year. Bolkov wasn't a fool. If a trap was being set this was the worst, most obvious tactic, so it was far more likely that the man was making an effort. He relaxed slightly, and waited.

Korotkov lit a cigarette and appeared to enjoy his tea, but the eyes betrayed his nerve-endings. Unless some striking new matter had broken entirely without Bolkov's knowledge, it had to be about Wolinski.

'About Wolinski ...'

'Yes?'

'Something's going on.'

'Something?'

Korotkov struggled for a few moments more, but it was out now.

'It's unheard of, that an internal investigation should be taken out of our hands.'

'You tried to take it out of *my* hands.'

'That would have been standard procedure. Section Chiefs don't investigate their own subordinates – it would have put you in an impossible position.'

You would have made certain of that.

'And it isn't just Wolinski. The day-today running of some of our best agents has been put under scrutiny, as if ...'

'As if?'

'As if Karlshorst was assumed to be entirely compromised.'

Bolkov shook his head. 'We had problems two years ago, but they were dealt with rigorously. Comrade Serov ensured that everything was seen to be put right, and in the right way.'

'I know.' Korotkov stared at the samovar, and actually chewed his lower lip. He wasn't even pretending to understand the situation, which was entirely out of character.

'It might be something else.'

'What?'

'Part of a process. You were NKVD, weren't you. Andrei Nikolaevich?'

Korotkov knew perfectly well what Bolkov had been, but this was an invitation to a conversation.

'Yes, from 1938.'

'Me also, 1941. We had a hard job back then, didn't we?'

'We didn't make too many friends.'

'No, but it had to be done. Our backs were against the wall, the Fascists on the brink of ...'

The Station Resident paused on the edge of a gross indiscretion. The Great Patriotic War had been a desperate business, but its outcome had not been in doubt for a moment. The Soviet Union could never have been vanquished by a degenerate philosophy like National Socialism. Bolkov, anxious to hear more, pretended that the slip hadn't happened. Somewhere deep in his thoughts, Korotkov struggled for a moment and continued.

'It isn't a secret that the General Secretary has reservations about his predecessor's record. We're tarred with that, to an extent.'

'But Khrushchev was NKVD too.'

'He was, and his hands were every bit as deeply in the business that needed to be done as yours or mine. That isn't the point, though. I get the feeling that we're in line for – what shall we call it, reformation?'

'The Berlin Station?'

'KGB everywhere. Have you noticed any pattern to senior appointments in the past couple of years? Not one new Directorate Chief is former NKVD; *all* were Komsomol at some point. Khrushchev thinks the old guard are mostly a breed of stupid field-executioners, and he's hinted with his peasant's lack of subtlety that he wants us replaced by younger, smoother, university types. Did *you* attend university, Andrei Nikolaevich?'

Again, the question was rhetorical. Bolkov's university had been the fields of Ukraine and Byelorussia, a blood-drenched canvas of steel and bone that only a lunatic would have studied wantonly. He said nothing.

Korotkov laughed, unconvincingly. 'I suspect he'd sooner we were more like CIA – a crowd of pipe-smoking theorists in shiny grey suits, whose hobbies run to chess and boating, not drinking heavily and singing old revolutionary songs.'

Rumours that parts of the Kremlin were looking to modernize KGB had been circulating for months, but Bolkov wasn't too worried. Experience counted for something, so the *process* that Korotkov feared would necessarily move very slowly (as did all change within Soviet institutions). Still, it didn't hurt to keep an eye on horizons. He shrugged.

'Well, we should both be getting our pensions before that happens.'

'I'm not so sure.' Korotkov gave his lower lip some more attention. 'For a while now we've been aware of … *movement* in Berlin that we can't account for.'

'What do you mean?'

'Things are getting back to Moscow other than through Karlshorst, by which I mean us. And by things I mean an intelligence stream – not very accurate, and not too sensitive, but intelligence nevertheless. And by Moscow I mean the Kremlin directly, not via the Lubyanka.'

'Are you certain?'

'I heard it from Serov himself. He wants it investigated, urgently. And then he wants it stopped, quietly but decisively'

If the Head of KGB was soiling himself even a little, it couldn't be dismissed as mere paranoia.

'You think this is linked to the other thing? The initiative to - what, reform us?'

'I don't know. How can I? Listen, I've mentioned this to you because if we're to investigate it I need your people. You know more about Soviet personnel in Germany than any other Directorate – it's what you *do*, after all.'

To be asked by Korotkov to collaborate in confidence was a novel experience, but Bolkov couldn't see any way to refuse.

He nodded slowly and was about to ask the obvious question, but the other man pressed on.

'I have to ask something, though, and it isn't usual. That's to say, it isn't protocol.'

'What, then?'

'If these things are linked, we can't know who in Moscow is involved. For the moment, may I ask you not to speak of it to your Chief of Directorate?'

Bolkov opened his mouth to refuse, but Korotkov was ready for it. 'Comrade Serov told me to refer you to him. He takes full responsibility. He'll speak on your behalf to Comrade Yudkin – when this is over, obviously.'

If there was anything about this that didn't surprise Bolkov it was that Serov was involved. He was the oldest of the Old Guard – one of Beria's favourites, who'd stuck the knife in his boss's back and taken his job. His most famous boast was that he could break every bone in a man's body yet not kill him, a talent that was looking very old-fashioned – quaint, even – in this new age. An influx of educated, forward-looking *apparatchiks* into KGB's senior ranks would make him stand out like an elk on Arbat Street.

'Very well. What do you need me to do?'

Korotkov removed a file from his desk drawer and opened it.

'I've been attempting to monitor telephone calls from Berlin to Moscow that don't go through the secure exchanges. However, even filtering out homesick *soldats*' conversations with mothers and sweethearts, we're left a mountain of work to do, and no resources. But then it occurred to me that raw intelligence finding its way directly into the Kremlin isn't necessarily – or even likely to be – routed through channels to which KGB would have easy access. Also, if it's first-hand information, then it needn't even pass through East Berlin. I think it's very possible that our mystery man or men in Moscow have contacts in the western city.'

'Might the source or sources not be run by *Stasi*? They're fond of ploughing their own furrow these days.'

'I doubt it. Clearly, we rely heavily upon them for intelligence from and on German nationals, so to that extent your suggestion makes sense. But Serov keeps a close grip on State Security's contacts with the Kremlin - *everything* goes through him, and he's put in place enough safeguards to ensure that the net doesn't get ripped. It would take a very courageous soul at Ruschestrasse 103 to attempt to disrupt or bypass the system - and ask yourself, why would they try? Look at it from the other direction, also - would whoever is going against Serov in Moscow use an organization in which so many people owe the man their jobs? He virtually *built* DDR's State Security.'

Bolkov nodded slowly. 'So again, what can I do?'

A photograph was lifted from the file and pushed towards him. 'Two unconnected sources allege that this man was formerly involved in Berlin operations run by MGB, the most recent of which occurred sometime in 1948, during the Berlin lockdown. As far as they know he was never KGB. He's a German national – this is the name that one of them gave to me, though he isn't entirely sure it's correct.'

Bolkov examined both the image and name. 'I'm not familiar with him.'

'He was living in Berlin eight years ago. We don't know if he's here still. I need your people to put the word around, both on the street in the city and at Wünsdorf. We need to find and interrogate him.'

'Why him in particular?'

'The man he reported to directly at the time was a Major in MGB, based in this very building. He defected to the Americans but then reappeared, and is now close to the General Secretary's office. In fact, I hear that Khrushchev invited him to dinner at least twice last year.'

'Remarkable.'

'That he wasn't shot out of hand? I agree. And this is where our two problems might converge. Comrade Serov told me he suspects that this traitor is one of those actively encouraging modernization – even reformation – of KGB.'

'Why would he do that?'

'It was the information he brought back from America that, more than anything else, put Beria in the ground. Perhaps he wants to finish the job and clear out the rest of the stable. Back then, of course, he and Serov were working to the same end; now, they may be facing each other directly across a battlefield. His name is Zarubin, by the way.'

'I've heard the name. So this man … 'Bolkov tapped the photograph; '... might be working for him still?'

'It isn't clear. At the moment he's our only *potential* link.'

'Alright. You said he was to be interrogated. But surely, if we do that ...'

'We risk flagging our interest, which may warn this Zarubin. Fortunately, there are plenty of places to put a body where it can't embarrass us.'

12

Returning directly home from the *Abgeordnetenhaus,* Fischer
was met at his front door by Frau Benner, who gave him a
week's notice.

'Your *friend* (she spat out the word as if it had bitten her tongue
on the way past) has turned everything on its head.'

Uncharacteristically, she didn't address him formally, nor offer
further enlightenment as to what constituted this inversion. For
want of any idea how to negotiate a change of mind, he patted
her arm and advanced to investigate.

The sitting room was being decorated. Clearly, Holleman had
plundered the garden shed for paint, and returned with the only
available shade (Teal Blue). Approximately half of one wall
had been painted already, though the wide spectrum-shift of old
and new colours suggested that several more coats would be
necessary before the transformation was complete.

Fischer's first reaction was intense irritation, followed quickly
by frustration. The new colour was definitely an improvement,
which killed any chance of his moaning convincingly about it.
Herr Grabner had been an anglophile – or rather, an admirer of
the English aristocracy – and having visited several stately
homes on pre-war visits to the country had returned with ideas
very much above his station. Accordingly, the sitting room's
walls had been stained a deep red hue that very large spaces lit
by many windows could wear comfortably but which anything
scaled more domestically could not. Fischer had often sat in its
most comfortable armchair, listening to his gramophone,

sipping wine, and imagined himself to be in a particularly civilized stomach. Even the brightest days managed only to raise the interior light to something resembling an arterial emergency, and in dull weather the electric lights needed to be left on throughout the waking hours. The partial job that Holleman had made of it so far promised to raise both light and mood tremendously.

'Freddie …?'

'Otto! I hope you don't mind. I 'phoned Kristin to report in, and she told me to make myself useful.'

'You might have washed the breakfast dishes.'

Holleman shook his head vigorously. 'Get in a woman's way? I tried that when I first entered the matrimonial state. Anyway, it would have taken a few minutes at most, and I'm bored.'

'Go home, then.'

'Why are you becoming a politician?'

'I've told you why.'

Holleman returned to his pot and brush. 'I'll need more paint.'

The room had been prepared carefully. Brown paper masked the floors close to the walls, and the window frames were taped. The room's furniture had been dragged away from danger, but on rugs so as not to mark the polished wood beneath. Had Fischer hired a reputable firm of decorators he couldn't have expected more, and had his housekeeper not sniffed her disapproval in his ear at that moment he might have felt obliged to make a positive noise about it. He turned to her.

'Never mind, Frau Benner. We'll stay out of the room for a couple of days.'

'I can't work in these conditions.'

'It won't be for long. And how nice it looks already!'

Another sniff, more contemptuous than the last. 'I've cleaned here for eighteen years, and it's never been decorated!'

'Then it's not before time. Please don't leave, Frau Benner – how will I ever find anyone as conscientious as you?'

'Well ...'

It was delicate diplomacy and needed time to breathe, but the schedule was kicked hard when Holleman began to sing *Erika* as he painted. This was not the semi-official marching song so tirelessly flaunted in Goebbels' newsreels, but a profoundly obscene version with which the heroes of the Lie Division had entertained themselves on most workday afternoons as they sank slowly to the *Silver Birch*'s filthy floor.

Hastily, Fischer guided Frau Benner out of the room with a hand on her shoulder. 'Look, why don't you think about it for the rest of the week. By then the room will be finished, the mess cleared – I promise – and perhaps Herr Holleman will have gone home to Trier.'

The three percussive beats that marked the end of each verse (the thud of boots on the ground replaced in the Lie Division's version by loud orgasmic grunts) sounded for the first time as Fischer closed the front door on his housekeeper. He returned to the sitting room.

Both *Erika* and the paint brush paused, and Holleman clambered painfully to his foot.

'I've been busy.'

'Yes, I'd noticed.'

'Not this. After Kristin gave me my orders I called Albi Müller. You remember Albi?'

The name was vaguely familiar, but as it solidified in Fischer's memory he told himself no, it couldn't be *him*.

'I gave him the name *Macke* and asked if they'd had a file on the fellow.'

'You called VolksPolizei headquarters?'

Holleman's eyebrows rose innocently. 'Why not?'

'You're a defector, for God's sake!'

'Yes, but this might be police business.'

'They'll trace the call to here!'

'Who do you think they are, the CIA? *Stasi* might have something that could pin it down to *somewhere* in Lichterfelde – though I doubt it - but VolksPolizei couldn't afford equipment like that, ever. Anyway, Albi wouldn't say anything.'

'Why not?'

'Because he's fond of me. And he's a coward.'

'So he'd try to cover his arse, surely?'

'Nah, he wouldn't want anyone to be reminded that he was brought into the force by a traitor. When he heard my voice he probably shat himself.'

'What did you say?'

'That we had a family of refugee East Berliners here in Trier – that was clever, eh? They'd been causing trouble, and I wondered if VolksPolizei had a file on them.'

'What did he say?'

'That it served us right for taking in scum like that. Then he remembered that *I* was scum like that, and he apologized. I told him that if their record was bad enough we could send them back. He said we – I mean, the Federal Republic - didn't do that any more, which is true, more or less; but I told him that we had a new policy, and that *real* scum, scum with police records for serious offences in the DDR, were to be scraped up and sent home so that VolksPolizei could get another stab at them. He said he'd have a look.'

'I presume you didn't give him my number?'

Holleman looked offended. 'I hope I'm not a total dolt, Otto. I told him I'd call back in a couple of hours, which is now'ish.'

'Alright.' Fischer thought for a few moments. 'But even if they have a file on Macke, we probably wouldn't send him back across the Line, not now that he's been given political refugee status. So what's the point of this?'

'Armed with the right sort of evidence, you could at least get him and his brood shoved out of Steglitz.'

'And dumped on some other poor bastards?'

Holleman smiled broadly. 'Exactly!'

'That wouldn't be right.'

'Otto, Otto – you have to *think* like a politician if you're going to be one! Other than with a gun, very few problems are solved more neatly than by dumping them on someone else. Probably, the next lot to get the Mackes will do the same, and the next, and so on. If the bastards never get to warm a seat before they're moved on, it'll be punishment enough for what they've done, won't it?'

'I suppose so.'

Satisfied, Holleman dipped his brush turned back to the wall, thought again and paused.

'And you had a call.'

'Did I? Who?'

'He wouldn't say. The conversation turned a bit cool when he heard my voice. He just asked me to say that he'd call again in the next few days with a message from home, so I assume he's from one of those shitty little villages on the Baltic. I didn't know you'd kept in touch with your old *heimat*.'

Home wasn't Usedom - it was Moscow, and the evasive caller was undoubtedly Globnow. Fischer had been given a full three days to get used the politician's life before first notice of execution was presented. He rubbed his eyes with a hand. Of course they'd move quickly. For days now, Berlin had been in an uproar because of Khrushchev's speech. In fact, they'd been

been on edge since Hungary, two years earlier, and for a profoundly obvious reason. Then, the Soviets had promised to negotiate with Nagy's new government, yet the moment he started talking about free elections they went in hard. Since that moment, no-one had believed that Khrushchev's alleged goal of a non-aligned, re-united Germany meant anything other than a Kremlin puppet-regime.

He had put the West on notice, and Moscow would be looking to every one of its turned men to undermine the resolve of the civilian front-line. Whatever time Fischer had hoped he might have to squeeze himself into a harmless role - housing, drains, the sweet Bonn posting – was gone already; Globnow was coming with Zarubin's instructions, and they wouldn't involve him staying small, or indiscreet. He was a cog in a machine that had to be disrupted – or, more likely, the bag of cement poured into its fuel tank. At best, he'd be a busy mouth, talk up the happy prospect of a city without Allied garrisons (and hoping that someone would be mad enough to be convinced); at worst, a virus assaulting the Municipal Body Politic. And either would remove any desire he might have to look willingly into another mirror, ever.

'You're *very* quiet today, Otto.'

'Only compared to you, Freddie.'

'No, really.'

'I'm … worried. About making a good job of this.'

Holleman snorted. 'No-one expects a politician to shine. Take the money, tread water, agree with whatever the rising men say, don't get caught in any married ladies and step down graciously before you're pushed. If you can manage all that, folk might even recall you fondly when someone worse comes along.' He applied another dab to the wall and limped back to appraise his work. 'And they always do.'

'I should be forgettable?'

'You should be *invisible*. Germans have had enough of interesting politicians. Look at Walter Ulbricht – he's as close to a dictator as either Germany has, and the man's as bland as milk soup.'

For once, Holleman's advice couldn't have spoken more closely to Fischer's instincts, but it missed the wider matter of what Moscow might require of the model dull politician. He would know soon enough, and though he might wish the moment postponed indefinitely he was beginning to sense the mixed feelings of a condemned man who's fifth appeal has failed.

If I hadn't bothered I'd be peacefully dead by now.

He rubbed his eyes once more. 'How much more paint do you need?'

Holleman pursed his lips. 'I want to say five litres, but that might be trimming it a little. Say ten, then, and if it's too much I'll do another room after this.' He turned and grinned. 'It might take that long to break you, but I will.'

13

Peter Globnow couldn't recall the last time he'd been worried. Anxious, yes – it was both inevitable and necessary that a soldier permanently stationed in enemy territory keep his nerves frayed, ready to be set off by the least hint of wrongness. It was why he was observant, furtive without seeming so – an auditor of every passage from one point to another when on business that didn't pay the rent or put food on the table. He enjoyed the illusion of ordinary, safe days without ever imagining it to be anything else.

Today, though, his nerves were alight, his dangerous tasks weighed further by what they might signify. He found himself in rare disagreement with his instructions, or at least puzzled to the point of wanting to understand more (a dangerous urge). In the eleven years since his leaving MGB, he had questioned neither the motives nor judgement of the man who had got him out, and now both seemed to him almost incomprehensible. He was perfectly aware that the world had changed since Khrushchev's speech, and that new circumstances required new strategies; but with all that he kept coming back to the same question: what game was Zarubin playing?

Globnow didn't like surprises, and he'd been surprised twice in as many days. First, he'd been apprised of the Wolinski business. Zarubin had never wandered close to active KGB personnel, and with good reason. To the organization he was a traitor still, someone who had fled to the Americans, survived a subsequent change of mind and then provided the dagger that had finished off Beria. He had thrived in Moscow since his return, but his high perch was piano-wire thin, and Soviet politics generated strong crosswinds. If Khrushchev fell, or even lost such support as to drag him back into the mass of ministers who currently deferred to him, KGB wouldn't waste an hour in putting right at least one outstanding affront. Yet Zarubin was now not only thrusting himself into one of their most sensitive internal investigations but may have manufactured it precisely for that purpose.

Why? Who *was* Wolinski? What possible utility could there be in shoving a boot up Karlshorst's fundament? Globnow didn't expect to share Zarubin's thinking, but a man who risked his freedom every day deserves to have at least a vague sense of how the ground lay. He had been told that he must meet this Wolinski and pass on the General's requests (if that was the way to put it), and perhaps then he'd have a clearer view of what good could come from it. In the meantime, there was the other surprise – Otto Fischer.

For more than two years now, Globnow had coddled the man, merely reminding him of his obligations to Zarubin without setting a single task to test the man's competence or commitment ahead of his employment. This was not usual procedure, but he'd obeyed his instructions to the letter, assuming that some long-game was being played for which no more obvious or practiced operative would do.

Fischer was hard to read. The conversations they'd had suggested that their broad view of the world and its poisonous corners aligned quite closely, which was unfortunate. It might be that his first assignment would lead to praise, prison or a long, weighted swim; it might equally reveal that they had all been wrong about his loyalties and capacity for playing two hands at once. Either way, Globnow's was the hand that would pat the back or correct the mistake.

What was required of every other one of Zarubin's men in Berlin had been clear for some days now. They were insinuators and subtle agitators, people in positions of trust who could quietly begin the work of making Berliners think about their situation. Was real freedom to be had at the end of an American dog-chain? Didn't Germans have the right to be their own masters once more, united by culture and temperament, yet also by political will? Khrushchev was offering that; the Americans offered only division. And so on.

In the *Abgeordnetenhaus*, Fischer would add usefully to these voices, or so Globnow had assumed. Zarubin had different thoughts, though, and – finally – had spoken something of them. It was absurd, even fantastical, yet Globnow was now on his way to arrange things, to speak to a man of whose spectacular treacheries neither KGB nor *Stasi* were aware, and for what? To prepare the way - like a clandestine John the Baptist - for the Coming of Otto Fischer.

How well did Zarubin know Fischer? To place so great a stake on him, to risk the exposure both of a golden asset and, probably, the General's own position at the Kremlin, seemed insanely hazardous. Of course, if it worked it would be a triumph; but how many pits lay between now and then?

In the office of Willy Brandt himself, a gentleman of impeccable reputation was going to be asked – or told, rather - to ignore more worthy applications and take on a political novice, a virgin. That done, he was to ensure that the path of his progress was swept clear. No doubt he would object strenuously (and Globnow wouldn't blame him), but his very sensible reservations would be similarly swept aside. However reluctantly, he would follow his instructions - not because they made any obvious sense, but because they came from General Zarubin.

Christ. Had in been up to Globnow the preferred candidate would have been an amalgam of Mata Hari and Leopold Trapper, not a half-faced war-veteran with the luck of a dog in a cat-food factory – a man who could stumble in a wheat field and land in cow shit. He had been burned, shot, betrayed more times than he could (probably) recall, and, most recently, lost his business to Lichterfelde's only gas-main explosion since charcoal had gone out of fashion. Globnow wasn't a gambling man, but a bet on some disaster falling out of this felt like money banked.

He had been almost relieved when Fischer didn't answer his telephone that morning. The stranger's voice had thrown him momentarily (particularly when it loudly demanded to know his business), but he wasn't worried that anything had been said, even to a twin brother. At least now he'd have a further day to think of a way of explaining the next step that didn't sound as mad as it was.

It was a symptom of his present disorder that he'd been walking for almost half an hour without noticing any part of the journey. He was now in Rummelsburg, not too far from his workplace and the small park where he often ate his lunch, though neither was his destination this morning. Normally, he put at least a portion of his mind on sentry duty, but his distraction rendered invisible both the grey van that had been matching his pace for almost five minutes and the two men who had jumped from it and were walking almost directly beside him on the opposite side of Schlichtallee. He was similarly oblivious to the uneasy, staggered halt of several pedestrians coming towards him, and to the moment that the men across the road changed direction to close down the distance between them and him, which made the hood that came down over his head and turned day into night a revelation of the very worst kind.

'May I ask what you're doing?'

Zarubin looked up. Levin's face matched perfectly the innocence of the question, so he almost certainly knew the answer already.

'I'm preparing a report for the General Secretary, on the likely American and British reactions to his ultimatum.'

'Ah. Did he ask for one?'

'No.'

'I doesn't sound like the sort of thing he'd request. I assume it was the First Deputy Premier's idea?'

Zarubin put down his pen, and, recalling his Mother's example at moments of stress, recited *Karl stole corals from Klara* three times, quickly, in his head. He had never enjoyed any insinuation that it wasn't he who had thought of something, and what made it worse was that Levin had put the arrow dead centre. Anastas Mikoyan had come unannounced to his office the previous day, before even the cleaners arrived, and settled himself on the battered leather sofa that kept an over-stuffed bookcase from falling forward. He was a pleasant, unaffected man for all the dried blood on his hands, and Zarubin enjoyed his company, usually. This time, however, a deep frown conspired with the heavy moustache to dampen the atmosphere before his first words were out.

'Did he speak to you before he did it?'

Zarubin hadn't needed to guess what *it* was. 'Not directly, no.'

'Nor to the Central Committee. Nor to any member of it, apparently. He certainly didn't bother to let *me* know what was in his head. This isn't how it's supposed to be done.'

It must have hurt Mikoyan not to be consulted. By several measures he was the second most powerful man in the Soviet Union, and had stood closely by Khrushchev only the previous year, when Malenkov and Molotov had tried to lead a palace coup against the man. Now, he was being excluded from a major foreign policy decision despite his enormous diplomatic experience.

Zarubin believed he understood the reasoning behind the snub. Mikoyan had a far subtler mind than Khrushchev, and believed that any confrontation was stupid when a sideways step and lateral thrust could do the job more effectively. During the Hungarian crisis he had argued that too heavy-handed a reaction would gift the Americans a propaganda triumph. He had been right, of course; the image of Soviet tanks crashing into protesters was an early Christmas present for Washington, but prescience was never well-regarded in the Kremlin, not when everyone else had gone the other way. No doubt Khrushchev had conceived his latest brilliant idea, feared being out-argued by the man he called *his rug-merchant*, and stepped off the cliff before he could be grabbed.

It was done, though, so Zarubin wondered why he was being graced by this visit. He cleared his throat. 'What do you think of it?'

Mikoyan snorted. 'Not much. The Americans and British won't move an inch - they know a bluff when they smell one, and how a bluffer looks when it's called. It's just like '48.'

'You think he wouldn't do it?'

'Hand over control of the West Berlin access routes to the DDR? Would you?'

It would effectively make Soviet war-planning a hostage to Walter Ulbricht's mood swings, so no, Zarubin wouldn't. He didn't bother to shake his head. No answer had been expected.

Mikoyan sighed and stared up at the ceiling. 'So, we put our slowly-improving relationship with the capitalists into reverse and encourage them to spend a few more billion dollars on long-range bombers and missiles. We'll be obliged to do the same, thus sticking a sharp rod into the economy's groin - which, God knows, it doesn't need right now – and all so that we can look like village idiots when the German situation remains exactly where it is.'

It was a masterful analysis, beyond contradiction, though Zarubin couldn't resist giving the stool a mild kick.

'You don't *believe* in God, Anastas Ivanovich.'

Mikoyan gave him a tired smile. 'He might believe in me, though.'

'So, what would you do?'

'Start from somewhere else.'

'That being?'

'Play to the Americans' palpable weakness, which is their ignorance of the world. We can't outproduce them, so we should make them squander their wealth and reputation in futile pursuits.'

'Reds under the bed?'

The smile was less forced this time. 'It's ironic, isn't it? The Americans have become convinced Trotskyites. They see the triumph of Communism as an inevitability, absent their clumsy interventions. All we need do is push a little - what does it cost us, to send a little obsolete hardware to out friends in the jungles and give loud speeches about self-determination at the UN? With a little intelligent planning we could spread the US as thinly as the British Empire, and make them as many enemies in the world.'

'You know the Americans well.' Mikoyan had been to the US, met Henry Ford, visited a self-service supermarket, and, on his return, introduced the Soviet Union to hamburgers, ice-cream and corn on the cob. There was no-one in the first rank of ministers who had a tenth of his understanding of the enemy.

'As do you, Sergei Aleksandrovich. Three years, wasn't it?'

'It felt like much more.'

For a moment it had seemed that Mikoyan might say something to that, but he held his tongue. Five years earlier, when the unhappy exile Zarubin had reverse-defected, a pat on the back or a head-shot had been equally in prospect. Khrushchev had supported him for self-interested reasons, but Malenkov's friendship had been tied to nothing – and that had been at a time, immediately following Stalin's death, when there was no advantage to having vulnerable friends. Perhaps, Zarubin had posited since, the older man felt some measure of kinship with a fellow-traveller. During the Revolutionary War, he and twenty-five other members of the Baku Soviet had been captured by the Whites. Twenty-five of them had been executed; Mikoyan had been allowed to walk away unscathed.

He had never explained his deliverance, not even to Stalin, yet to have survived he must have displayed an elasticity of conviction every bit as great as Zarubin's. For a man who didn't believe in God he carried a weight of guilt on his soul – not least for having gone on to sign every death-warrant that Stalin had shoved under his nose, for offences so light as to be hardly worthy of the name. Perhaps his patronage of Zarubin had been a little late penance, for sins unacknowledged.

And here came the first favour that he had ever asked in return. 'He trusts your judgement.'

'And yours, Comrade Premier.'

'No, he *admits* to mine - I don't think he's ever wanted to hear what I think. I need you to draft an opinion paper – only three or four pages, he doesn't like to read – on how you see the Americans reacting to his speech. Be honest. Don't dip it in honey. And don't worry, I'll defend it loudly.'

'But it's too late.'

'The speech can't be unsaid, but we can try to limit the damage. Already, he's having doubts about the wisdom of what he's said, so it shouldn't be too difficult to move him further – with your help.'

'Are you certain?'

'He's asked me to go back to the US, to reprise my Lovable Soviet act and calm them down.'

'What did you say?'

'I told him it was his fucking mess and he should go himself. He won't though, so I'm packing a suitcase. Your paper will reach him while he still feels he owes me something.'

So here Zarubin was, explaining himself to his secretary instead of writing the thing (which admittedly, could almost write itself, being merely an exercise in common sense).

'Yes, it was Mikoyan's idea.'

Levin nodded, his eyes on the floor. 'Serov won't like it.'

'Of course he won't like it. *All* intelligence on the Enemy should come from or through KGB as far as he's concerned. He doesn't want anyone to have a world-view he hasn't shaped.'

'And yet ...'

'What?'

Levin looked up and smiled. 'KGB are wrong about almost everything.'

Zarubin was about to tell him to shut his over-loose mouth, but he couldn't fault the sentiment. KGB did an excellent job of catching enemy spies and running their own in hostile territory; yet their processing of data was tainted by preconceptions, partialities and a rigorous refusal to present the finished product without applying a thick coat of prescribed ideological thinking. He couldn't recall the number of times he had waded through reports on military, political, economic and social developments in the West which horribly exaggerated their negative impact. Had half of them been nearly accurate, the most dangerous threat to the Soviet Union and its allies would be hordes of tattered, starving *wessies*, clamouring for bread, iodine and penicillin at their borders. In the past few days, he had given a lot of thought to the grounds upon which the General Secretary had decided to make his provocative speech, and couldn't get beyond one possibility - or rather, probability: that Serov had listened to Khrushchev and then given him what he wanted to hear, rather than what he should have heard.

'Levin, have you considered that this office *might* be wired?'

'Naturally. But I've searched it occasionally and found nothing.'

'And you know what to look for?'

His secretary shrugged. 'Not really. I assume that you've done a better job of it already.'

In fact, Zarubin had the office swept every fortnight (by a former NKGB specialist whose son, formerly serving in the Murmansk Fleet, had magically obtained a transfer to Sevastopol), but he couldn't bring himself to offer Levin that peace of mind when his own was so unsettled. This paper – whether its authorship was plain or not - would allow Serov to further narrow down his list of whoever might be poisoning minds against KGB's Old Guard, and for all of Mikoyan's promise of support it would leave Zarubin dangerously exposed. He enjoyed his rank, role and continuing health solely at the dispensation of Khrushchev, yet the man was equally beholden to Serov, whose unexpected defection from Beria's camp in '53 had been the anvil to Zarubin's *faux*-CIA Intelligence hammer. Given the General Secretary's renowned fickleness, offering him – in fact, forcing upon him – a choice between two polar opposites wasn't the safest strategy.

The cynic in Zarubin wondered if Mikoyan might be setting him up, but he couldn't see a motive. The man's lack of ambition for the very highest rank was legendary - it was what had kept him alive while successive generations of more competitive creatures had died against a wall, still feebly shouting *Long Live Stalin*. It was no secret that he had been up for the same treatment when the old bastard died suddenly (no-one knew why, though Stalin never needed an excuse), but *nearly* didn't count when it came to a firing squad. As far as Zarubin knew, Mikoyan was content to serve out his the rest of his time dutifully, retire safely and make no further enemies.

Still, this was extremely unfortunate. Zarubin had fondly imagined that he'd be able to play the game at his own speed, but first Khrushchev and now Mikoyan had nudged his elbow, giving Serov sight of what should have come upon him too slowly to be noticed. A contest that had been unequal from the start was beginning to resemble a puppy-drowning, and Zarubin feared that his was the wagging tail.

Levin cleared his throat. 'What do we have on Director Serov?

Zarubin looked up from his half-started briefing paper. 'On?'

'Dirt, I mean.'

'Apart from liking the ladies, I'm not aware of any personal faults. Professionally, he's deported everyone he ever met who wasn't nailed down. Or beaten them to death with his own fists. Or had them shot. Or betrayed them, if they were particular friends. I can't see what I could make from any of it.'

Levin frowned. 'It's difficult. When you're *that* reprehensible, accusations tend to raise laughter rather than outrage. Perhaps ...'

'Yes?'

'Perhaps you should have chosen a different enemy?'

'I didn't *choose* him - he was there, waiting for me. When Beria fell I was newly returned from America, half in and out of the fire, and had no say in who'd replace him. Serov schemed with GRU to get his own arse into the chair, and I suspect that since that moment my name's been on either his deport, beat, shoot or betray to death list. Or all of them, possibly.'

'Perhaps *I* should have chosen a different employer, then.'

'It's of a piece with your judgement generally, Levin. At least you won't need to worry whether your pension will stretch. Now, let me write this damn thing.'

15

Fischer looked back upon his first morning in the job and found no reason to complain. After breakfast he had walked briskly up to Körnerstrasse to give Paul Heinkel the damning history that Freddie Holleman's former VolksPolizei colleague had dug out on Herr Macke (burglary, aggravated assault and fraud, all unpunished thanks to a moonlight flit across the Line), and invited him to use it at his discretion. That had earned him the day's first handshake. Then, at Rathaus Schöneberg, the hand had been grasped a great deal more, and more robustly, and his back slapped heartily (almost always on that part of it comprising burnt tissue), and the reason for his face being the way it was demanded more and more loudly than was polite; but the rest had been almost pleasant. At nine-fifteen, he and thirty-four other new Representatives had lined up to swear their best efforts to uphold the constitution and ethical standards of Berlin's *Abgeordnetenhaus*, following which a welcoming breakfast, hosted by Brandt himself, greased their bellies for the coming shift at the coal-face of local government.

To his surprise, his tentatively-expressed desire to be considered for one of the Housing Committees had been heard already, and snatched at like a limb in a shark-tank. He had hardly drained the last of his coffee when a clutch of suits surrounded him in the state dining-room. The largest and sleekest of them ('call me Klaus, please, Otto') told him that there were at least two empty chairs in three of the four Committees (the fourth – a group liaising with Bonn in the forlorn hope of ever realizing the *Hauptstadt* Project for rebuilding all of central Berlin as the capital of the Federal

Republic – was, of course, much fought over as a forever-job), and that as an actual volunteer he could take his pick of one - or perhaps two? Why not all three, if he didn't mind not sleeping nights (hearty laughter, more slapping of a fragile back)?

Fischer had no intention of sipping from more than one poisoned chalice at a time, but to show willing he offered to join whichever committee most needed a new man. This started a brawl among the suits, all of whom thought that his was shouldering the greatest burden; but Klaus calmed it by suggesting that they might explain in detail each committee's remit and leave it up to their new hero to decide. Three plaintive presentations later (gratifyingly, no-one made even passing mention of drains), Fischer settled upon the Standing Committee for Non-essential Buildings, a beggars' purse body that hovered around the back of every new budget negotiation, hoping to divert funds from frivolous causes (housing, roads, sanitation) to finance the preservation and restoration of historical but unspectacular buildings standing in the way of the city's many redevelopments. It bore all the marks of a lost cause, and suited him perfectly.

Three hours later, another pleasant piece of news was delivered by Herbert Lamm. One of the representatives with whom he shared an office had lost a recount in his Borough, and if Fischer cared to move quickly he could claim squatter's rights. Within ten minutes he had met the other two members of their one-room community and passed whatever citizenship test they had set him.

'Let's have lunch!'

Lamm led them out of the Rathaus, to the fascist-owned restaurant he had praised to Fischer on their first meeting. The criminal in question was a small gentleman of courtly manners who welcomed them at the door with a fistful of menus and a half-bow before settling them at the establishment's best table. Fischer glanced around. On one wall was a framed print of Picasso's *Guernica*; the others were decorated with a selection of posters in the heroic Soviet style, proclaiming *¡No pasarán!* or exhorting the reader to greater efforts *por la Revolucion*. He turned to Lamm.

'This is a fascist?'

'Did I say that? Well, one can never tell with Spaniards.'

'Perhaps he fled Franco?'

'Possibly. But he fled to *Germany*, didn't he?'

Lamm turned and beamed at his host, who was at his elbow with a pitcher of water.

'Jorge, I hope you've held on to at least a couple of bottles of that wonderful '52 *Gran Reserva Rioja*?'

Jorge (who almost certainly had overheard something of the speculation regarding his past) returned the beam and went to excavate his cellar. Lamm leaned towards Fischer.

'It's sublime. Let me also recommend the steamed sea-bass. It won't be on the menu, but Jorge always obliges his Rathaus customers. And his *Jamon Iberico* – mmm!'

Fischer smiled and said nothing. If this was the left-wing of the SPD at the trough he wondered how Willy Brandt's faction took the edge off their appetites, absent a reliable supply of Beluga caviar from the General Staff canteen at Wünsdorf.

Jorge opened the brace of *Riojas* at an adjacent table and left them to inhale while he came to take orders. In the momentary pause as each man wondered whether to lead the pack, Fischer closed his menu and flattened the epicurean mood.

'Just the *fabado*, please.'

One of the two representatives he'd just met, a pleasant young man named Robert, shuddered slightly. 'It's made with blood sausage.'

'I like blood sausage.'

Lamm laughed. 'It's Otto's first day. He wants to be seen to be of the people. I'll have it, too, please, Jorge.'

With the fourth man, Dieter, following the consensus, Robert settled on the meatballs, an equally proletarian choice. Fischer hadn't yet checked whether a representative's remuneration included a lunch allowance; if it did, his example had probably saved West Berlin the cost of a hundred metres of dual-carriageway.

Pretensions of refined palates fell the moment the food arrived. Lamm and his colleagues paused long enough to push napkins into shirt collars and then fell upon their victuals like the guests at Breughel's *Wedding Feast*. Fischer's, halfway to his lap, was redeployed, and he made a slower start on his own stew. He felt strangely out of place - he was now one of them, yet knew nothing of what consumed their attention or schedules. They might have been bankers, or actuaries, or a gaggle of ministers on a fact-finding day-trip to Babylon for all he was able to read their moods, yet he was expected to be so thoroughly of their world that no heads would turn in his direction when the betrayals demanded of him by Moscow commenced. How did the best of traitors earn their invisibility?

By learning their trade. When the feeding frenzy had abated to something merely frantic, he cleared his throat.

'What do we all think of Khrushchev's speech?'

'Oh God!' Robert paused in his evisceration of a meatball and rolled his eyes at the ceiling. Lamm placed a hand on Fischer's and looked gravely around the table.

'We are the German Resistance!'

Everyone laughed. It was the Governing Mayor's favourite phrase these days, deployed during every speech about the city's uneasy relationship with the East - a curious choice of imagery, when one considered how *resistance* had been treated by the former German regime.

Fischer persisted. 'I mean, what do you think he intends by it? He can't believe the Americans and British will roll over, can he?'

Lamm shook his head. 'Who knows? We don't even know who he was talking *to*. Was it the Allies? His own Politburo? Us? Ulbricht? You asked the question, Otto – what do you think?'

What *Otto* thought was probably the same as anyone who had devoted more than a minute but less than three to the matter. He shrugged.

'I wonder why it happened right now. There's no particular event that's incited it – no confrontation that needs a threat, or gesture. But that's worrying in itself.'

'Is it?'

Fischer glanced around the table. 'Both the Soviet Union and the DDR are struggling economically – everyone knows that. And in the past few months several big men in Moscow have made public statements about the missile gap. Khrushchev hasn't had his feet under the table for long, so what if this is his moment to make a mark, before the West gets too far ahead to challenge?'

'You mean, it might not be a bluff?'

'Does it matter? Bluffs tend to get out of hand. How much face can he afford to lose, if the Americans tell him to fuck himself?'

Dieter, staring into the remnants of his *fabado,* nodded glumly. 'And they will. They have to. Eisenhower's made too many speeches about Berlin being the front-line for him to just pack up and pull back to Frankfurt.'

Fischer nodded. 'Yet what can the Americans do, if it isn't a bluff? West Berlin isn't defensible. If it comes to war, whoever wins – if a war *can* be won, these days – the city's going to be overrun by the Red Army, at least until there's an armistice.'

Lamm sighed. 'And who'd be first against the wall?'

Robert looked up hopefully. 'Brandt and the Senate?'

'Second, then?'

A slight pall settled over the company. Lamm turned, gestured to Jorge, pointed to the empty bottle beside him and raised two fingers. Fischer frowned.

'Should we …?'

'Probably not. I have to say, Otto, you can kill a mood better than Julius Streicher at a *bar mitzvah*.'

'I'm sorry. I thought it was something we should be considering right now.'

'Why? We can't do anything about it. Our job is to rubber-stamp decisions made by the Senate, or by the Americans and British after the Senate have rubber-stamped them in turn. The only initiative we're allowed is whether or not to order the sea-bass.' Lamm pulled a face. 'And I wish I had, now.'

A little later, the four men walked unsteadily back to Rathaus Schöneberg and squeezed into their two-desk, two-chair office. Waiting for them on one of the desks was a small pile of paperwork. Lamm groaned.

'What is it?'

'Unless I'm being a rank pessimist, it's the amended performance and indemnity provisions for the Neukölln street-lighting contract. We're voting on it tomorrow morning.'

Fischer took his copy and turned to the last page, number twenty-two. He looked up. 'If we're just rubber-stampers, do we need to read it?'

Lam shrugged. 'It's your choice; but being able to demonstrate an understanding of what's before the House is the accepted way of getting noticed. How will you be known as an up-and-comer otherwise?'

As the junior tenant of the office, Fischer assumed that he wasn't entitled to one of the chairs. He perched on the end of a desk and began to read. A few minutes later he had satisfied himself that, even allowing for too much wine with lunch, it was every bit as impenetrable a piece of writing as he had feared, and this was a partial comfort. If he was to be a bad man, he should at least suffer for it.

16

When Bolkov received a second invitation to Korotkov's office it struck him that he really didn't want to be kept in the picture.

The operation had been carried by a small Special Purposes team dressed as German workmen, and the package taken immediately to Leistikowstrasse prison. That belonged firmly in the I Don't Need to Know file, but Korotkov had given him the details anyway – a fairly obvious indication that the man wanted company for the blame if anything bad came of it. Two days had passed since then, which was ample time for information to be extracted and the package misplaced, so Bolkov had little doubt as to what the Station Resident wanted to discuss.

His heart had been further tested by Chairman Serov's telephone call from Moscow the previous evening. A man didn't need to strain to parse *utmost confidence, full support* and *absolute discretion* when the old butcher deployed them in his most comradely manner (he wore it as comfortably as a sow did a bodice). He might equally have sent a picture of an execution cell, captioned with a line of dots and a question mark. Bolkov had got, absorbed and been made thoroughly queasy by the message.

He found Korotkov poring over a piece of paper, which he assumed to be the unfortunate bastard's statement. The Resident looked up as his door closed.

'Ah. I've just received this from ...'

'Did he talk?'

'Hardly at all. And they pushed hard - the man actually died from heart failure. I've arranged for the body to go into the Spree tonight, pockets emptied. There's bruising, but nothing that can't be explained by a short voyage'

Bolkov suppressed a wince. Despite his wartime service in NKVD he had never reconciled himself to dispassionate cruelty. When the enemy was breaking through and your men's courage had crumbled, examples had to be made – that was obvious, even to a priest. But coldly putting a man to the question in the cause of an inter-service feud was far too Italian City-State for his tastes.

'No names, then?'

'Not of anyone substantive.'

'Not this fellow he use to report to? What was his ...'

'Zarubin? No. They concentrated on his chain of command but he didn't break. Towards the end he gave one name, but we don't know what it signifies.'

'Whose?'

'A German, Otto Fischer.'

'Not an uncommon name.'

'Hans Schmidt wouldn't have been more unhelpful. But think about this - our dead fellow was a local man, so if he's being used by someone in Moscow he was probably at the retail end: running informers, secret socialists, men susceptible to a promise of Soviet pensions. It's more than likely that this Fischer is also a Berliner, and active still.'

'Why do you say that?'

'In extremis, the mind involuntarily gives priority to recent memories. Perhaps Globnow was on his way to speak with this Fischer when we took him. He was moving westwards, towards the Line, so we may assume that we're looking for a *wessie.*'

'And we'll narrow down the hundreds of Otto Fischers we'll find …?'

'In the same way that we came upon Globnow – by referencing the past. Did this Fischer ever find his way into NKGB, MGB or KGB files, and why? And, most pertinently, who put him in there?'

Bolkov nodded slowly. 'Is it likely, though, that Fischer – if he is a mere street-runner – will have any idea who in Moscow is undermining KGB?'

'If he's no more than that, no.' Korotkov pulled a face. 'And if that's the case, at least we can tell the Director that we've exhausted all possible leads at the Berlin end.'

'An energetic, exhaustive failure?'

'The only acceptable sort. Serov will then have to push the thing in Moscow.'

'Of course, that may well flag his efforts to the people he's trying to pin down.'

It was probably a symptom of how Korotkov's own nerves had been shredded by this business that he entirely forgot to be discreet.

'Well, as it's him that any plan to modernize KGB most has in mind, perhaps it's time he led from the front.'

Bolkov looked out of the window, at a tree that almost touched it. For a moment the mental image of a discomfited Serov was pleasing, but then the other matter returned to give his stomach another turn.

'I spoke to my Chief this morning.'

'Yudkin? Christ! He hasn't got word of this, has he?'

'No. I mean, I don't think so. It's about Wolinski.'

'Your traitor?'

It was a not-so subtle reminder that Korotkov was on Bolkov's side for a specific reason only, and for as long as he needed to be. Otherwise, he might have claimed a share of Wolinski for Karlshorst as a whole.

'No, apparently. The investigation is complete. The story about a brother in the Americans' employ was just that, apparently, and the original accusation is now determined to be an anonymous slander, as yet untraced. I'm to expect Wolinski's return this week.'

Korotkov's mouth dropped open. He recalled himself and coughed. 'Really? There's no …?'

In both their experiences, this didn't happen. Over the Soviet decades, any number of innocents had been determined to be probably or almost definitely so, and it had hardly mattered. As with the Catholic Church, the system relied upon some future, unseeable power to correct earthly injustices and flushed its conscience accordingly. A slur might be discovered and regretted eventually; it was never simply ignored.

'I got the impression that Yudkin couldn't believe it either. What Serov thinks about it God only knows. He hasn't attempted to have the decision reviewed, though where it came from ...'

'It *had* to be the Kremlin.'

Korotkov and Bolkov stared at each other as the obvious thought occurred. They were about to welcome home to Karlshorst someone who had effectively been labelled untouchable – a relatively junior officer, moreover, around whom everyone would now need to wear ballet shoes. What that signified couldn't be determined absent further information that wouldn't ever be forthcoming, so the best option would be to get Wolinski transferred to another continent – and they couldn't do that, either.

Korotkov tapped his table. 'This arm-wrestling business in Moscow – it's just opened an office here.'

Bolkov swallowed hard. 'So if the man we've just interrogated to death *was* connected to whoever in Moscow is going up against Serov ...'

'Don't say it.'

'Fuck! Can we afford to chase this Otto Fischer?'

'What choice do we have? Should I call Chairman Serov and tell him that, having assessed the exposures, you and I will be cheering him on from the sideline?'

'Probably not, no.'

'I'll have two junior officers from First Directorate live in the file-rooms until we find or write off this Fischer. In the meantime, if you could speak to one of your contacts at Wünsdorf and have GRU do the same – make up some plausible reason for it – we'll have covered all our sources.'

'What about MfS?'

Korotkov frowned. 'I don't like to ask Germans to chase Germans – you never know how much they'll give you, even if it's for their old friend Serov. No, let's see what we have first. It might be nothing, in which case we put him from mind. If it's more than that ...'

'What?'

'We can hope that he won't be as stubborn as Globnow. Or if he is, that his heart's up to the job.'

17

Friedrich Melancthon Holleman considered his situation as a
self-incarcerating inmate of Lipaerstrasse 87 and decided that it
barely trumped his infamous attack of piles.

Two years earlier, heavy-hanging grapes had confined him to
his home for almost three weeks - an interlude that, even now,
resonated unpleasantly. The constant pain, re-invigorated by
any badly-thought-out movement, had been almost the worst of
it; but boredom, his darling wife Kristin's startling lack of
empathy and the easy assumption by colleagues at Trier Police
Praesidium that he could function professionally from a prone,
belly-down position on the sitting-room carpet had nosed ahead
of the actual agony to take the Turd Trophy. He didn't like
pain, but he detested being rolled over.

At least *this* had been his idea, if not quite his best. In a perfect,
Freddie-friendly world, his dear friend Otto would have
welcomed him, poured a beer and succumbed to the first
enquiry as to why the fucking fuck he was entering Politics. It
wasn't, though, and he hadn't. In other circumstances it might
not have mattered; pressure could then have been applied
during every waking minute until resistance crumbled or a
crack of sufficient width opened to allow the clues to tumble
out. Every waking minute wasn't available, though. This was
Berlin, where Otto Fischer could come and go as he pleased but
the handsome Holleman face couldn't be seen abroad (it being
the unfinished business of VolksPolizei, *Stasi* and at least two
retired Interior Ministers, all of whom probably still scanned
reports daily in the hope that a tall, one-legged former
Inspecteur had wandered within cacking distance).

The same had almost certainly occurred to Otto, who seemed to be taking heavy advantage of Outdoors. This morning's excuse had been his required attendance at the *Abgeordnetenhaus*, which, though fairly convincing, left Holleman with another stretch of hours in the company of Frau Benner and nothing to do except stare at another wall or transform it from its dungeoned *chic*. He preferred to be busy, but the lady had made it clear that she didn't like teal blue, so further efforts in that direction might incline her to interfere horribly with his lunch.

He picked up a newspaper and read it for a while, but he'd been too long out of the city to be interested in its small-talk and occasional corpse. The Khrushchev business was big news, obviously, and much-covered; but as the man's motives were unknown every word was necessarily speculation, if not a coin flipped. Holleman was perfectly capable of forming his own, wild opinions; in any case, as a former SED politician he was perfectly aware that even the Party faithful were rarely informed of reasons for policy swerves.

The newspaper went back into its little rack (a bespoke domestic device, made of rustically-fashioned wood – that at least amused him for half a minute), and he glanced around for further distraction. He couldn't call home (Kristin would scold him for piling on Otto's 'phone bill) or work (he'd have to explain why he was interrupting his alleged holiday on the Danube), and the few friends he'd made in Trier would wonder why a sober Freddie Holleman was in the mood for a conversation, and during daylight at that.

His only other immediate recourse was Frau Benner, but attempting to engage her in conversation was breath wasted. He suspected that he'd been over-excited when first he arrived (not having seen his best friend for more than five years), and his language - never too carefully regulated – may have been more suitable to a parade-ground than suburbia. That sort of mistake couldn't be walked back, not with an elderly woman of genteel manners. She was making a point of avoiding him, and Lipaerstrasse 87 had enough rooms to make the task easy.

The nearest wall offered no better suggestions. What did Otto do with his empty time? He listened to his gramophone, probably, and read books. He definitely thought a lot – when nothing pended on his schedule he could stare at a blank surface and lose himself for an hour or more while his head wrapped itself around something. To Holleman, a brain was like an elbow – very useful for certain things but not to be sprained by over-exercise. As for reading and music, they were the toys of folk whose wife didn't have a list of outstanding jobs for when they returned home in the evenings. He had little experience of that particular vacuum.

Oh, for God's sake. He told himself that he was a detective, so what was wrong with detection? The mystery of Otto Fischer and political office would certainly be resolved by a successful interrogation; but failing that, what about the paper-trail?

With as much stealth as his tin leg allowed, he tip-toed to the kitchen and reassured himself that Frau Benner was fully occupied with the household laundry. Then, he retreated to the fancy dining room – where, presumably, the late Herr Grabner had entertained guests whose status made the standard, everyday dining room an insulting prospect. In one of its dark corners he had noticed a roll-top bureau, and he would have wagered his last month's salary on it not being locked.

A quick tug on its lower edge confirmed his mistake. He breathed hard and reminded himself that this was Otto Fischer's workplace, so how hard could it be? A small metal replica of a JU88 sat on the flat rear top; he lifted it and found nothing beneath. In the left-hand of two drawers immediately beneath the roll-top, a mass of rubber bands, paper-clips and assorted half-chewed pencils discouraged closer examination. Its twin was empty except for a small key.

Cock.

One pile of papers, tucked into the roll-top's corner, was neatly stacked. Holleman glanced at it, satisfied himself that this was Otto's soon-to-be monumental operational history of the *Fallschirmjäger*, and put it from mind. The rest was ordered to some form of chaos protocol, threatening an avalanche on to the floor of the dining room. He pushed that useful elbow against them and pulled out enough of the excess, one handful at a time, to ease the pressure. A 1904 copy of the Imperial Board of Health's *Hygiene and Sanitation*, propped at an angle, relieved the elbow and allowed him to examine his haul.

Most of it seemed to be shit-pipe related, a legacy of Otto's time as Drains Führer for the local SPD branch. On several occasions during his pre-war career as an *OrPo* street-pounder, Holleman had chased felons down into and through Berlin's sewers, and a couple of the diagrams stirred nostalgic recollections of a time when paperwork had been a negligible burden. As he read, it occurred to him that this had been a *real* job, political but worthwhile; yet Otto had dropped drains and then the refugees business to become a nodding-head in the *Abgeordnetenhaus*, where dictats were debated as if anything might be done about them. Looking back at his own time as an SED deputy, Holleman could reassure himself that at least the DDR made a proper, bare-faced pretence of democracy, rather than this shameful pretence of a pretence.

A deeper rummage excavated more recent correspondence regarding Otto's selection as a representative, which made him pause. It should have been at the top of the pile, not in its recesses, so it had been pushed deliberately where it was harder to find - to hide it from prying eyes, or a tender conscience?

One item in particular caught his attention. It was a brief, congratulatory note from the local Party, dated a few months earlier, informing Otto that he had been recommended for one of the allocation seats, should the SPD increase its proportion of the overall vote at the next House elections. Holleman was no expert on West Berlin politics, but it struck him that a seat a man wasn't required to fight for on the streets was probably much coveted. How did someone get thrust to the front of what must have been a very long queue, and whose hands did the thrusting? Otto had *no* connections, much less the right ones, unless …

Holleman wondered if he had been thinking this through from the wrong end. What if Otto's ambitions to be a politico were someone else's? And if they were, why Otto? Who would want to plant an arse in the *Abgeordnetenhaus* that wasn't his own, and do it in such a way that removed any risk of failure in the voting booth? Everyone knew that the SPD was going to increase its share of the vote this time – hell, the news had even carried as far as Trier (a town that cared only about what was going on in the Moselle region), so the clamour for the extra seats must have been immense. Who would put Otto Fischer in one of them?

Someone with a great deal of influence, obviously. He wondered for a moment if the culprit might be the *Bundesnachrichtendienst,* but that thought almost raised a laugh. Its name had changed but the organization was run still by Reinhard Gehlen, and the only post he might have considered for Otto was one at which rifles were pointing. In any case, why would the Federal Intelligence Agency plant a man in a friendly parliament? And if it *could* conceive of a reason that escaped Holleman, surely an important body like

Berlin's Senate would have been targeted, rather than the toothless *Abgeordnetenhaus*?

No, that was a mad idea. Nevertheless, Holleman couldn't help but entertain a vision of General Gehlen, his teeth gritted tightly, welcoming Otto back to the Org with a handshake. It was one that a man could die or get drunk happily with, and it took the edge off his boredom for a few minutes. He wasted a few more after the postman delivered his letters, checking the franks and postmarks carefully for clues. At eleven o'clock, Frau Benner brought him a coffee and a slice of *honigkuchen*, frowned at the mess he'd made of the bureau but retreated without a word. He had just finished his cake and was picking a fragment of almond from his teeth when another thought came to him, and killed his appetite.

What if, as Holleman came west, Otto had gone the other way? *That* was mad, too - but Christ, how many Germans were something other than what they seemed? It was an open secret that *Stasi* had used the westward exodus of their people to massively infiltrate the Federal Republic with undercover operatives, taking the only advantage that humiliating circumstances offered. What if they'd also reached out to clasp the collars of westerners they knew already? Otto had spent three years in Sachsenhausen, a guest of MVD, and his release, secured by Holleman when the Soviets handed over the camps to the fledgling DDR, had used up any goodwill he'd had in the new Interior Ministry. Could they be calling in their chits?

He wished now that he hadn't eaten that slice of *honigkuchen*. It was an awful thought, yet how better to explain why a man who had never shown the least inclination to trust *any* politician should now, apparently, want to climb into the sty? He wasn't doing it for the salary, didn't care two pfennigs for his standing in Lichterfelde's society, and if he was serious about wanting to make some sort of contribution (Holleman didn't believe it for a moment), why didn't he donate money or time to the Inner Mission, or a stray dogs' home?

This would need to be chased carefully. If Otto got a scent of what Holleman suspected he would close up more quickly than a startled hedgehog. It had to be circled, crept up upon, kept upwind of the slightest suspicion until a weight of evidence made denial impossible. Then, they could both make a start on what to do about it. It wasn't as though they hadn't faced this ...

The front door slammed, and West Berlin's newest time-server stepped into the fancy dining-room, regarded the mess spread widely across the polished floor, and sighed.

'Freddie ...'

'Never mind that. Otto, are you spying for *Stasi*?'

18

'Where the hell is Globnow?'

Assuming that he wasn't being asked, Levin said nothing as he placed three reports on Zarubin's desk. The General had a strange temper – it never quite touched the extremities either way, but a sensible man didn't test his luck at times when normally reliable things moved in unpredictable patterns.

'Is he sick? Taken a holiday, perhaps, and forgot to tell me?'

This was something Levin could comment upon, and he did so carefully.

'I told you I spoke to his factory. If it's a holiday they'd know - and if he was sick also. He hasn't contacted them.'

'It's been more than thirty-six hours since he was due to brief Fischer. When I told him that I wanted confirmation and details of their meeting, did he misunderstand?'

It wasn't like Zarubin to ignore even subtle implications. If Globnow hadn't been to work, and hadn't explained himself to to his employers, then …

The General had picked up the first report, read its title and dropped it in disgust. 'An accident, then. Get a list of Berlin hospitals, east and ...'

'I'm arranging it.'

'And ...'

'I'm checked the mortuaries also.'

'Perhaps he's defected.'

'A man who doesn't believe in *anything*? Who can't be blackmailed or threatened?'

It was difficult for Zarubin to remain angry. There wasn't another secretary in the entire Kremlin who could think three correct moves ahead they way that Levin did on his bad days. He sighed and deflated slightly.

'If he hasn't spoken to Fischer, he probably hasn't told Sparrow to ease the way for him. Shit!'

Sparrow was the code-name of their man at Rathaus Schöneberg, a German national who had scraped a living in the immediate aftermath of the war by betraying his American-financed countrymen to the Soviets and the communists to Gehlen. Being under suspended sentence of death just about everywhere, his MGB files had been destroyed by Zarubin in the confusion of the organization's transmutation to KGB and the man himself snatched up as the perfect long-term sleeper – so perfect that his real name was hardly ever uttered, lest some malign conjunction of currents allowed it to catch in the wind and carry a thousand kilometres westwards to where it might cause damage.

'And Globnow was going to brief Wolinski, too. It seems to me that ...'

'Be careful, Levin.'

'You rely too much upon the one man. What about the others? You have, what, five ferrets in Berlin?'

'Other than Sparrow I trust only Globnow to be discreet.'

'The others wouldn't be?'

'None of them would *willingly* disclose information.'

'Ah..'

'Blast!' Zarubin clutched both sides of his desk and breathed hard. Levin was right, obviously. To have every aspect of his Berlin manoeuvres in the hands of just one man was almost to invite an enemy to take the single shot. In hindsight, Fischer should have been reeled fully into the net several years ago. Like Globnow, he was as reliable as rain in Spring, a man lacking any ties of loyalty or belonging - an intelligencer's tabula rasa, ready for any purpose to which he might be committed. Zarubin knew that he had been indulgent, or weak, allowing a mild feeling for the man to put off the moment – which was something of an irony, give his plans for him.

There was a schedule and it couldn't be stretched; but unless Globnow resurfaced Zarubin didn't have the means to implement it. If Fischer had been activated he could have briefed Wolinski, or vice versa; as it was, Berlin was presently hosting a tiny colony of blind operatives-in-waiting, none of whom had any idea of what came next.

'Could *you* go back to Berlin?'

'No, Levin, I could not. My recent visit was too much like rubbing the wolf's nose in the dust and then presenting my bare arse. I got away with it, and don't intend to push my luck further. However, I believe that you have excellent German?'

'It's … you're not serious, Comrade General?'

'Why not? You understand every detail of what needs to be done. You aren't known in the city, not even by KGB, so you can visit Globnow's home and workplace without making eyes turn. If anyone asks the question, you're an old friend – from what's now Kaliningrad but wasn't then, which would explain the faint accent. Don't worry, your identity papers will be excellent.'

'But I'm not a ...'

'Spy? Who is, by trade? It's an accidental profession, much stumbled into. You're certainly better prepared than any of the poor devils we recruit, so you'll be able to discharge this simple task with ease and confidence. Find Globnow. If that isn't possible, contact Sparrow and tell him to proceed. Then, give Otto Fischer his instructions, and while you're at the gallop still, arrange to meet Wolinski at one of our safe-houses and explain precisely what's expected of someone we've managed to raise like Lazarus. With proper planning, you can be in and out of Berlin in twenty-four hours – thirty-six, at most.'

For a few moments, Levin struggled with one or more of his emotions, steadying himself against the desk and clearing his throat. Zarubin kept his own face blank. Though this was the only perfectly shining moment in an otherwise filthy day he didn't want to give the impression that he wasn't being serious - he was, entirely so, and now that his thinking had followed the thought he couldn't think why he hadn't thought of it before now. Levin was almost genetically suited to the task - he was forgettable, naturally devious, a man who could walk across a high-wire and no-one he passed along the way would recall it. Even his lameness would be an asset in a nation where able-bodied men of a certain age were in a minority. He would be a herd animal, indistinguishable in the press.

'I wouldn't be much use in a fight.'

Briefly, Levin looked so pitifully hopeful that Zarubin almost didn't enjoy snatching away the rug.

'A fight? Dear me, Boris Petrovich, what an imagination you have. If Gehlen's people find you they'll arrive as a small mob, so your martial abilities won't be an issue. Or they may employ a sniper to shoot you at a decent distance, in which case ditto. Espionage is the art – if it *is* an art – of passing unseen in enemy territory to best effect. A fight is the last thing you should be looking for.'

This clarification was only half-delivered when Levin's shoulders slumped. As a career paper-processor he must have expected to risk bad (or, rather, worse) posture and the occasional tiny but exquisitely painful wound to a fingertip. A clandestine trip to Berlin held out a promise of something more, however. It wasn't that he was a coward, or even a stranger to parlous dangers. He had served with Ist Guards Tank Army during the war, but the sound of gunfire hadn't overly disturbed his sleep until the final days, when Colonel-General Katukov had moved his Headquarters (in which Levin heroically shuffled requisitions, orders and the plaintive requests of front-line troops to be allowed to use their initiative) to the south bank of the Teltow Canal. A return to the scene of his epic final victory, even in these happier times, was a pleasure he would have wished postponed indefinitely.

'When shall I leave, Comrade General?'

'Speak to our man at Khodynka aerodrome. If he can manage to arrange a flight quickly, go this afternoon. If not, evening will have to do. Take some American currency from the cashbox for a hotel tonight - but please, nothing five-star.'

19

Scanning the list of West Berlin's historic buildings under threat of demolition or radical alteration, Fischer couldn't but think that the RAF, USAAF and various Red Army artillery units might have tried a little harder.

He hadn't witnessed the city's final days of war, nor its first year in what had whimsically been labeled peace; but as late as the early 1950s, a tour of Mitte and Berlin's former industrialized areas had given a strong impression of annihilation – of a place wiped entirely clean of its awkward past.

The worst will in the world could only do so much, however. Within (and considerably beyond) the area formerly enclosed by the Customs Walls, hardly any venerable structure had escaped heavy damage; yet well-built stone architecture was stubborn when bombed or shelled, and a great deal of persistence was required to erase it entirely. Not every old building in Berlin was a skeleton, and not every skeleton was beyond hope of resurrection.

What spite hadn't destroyed, however, town planners were perfectly capable of expunging. Blending old and new successfully was difficult enough without awkward history, tight budgets, foreshortened schedules and architects' egos conspiring to confound the attempt. Fischer had the district of Hansaviertel (though he wished he hadn't) as a perfect prior example of how bulldozers could clear priorities as easily as rubble. It was his job now to lie in front of them, to give second thoughts a chance.

The Standing Committee for Non-essential Buildings' jurisdiction was all of West Berlin, but his eye was caught by the threatened buildings close to his adopted *heimat*. Given that Steglitz and Lichterfelde were dragged into Berlin only within living memory, there was not a great deal of major historical heritage to fret about, but more modest tokens of past times were plentiful. Minor churches, charity schools, redundant graveyards and fine but outdated Second-Empire shopping facilities lay too often in the path of plans for something more necessary to the modern age. Nostalgia wasn't sufficient to protect them, so if nothing else it was the task of the Committee to remind Berliners of what they had before it was gone.

A thick finger disturbed his right-side vision and tapped the list.

'They're never going to tear down the *Matthäuskirche*, surely?'

'*They* might not need to, Freddie. The renovation budget's almost gone, and the Diocese can't afford to make up the shortfall, apparently. If it's decommissioned, who knows what will happen?'

'Tsk. That's a shame.'

'When were you ever in a church?'

'Plenty of times, when I couldn't avoid it. Can you help them?'

'It probably doesn't fall under our remit. The list is meant to be comprehensive; many of the buildings are the responsibility of their owner-organizations, not the City Government.'

'What's your budget?'

Surprised, Fischer looked up. 'We don't have one.'

Holleman scratched his cheek. 'So, your job is to make it look like Willy Brandt thought seriously about each case before saying No.'

'Very possibly. Why are you hovering, Freddie?

'Are we going to eat soon? I'm hungrier than a kitten.'

In the twenty-four hours since dropping his explosive question, Holleman hadn't returned to the matter of political motives. A mere *don't be absurd, Freddie* had done the trick, apparently, but Fischer wasn't fooled for a moment. This was the wrestler stepping back slightly, biding his time, manoeuvring, looking for the next opportunity. Fortunately, the pregnant question had been directed at the burned, right-side of Fischer's face, so his shock hadn't been too obvious, but the very near-miss had thrown him badly. Spying for *Stasi* – it was actually *more* plausible than the truth. If State Security ever discovered that Moscow was running a man in the *Abgeordnetenhaus* without notifying their German cousins (much less sharing his intelligence), they'd howl to the rafters of Ruschestrasse 103 and demand that the body and the paperwork be handed over immediately. It was *their* job to run their compatriots in West Berlin and the Federal Republic; *their* business to throw a rock into near-capitalism's machinery. If Fischer understood one thing about espionage agencies, it was their rabid territoriality.

The thought had made him shudder. Ruschestrasse's howl would be directed at Karlshorst, where hands would be thrown up and everything denied (truthfully). Then, *Stasi* and KGB would link arms and go looking for the cuckoo in their collective nest, and unless General Zarubin was more quick-witted even than he believed, his remaining fingernails and most of his teeth might be heading for an interrogation room floor. As for what his hapless foot-soldier would lose …

What the hell was Zarubin's game? He'd admitted to not being KGB these days – or at least to sitting across the table's long side from whoever ran the Lubyanka – so whatever he was planning was bound to crash through someone else's playground, and for what great prize? He was about to employ a man who knew nothing about subterfuge, to infiltrate the least important instrument of government in Berlin, and to what possible end? To secure advanced warning of where traffic-cones would be deployed at vital road junctions? To give Moscow the nudge regarding changes to how local business rates were calculated?

And what the double-hell was he waiting for? It was now almost a week since the elections had raised Fischer to the faint Purple, yet his messenger Globnow – who had been a regular visitor to Lichterfelde when he had precisely no instructions to give – was missing in inaction. It was as if Zarubin assumed that the city's administration could be paused while he made a careful decision about where to place Otto Henry Fischer within it.

The finger tapped the paper once more. 'Oh, look! Not the old *Salomon Freischule* on Augsburgerstrasse, surely?'

It hadn't been that since 1934, obviously. A Jewish presence in such a genteel district had been particularly offensive to the National Socialists, so the Christ-murderers had been expelled, the place disinfected and gentile pupils invited to take their place. After that, war damage had left the modest little building in permanent danger of town planners or a gentle north wind - Fischer was mildly surprised that it had survived this long, and more so by the slight flattening of Holleman's pronunciation, as if he were trying to honour its older purpose. He wasn't usually sensitive to other cultures.

'I didn't know you knew it, Freddie. Were you ever on the beat south of Tiergarten?'

'Nah. My aunt Rachel was a pupil there, before the First War.'

'Your au … ' Fischer gaped at his friend. 'You're *Jewish*?'

For a moment, Holleman stared at him, saying nothing. Then he climbed clumsily to his feet, unfastened his trousers and removed an object. He looked down at it, fondly.

'I owe it to Mother. She and God fell out after Uncle Joachim died at Agadir, so I didn't go through the usual.'

Even distracted by the startling revelation of Holleman's secret history and perfectly *goy* cock, staring him in the eye from less than a metre away, Fischer was struck by a jarring, lateral thought.

'There was no fighting at Agadir.'

'Joachim was a rating, on *SMS Panther*. He went over the side while she was in harbour there - pissed, probably. They never found the body.'

'Right. And you survived the Third Reich … how?'

Carefully, Holleman tucked away his closest unmutilated friend. 'It helped that Mum had married out of the Faith, and that Dad's family was so enthusiastically Lutheran as to lumber its sons with *Melancthon*. And that their first house burned down in 1911, of course.'

'With her papers?'

'Yeah. Until he was convicted, Dad was in the duty-free cigarette business. He happened to know a good papers-man who could give her a new, not-very-Jewish birth certificate.'

'Why, though?'

'Berlin wasn't the best place to be a Jew even back then, with the DSP and such like ranting on. In any case, Mum had been shunned by her folk for not having me snipped, so it seemed the sensible way to go. Her family name – Birnbaum – became Bauman, and after we moved to Moabit to be closer to Dad she made a point of dragging me to the Johanniskirche every Sunday. To our neighbours, we were as Christian as communion wafers.'

For more than half a century, Friedrich Melancthon Holleman had gulled the German nation. Whether as school dunce, *OrPo* street-pounder, fighter-pilot, Lie Division dissembler, senior VolksPolizei officer, Communist politician or, latterly, a medium-ranking officer at Trier Police Praesidium, he had somehow managed to make his comrades, friends, work colleagues and the occasional genocidal Regime look the other way on the matter of his being a member of the Twelve Tribes. For a moment, Fischer wondered how it could be done, but then the obvious fact of Freddie Holleman asserted itself. To be Jewish, you needed to *be* Jewish. Not only did he fail to display the merest symptom of the condition, he did so brashly and with particular care to draw attention to himself. How likely was it, that the loudest and foulest presence in any room could ever be suspected of the sin of discretion?

'Does Kristin know? Your kids?'

'No! Her parents hated Jews – hell, they hated everyone – so I didn't try to make a hard job any harder. Besides, by the time we got hitched it wasn't something sensible to mention.'

'You never mentioned it to *me*, Freddie!'

Holleman shrugged. 'Why would I? It's not important.'

'You don't feel even a *little* Jewish?'

'As much as I do Protestant. *Can* we eat, Otto? I'm starving.'

During lunch, Fischer tried to keep his mind on what he knew of the city's planning processes (which was very little, though more than a week earlier), but Holleman's casual revelation wouldn't get out of the way. He picked at pork knuckle and watched his friend noisily devour his own portion - which added to an unreasonable sense of outrage – while wondering how someone with even a tenuous link to the home side could shrug off such a historic hammering. But then, a lifetime spent denying something had to warp any …

'Herr Fischer.'

He almost dropped his fork. Three thoughts occurred almost simultaneously: that it hadn't been a question; that Frau Benner had gone home more than ten minutes earlier after serving up their lunch: and that the front door had a mortice lock with no external handle.

The threat wasn't immediately apparent. It came as a slightly-built fellow, about fifty years old, who favoured one side of his body more noticeably than Holleman did his half-missing leg. He looked more nervous than a house-breaker should, though when he noticed the other person at the table he started and then brightened.

'Friedrich Holleman! How very … odd.'

The accent was slight but allowed Fischer to placed it well east of the Vistula. He was still struggling to find an appropriate form of words when Holleman cut through the awkward pause.

'Who the full, ripe fuck are you?'

'Levin. May I sit, please?'

The gentleman obliged himself without waiting for a reply, lifted a small briefcase onto the table and removed a sheath of papers. Thoroughly disoriented, Fischer watched but said nothing. Holleman glared suspiciously at the newcomer, who, looking up and noticing it, smiled pleasantly.

'I've never been to Trier, but being a student of early church architecture I've read a great deal about the Cathedral and Constantine's Basilica. You must be enjoying your exile there.'

'How do you know about that?'

'General Zarubin must have mentioned it.'

Fischer and Holleman almost left their respective chairs, though Levin continued as if the pin was in the grenade still.

'Given Herr Holleman's situation, I assume that I don't need to be discreet? You've told him about our arrangement?'

'Situation? Arrangement?'

Holleman wasn't the prettiest species of parrot, but Fischer was grateful to be allowed a further few moments' frantic thinking-time. Why was this man doing Globnow's job? What was Freddie going to say – do – when he realized what this was about? And what sort of potential suicide plot did those papers contain?

'*What?*'

He'd missed the start of the explanation, but Holleman's furious gaze was passing between the two men. Fischer couldn't think why he looked so shocked – he'd half-guessed the truth already. It couldn't be outraged at the thing itself, not from a man who'd happily served both the East German State and Zarubin for a number of years.

'Why didn't you *tell* me?'

Pique, then, because a confidence hadn't been shared. Fischer shrugged. At least he could be honest on that point.

'Why? I didn't want to *think* about it, even. What use would it have served, any more than you telling me that you were one of the Chosen People?'

'At least ...' Holleman paused. It was a difficult question, give that his only advice would have been *run* - something that, presumably, had occurred to his friend already. He shook his head.

'*Why*, then, you *muschi*?'

Levin (whose gaze had been following the dialogue) coughed gently and interrupted.

'There was a degree of duress. It was made clear that Herr Fischer's closest friend – a man whom General Zarubin himself had once trusted, but who had fled traitorously to the West – was not entirely safe, even now; that *Stasi* might discover his real name, and come looking.'

'*Zarubin* fled to the West – and as far as fucking America!'

'Ah yes, but he returned. You haven't – yet.'

Levin was treated to another Holleman glare, but Fischer was almost grateful. It was a lie, of course – nothing had been said to him about consequences, because Zarubin had known his man – but even a professional shrew like Freddie Holleman could hardly damn him for being altruistic.

The Russian pushed the sheath of papers across the table. 'You'll need to make yourself familiar with this.'

'What is it?'

'A briefing paper, on the Politburo's thinking about Berlin and its future relationship with the Federal Republic.'

'Is it accurate?'

'Who knows, when they don't know themselves? It was drafted by the General, so it's at least plausible.'

'And why does it need to be?'

'To convince Mayor Brandt's office that you're an expert on Kremlin affairs.'

'But ...'

Levin interrupted whatever Fischer hadn't yet thought to say on the matter. 'You need to move quickly. Brandt's in Paris at the moment, speaking to NATO foreign ministers about the crisis. He'll be back the day after tomorrow, by which time you'll have met a gentleman from his office. Don't worry, he's one of ours, so your introduction will be a favourable one. You're going to become indispensable to the Mayor, and at short notice.'

'How short?'

'He's going to Strasbourg next month, to speak to the European Parliament. You'll either be accompanying him or contributing to the speech he'll deliver there. After *that*, in February, he's embarking upon a world tour, to rouse all of humankind on behalf of plucky little West Berlin.' Levin smiled broadly. 'If you make an impression you might get to see places, Herr Fischer.'

Fischer gaped at Freddie Holleman (who appeared both to be angry and smothering a laugh) and then at Levin. 'I don't know the first thing about the Kremlin!'

'I must contradict you. You worked for Luftwaffe Intelligence *Ost* durng the war, yes?'

'Yes, but ...'

'And then served briefly with the Gehlen Org?'

'That was ...'

'And then, between 1947 and 1950 you studied Soviet Politics at the University of Bern.'

'Wha ... I was a prisoner, in Sachsenhausen!'

'And therefore entirely untraceable. Here ...'

'What is it?'

'Your degree certificate, your expired passport - with Swiss stamps - and a list of your professors, which you should memorize. Again, you needn't worry. All but one of them are dead; the exception is presently working in Moscow. Your name, details and attendance record are of course on file at the University's registration office.'

Fischer picked up the certificate (which appeared to his untrained eye to be the genuine article) and stared at it. 'How do I explain almost seven years spent subsequently as a time-piece repairer? I was in the Berlin business directory, so you can't wipe ...'

From Levin's briefcase came a weighty, bound mass of paper, which landed on top of the distressed passport.

'You've been writing this all the while – possibly the definitive study of Stalin, from the purges to the end of the Great Patriotic War. It's a donation, from someone who was discovered writing it and therefore has no use for stuff anymore. We've had it translated into German, and then typed up, badly. You'll probably want to familiarize yourself with your work - though I have to say, it's somewhat dense.'

'It's ...' *not feasible.* Fischer's mind grabbed at a dozen fleeting possibilities, all of which could rip off his cover faster than a bridegroom's socks. How many people would he meet who had infinitely more understanding of Soviet politics than him? How would he argue a challenged briefing? What if he bumped into someone who'd actually *been* to Bern and wanted to talk about the good old university days? And why would any of Brandt's people accept his credentials without making a stab at digging out the past?

Herr Levin had already displayed symptoms of competence. To that he now added clairvoyance.

'I know, you don't think you can convince people; but you'd be astonished at how readily a first impression can cement an opinion. Our very brief acquaintance has allowed me to decide that you are a serious, thoughtful man, and they, too, will conclude this. Being sensitive to one particular aspect of the past, they will examine what survives of your military records and see that you fought well and honourably, and that were awarded the Knight's Cross, an uncommon achievement. Most pertinently, they will see your face and wonder how it is that a man so afflicted didn't just give up and die. Brandt himself has a particular weakness for heroes, given that he fled the Nazis and spent the war in comfortable exile. All of these things will persuade. Politics is a performing art, and you have the necessary props in place, even before the matter of your expertise is considered.'

Aghast, Fischer deployed his final, weak thrust. 'But I've already joined a committee ...'

'Ah, yes, our man in Brandt's office was told to keep his eye on appointments. You can continue with it, if you wish – it isn't as though you'll be *doing* anything there. Please attend the Rathaus tomorrow. The man's name is Brecker – Othmar Brecker. He'll brief you on what Brandt likes to hear from his new boys.'

That was it, then. Fischer had expected to be pushed, squeezed, used up and discarded callously, but none of it prominently. Had he thought about it, the prospect of his treasons being relatively anonymous would have been a mild comfort – a chance to avoid having his sins eternally recorded upon on a headstone, or in the newspapers. But as an aide to West Berlin's Governing Mayor, a man who was rising to national prominence as the face of German resistance to Soviet ambitions, the most anonymity he could hope for when it all came out would be a quiet head-shot in a convenient forest. He glanced down at his homework, at Holleman's still-stunned face, and finally at Levin.

'May I ask one thing?'

'Of course.'

'What's the *purpose* of all this?'

Levin frowned severely. 'Really, Herr Fischer. As a paratrooper, were you in the habit of demanding to know why you were being tossed out of a 'plane?'

20

Bolkov listened to what Korotkov's files had on one Otto Fischer and then asked the obvious, if forlorn, question.

'Are you certain he isn't *Stasi*'s?'

He was aware that there was a plaintive edge to his voice, but he was beginning to hope intensely that this would turn out to be one of the anxiety attacks that struck periodically at every intelligence agency. A dying man had uttered a name – was it important? It might have been that of his dentist, the failing brain recalling an appointment that couldn't now be cancelled, or the fact that the man had bedded his wife. It didn't have to be what they feared it was.

The Station Resident shook his head. 'They were able to tell us very little about the man – merely that someone of that name was released from Sachsenhausen in 1950 – which, of course, we can corroborate. It's a common name, but there's mention of facial mutilation in our files, and the gentleman of the same name who was recently elected to the *Abgeordnetenhaus* is certainly blessed in that regard.'

'Why was he in a Special Camp?'

'The record doesn't specify.'

Bolkov winced. 'That shouldn't be possible.'

Like their Cheka, OGPU and NKVD predecessors, MVD had kept copious and precise paperwork on the wretches they processed. Sachsenhausen – MVD Special Camp no. 1 - had been a holding facility for those members of the National Socialist regime whose crimes hadn't warranted a show trial but who had earned more than a smack to the head and a warning to behave next time. Typically, they had been military types of sufficient rank to be guilty of *something* (even if a decision couldn't be made upon what, exactly) or politicals with low Party numbers, leavened by a mass of unfortunates who fell imprecisely between two or more degrees of culpability. Most had been dragged off to camps in Siberia, released or transferred to German prisons when the newly-formed DDR took over the Special Camps; a few had been tried very publicly and then executed to prove the anti-Nazi credentials of the successor state. All, whatever their offences, had been attached to extensive stationery recording the same.

Korotkov shook his head. 'I know, but it doesn't. There's a note to the effect that Fischer was interviewed – twice – by the Commandant, but the transcript of their conversations either wasn't set down or has since been extracted.'

'Twice? Personally?'

'The man was curious, obviously. About what, I can't say.'

'Who was he?'

'Vaisman, Kyril Ivanovitch, Colonel of MVD.'

'I don't know him.'

'Nor me. He died of lung cancer, six years ago, so we can't ask him the question.'

'Does it give the date of Fischer's release?'

Korotkov consulted the file. '10 January.'

Bolkov started. 'That was … four days after we handed over the camps to the Germans. How the hell did he get sprung so quickly?'

'He had allies, obviously.'

'Are you *sure* he's not *Stasi*? Now or formerly? They'd tell us, wouldn't they?'

'I can't think of a reason why they wouldn't.'

'No.'

Both men devoted a little time to examining the walls of Korotkov's office. If Fischer was being run by CIA, SIS, SDECE or BND, he was in the wrong place, doing the wrong things. If he was an agent of friends other than *Stasi* – SB or StB were the likeliest suspects – they would have volunteered the information already and offered to share anything valuable (hoping for a quid pro quo from the infinitely better-resourced KGB). What remained was either a matter of no, or infinite, concern.

Bolkov broke the silence. 'It's circular. Globnow gave us nothing before he died other than Fischer's name. We assume the latter is a player only because we assumed the same of Globnow.'

'But Globnow is – or was – associated with General Zarubin, whom Director Serov has identified as a person of interest. If he's correct ...'

'He may not be. Serov doesn't dance around a thing he's convinced of - he crushes it.'

'True, but we can't press Globnow further on the matter. The few things we know about Fischer throw up questions, rather than bed them down.'

Bolkov nodded slowly. As winsome as the Soviet system could be, it didn't usually incarcerate a man for no reason – bad or erroneous ones, certainly, but not for the crime of wilful innocence. And having put him away, it didn't then take care to erase the cause. If an egregious mistake had been made and realised subsequently, Herr Fischer would have been one of the first inmates of Sachsenhausen to be loaded on to an east-bound train when jurisdiction was transferred to the DDR (because errors were never, ever admitted, even to allies). Yet not only had MVD washed their hands of the man, State Security had then released him as soon as the paperwork could be drafted and signed. Since then, almost nine years had passed – about and during which they knew only that Fischer had lived either as an innocent man or a very careful sleeper.

Korotkov sat up. 'We can't just snatch him – as a new House Representative he's too visible. But we need to be certain.'

'You're going to put eyes on him?'

'A team of eyes. I want continuous surveillance until we can be absolutely certain that he's nothing more than he seems.'

'And if he is?'

'We refer it to Serov. *He* can make the decision.'

It was the first thing Bolkov had heard with which could heartily agree. The Director was a hard bastard with failure, but even he didn't move against men who'd merely enforced his orders. In the meantime, they'd be moving as decisively as the situation permitted, which was the most that …

He paused, thought it through briefly and smiled at Korotkov. 'I've just had a pleasing notion.'

'Really? I'd be delighted to hear *something* pleasant.'

'We've been wondering what to do with our traitor-who-isn't-a-traitor.'

'Wolinski? Hadn't you decided upon death by back office?'

'I had, but it looks too much like what it is – us running scared of something we don't understand. Wolinski has good form with surveillance – though of suspected Red Army personnel, usually. I would have thought that tracking a German civilian would be straightforward by comparison.'

'And with Wolinski in the field-team, we can …?'

'Maintain our own surveillance, without suspicion of doing so from whoever in Moscow is Wolinski's particular friend. I imagine that Director Serov would approve the initiative – hell, he'd shake our hands, if it were possible.'

Korotkov took a great deal more time thinking it through, but eventually he nodded. 'And if it turns out that our two problems are related, we've at least put the one where it might expose – or be exposed by - the other.'

'In either case, who could complain that procedures hadn't been followed correctly?'

'Or proper diligence displayed?' Korotkov smiled and held out his hand, and Bolkov took it (though he hated and feared the man). For once, their interests were moving in the same direction. They had insulated themselves against a search for scapegoats, should Serov's modernizing enemies in Moscow gain the upper hand – and, without giving a hint of his true motives, Bolkov had pre-empted Korotkov's use of Wolinski as a weapon to discredit him and his Section. It was the best morning's work he could recall, and if his sense of being caught between the Cyanean Rocks persisted, at least he'd managed to raise sails without the mast going overboard.

21

Wolinski had long held to a philosophy of sorts, a rule for getting through life, which was to see every day as a randomly scattered field of spiked pits and wired pressure-plates, negotiating which required that a mind not wander for longer than it took to stretch out a stiff back-muscle, or consider the menu in Karlshorst's junior officers' dining-room, or think of a good excuse to refuse a tennis invitation, a game of chess or - especially – a couple of vodkas after work. Drinking with Russians was not the best way to keep one's attention on anything other than a floor.

How had that iron vigilance slipped? You lived with a thing for long enough and it became a skin, an instinct almost, not something that might be caught and snatched out of reach by a gust of wind. Yet Wolinski's reaction to an eminently foreseeable event had been dull surprise, followed by a paralysis of inspiration that might have been chemically induced. *That* thought had stayed for a while. The modern KGB was very fond of its medical bag of tricks.

Obviously, this had been engineered precisely to achieve its result. An accusation had been made, the reaction – swift and correct – had offered a brief, unpleasant taste of the luxurious facilities at Leistikowstrasse and then an offer had been made, considered and accepted in the time it took to glance sideways at the alternative. The only extraordinary aspect to the process was the weight of whatever it had taken to brush aside procedure and restore the accused to favour. The string-puller had taken great risks to land a very small prize.

Wolinski was about to face two ways, for what should have been the same side. Duties at Karlshorst would proceed as before, but things were going to leak eastwards, avoiding the usual channels – which meant the Lubyanka. People here would be nervous, wondering who it might be who dared to go against KGB. GRU would probably be the first suspect, but the organizations' interests only overlapped occasionally, and neither could gain anything by the other's embarrassment. In any case, GRU was headed by Mikhail Shalin, who had once been Serov's boss - and, like almost everyone else, had treated the man as if he were a half-tamed wolf. The last thing he'd want would be to poke a stick at it.

Who else, then, they would ask. Who would have the balls or delusions of immortality to poke Chairman Serov in his most sensitive parts? Personalities counted for far more than nameplates in the Soviet State, but they would have to assume that if the Council of Ministers, Politburo or the General Secretary himself wanted to move against the KGB Chairman they could do so without indulging in spies' games on one of the Empire's frontiers - games at which, furthermore, Serov was likely to be far more adept than they. It was a conundrum, and heads would ache,

Wolinski's head would ache too, for different reasons. This was a game, but only to those who weren't caught in the cross-fire. A promise of full exoneration had been made, but could it be kept? Wolinski had been caught like a fish, yet had never met an American, much less conspired with one. It hardly mattered. What course was there, other than to pretend to be grateful for a false deliverance, do exactly what was required and hope for an unlikely best?

It was almost laughably ironic, that such a lazy, unimaginative accusation had been made. The Third Directorate didn't have any foreign counter-intelligence role, so it was only the innate and immoveable paranoia of Soviet Intelligence that had made it stick. If Wolinski's accuser had known the true nature and extent of his victim's crimes against the State he might have thought twice about using it - in fact, he would have done well to turn and run as a far and as quickly as would put ground between himself and radiation poisoning. If there was a kernel of consolation to be found in this mess, it was that when things went wrong it might well be the foot-soldier who did the dragging down.

22

'This place wears its sins still.'

'It's been fourteen years, Freddie.'

When Fischer had tired of Holleman's arguments (if the incoherence flood could be so flattered), he had escaped to the Botanical Gardens. Unfortunately, his tormentor had escaped with him. It was a symptom of the other man's agitation that he was willing to be seen outdoors, though he had taken basic precautions. His 'disguise' comprised a walking stick, borrowed from the estate of the late Ferdinand Grabner (one of the deceased's English-gentleman affectations), and a fur-trimmed Ulster (ditto), the edges of which almost met across his barrel chest. To a half-blind undercover *Stasi* officer he might have passed as a Lichterfelder of some means and taste, though with either a bad leg or chronic drink habit.

'Yeah, but old ladies stick in the mind.'

'They were only as old as we are, now.'

Holleman came to a halt, frowned and shook his head. 'Fuck.'

'Neither do I.'

'What?'

'Know where the time goes.' Without inviting his friend to join him, Fischer sat down on a bench, lifted a pack of cigarettes from his pocket and lit one. The first drag made him cough, but he persisted. Holleman sat on the upwind side.

'When did you start again?'

'I haven't.'

For a while they both examined the near-field. It was a bright day but cold, the wind bringing an early taste of January. A few people were visible, cutting through the Gardens at speed rather than taking the air. Fischer hunched in his own overcoat (though this was only partly the temperature's doing) and scowled at the visible Germany. The cigarette lasted a minute more before revulsion cut through his preoccupations. He dropped and ground it with a foot.

Not comfortable with any species of silence, Holleman broke first. 'You're in a mood.'

'A vise, rather. The last of my luck seems to have gone missing.'

The big man snorted, depositing flecks of mucus on to his fur collar. 'When have you ever had the slightest ration of *luck*?'

'It doesn't just bring cake, Freddie. It's as welcome when it holds off the avalanches. Only this time ...'

'He's a bastard.'

'Who?'

'Our mate Zarubin.'

Fischer watched a gull, confused by the curved face of the Great Pavilion, abort an attempted landing and complain loudly. 'He's fond of games, for sure.'

'He shouldn't be such an ingrate. You got him back to Moscow unexecuted.'

'He saved Marie-Therese's life before he ever knew me. He didn't have to do that.'

'A man shouldn't get credit for being human.'

'He did the same for Rolf Hoeschler.'

Holleman considered this. 'Yeah. But he put him in the shit in the first place.'

'Yet he didn't drop you in the same when he discovered you weren't Kurt Beckendorp.'

'No, but he got plenty of use out of me after that. K-5 didn't scratch their arses without him knowing about it two minutes later.'

Like a long-lost sibling at a will-reading, Sergei Aleksandrovich Zarubin was impossible to read accurately. His capacity for good or ill was open-ended, and if his inclination was usually to go with some middle ground, no-one with a working head would ever assume that sentimentality was likely to override whatever the moment required. Over the past two years, a looming career as a traitor pressing on his morale, Fischer had often imagined himself tied to a firing post, getting a last regretful squeeze to the shoulder from the man before he nodded on the business at hand.

'You need to run, Otto - far away, where folk can't place Germany on a map.'

'And what would you do, when *Stasi* came knocking on your front door?'

'He wouldn't do that.' Holleman sounded certain about it, but his face darkened.

'You couldn't risk it. Kristin and the boys ...'

'Fuck! We should kill him, then.'

'I'll get the flight schedules for Moscow, shall I? Once it's done we can have a week's holiday, see the sights.'

Holleman slumped forward and rubbed his face. 'You know she won't let me back in the house until I sort this for you?'

'There's nothing to be done, Freddie. Tell her that Otto said so.'

'She wouldn't listen to you any more than me.'

That was probably true. Fischer hadn't spent much time in Kristin Holleman's company, but there was plenty of anecdotal evidence of a Bismarckian iron-will, softened only slightly by the pleasing view. Even the fearsome Gerd Branssler had been known to blanch at the prospect of disappointing the lady. Still, an impossible demand remained just that, no matter the consequences of failing to meet it.

'Well, have her find a strategy to deceive KGB and the Kremlin *and* keep me above ground, and I'll gladly run with it.'

'Don't be silly.'

'What's silly about it?'

'I mean, that's what she'd say if I gave her the message.' Holleman rubbed his hands together and followed a passing pram-pusher with his eyes. 'The Russian, Levin – he didn't actually say what it was that Zarubin wants from you.'

'It can't be trivial, if I'm to be anywhere close to Brandt.'

'They don't like him, do they?'

'He's another Ernst Reuter – a popular pain in their arse.'

'So you'll be fitting him up with a drug habit, or prostitutes?'

Fischer sighed. 'It won't be that obvious - or easy, I expect. If it was, they'd have done it by now.'

'Something financial then, to make out that he's corrupt?'

'It's an open secret that the Americans threw money at him a few years ago – and that it didn't go further than his pocket. I don't believe that anyone cares any more about what's in his bank account.'

Holleman shook his head. 'Character assassination didn't used to be this difficult.'

'Perhaps that isn't what Zarubin has in mind. He might just want ears in Brandt's office. Everyone thinks he's likely to be Federal Chancellor one day, so it would be a brilliant coup.'

'Or maybe have you become so indispensable that when they bring him down, you'd be his natural successor.'

It was meant to lighten the mood, but Fischer shuddered. 'Having an entire nation keep me from sleep wouldn't be preferable to a noose.'

'I'd vote for you, probably. Where do you stand on the Common Market?'

'Shut up.'

For almost ten minutes they sat silently, letting the view distract them. The Gardens were winter-bare by now, but evergreens provided enough colour to raise less flattened spirits. Most of the other visitors had their heads down as they passed, and though a middle-aged woman gave them more attention than they deserved, even Fischer's stretched nerves couldn't interpret it as surveillance (in any case, Holleman's habit of returning stares with interest almost certainly prolonged the moment). A church clock, chiming somewhere to the west, woke Fischer from his contemplation of an old companion, recently returned.

'I'm tired, Freddie.'

'Didn't you sleep?'

'I mean long-term, drained-to-the-floor tired. Do you ever think how wonderful it would be, to drift off to sleep and just forget to wake?'

Holleman shook his head firmly. 'Don't do that. You're not too cold, you haven't been diagnosed with something and the Ivans haven't encircled you - well, not entirely. You're just in a tunnel, and not seeing things right.'

'It's a very long tunnel, and not vented.'

That earned Fischer a slap on the back, which nearly dislodged his skull from his spine. 'Don't worry, Otto! We'll find the other end. If the Third Reich couldn't finish you off, what chance has Zarubin?'

'Rather more for my being the centre of his attention. Let's walk.'

They moved northwards towards Dahlem, losing most of their thin company. That didn't stop Holleman from checking around him, pantomime-fashion, before speaking.

'When are you going to contact this fellow in Brandt's office?'

'I spoke to Herr Brecker this morning, before you'd finished snoring.'

'I don't snore.'

'Before Lichterfelde's first ever seismic event subsided, then. I'm going to meet him tomorrow morning, before the Rathaus fills up. It would be better not to have too huge an audience.'

'I wonder what he'll tell you.'

'To be convincing, I expect. To incline the Mayor to trust my judgement, though how I'll do that God alone knows. And, I suppose, to shake his hand and say good morning, Herr Brandt - not click my heels, throw back my shoulders and shout *Sieg Heil*.'

Holleman laughed. 'It might get you out of the job tidily. Seriously, if you really messed up first impressions, what could Zarubin do? What would he ever know about it, other than that Brandt didn't take to you?'

'I get a feeling that my competence is expected. If I disappoint him, he might find something worse – even – for me.'

'Yeah, there is that. On the face of it – I mean, if you *have* to be a politician, and setting aside the fact that you're a traitor - working for the Mayor will be a sweet posting.'

'Sweet until the ground opens up and swallows me.'

'Well, if you won't run, hide or confess to Gehlen's mob ...'

As they exited the Gardens on to Altensteinstrasse, Holleman leaned on the railings to adjust his artificial leg. It had done a week's normal duty already that day, and the hobble had become more pronounced as leather rubbed on tissue. Fischer waited, hands in pockets, and either a stab of common sense or the noise of traffic suddenly in his ear, flushing the dullness from his head and restoring a small degree of perspective. Freddie was right. If he couldn't or wouldn't take any of the obvious measures to preserve the self, he needed to come to terms with his new, twin career. If he carried it off he might survive long enough to conceive some as-yet obscure escape plan; if he didn't, all his worries would soon be dissipating in air.

23

When Zarubin returned from the Intelligence Coordination Committee meeting, Levin was waiting for him in his office. Normally, he would have thought nothing of this – the man's job, after all, was to fetch and carry, bring and convey, report and take orders. Today, though, Zarubin had been put into a foul mood, and didn't want to make the effort to be courteous.

He had expected Serov to attend the meeting. As Head of KGB it was his place to do so, and the men never missed an opportunity to turn the ostensible relationship between himself and the committee members on its head. They were there, they imagined, to quiz him on his organization's ongoing business; to monitor operations in which the Council of Ministers had expressed an interest and to report upon progress or lack thereof. Serov, in contrast, was there to quash their self-importance.

Zarubin couldn't recall when – if – the Chairman had ever answered one of their questions in such a way as to illuminate. If he was minded to indulge his inquisitors he would apologize and explain that the present, delicate stage of a particular project made it impossible for him to offer details, for which failure he begged their understanding. If he wasn't, a smirk and brief shake of the head was all they got. Reminders that the Committee reported directly to the Council only brought a cold glare, and more silence.

A variation of that glare had been directed at Zarubin many times, and didn't require a cause *du jour*. Five years earlier the two men, more than any other, had been responsible for Beria's fall; but that hadn't been the result of, or the opportunity for, any sort of alliance between them. Back then, Serov had been biding his time, watching other members of the Politburo as they tried to drag their most dangerous colleague to the cliff's edge, at which point he might have stepped forward, administered the shove and earned their gratitude. Zarubin's return from America with (spurious) evidence of CIA approaches to Beria had forced Serov's hand, however. He'd been lucky to survive and replace his old boss, and had never forgiven the man who'd made him look like a craven, last-minute fence-jumper. Since then, everyone had known – had it not been apparent already - that Serov was to be trusted as much as any creature with scales for skin. They knew also that they didn't dare do something about him. It was an unfortunate corollary of the KGB Chairman's role, that he happened to have all the very wrong information on the right people.

At today's meeting, a question went to Zarubin regarding the CIA's likely reaction to the Viet Cong's infiltration of South Vietnam (it being his responsibility, absent effective KGB representation in Hanoi and given his prior work with the Americans). He responded as best he could (though nothing he said was tremendously enlightening), and as he spoke Serov treated him to a lingering look that managed to combine amused contempt with a faint promise of unpleasantness, should the chance ever present itself. The meeting moved on to other matters but Serov's attention didn't, and Zarubin began to feel a little like a pretty teenager in a prison yard. He'd known for a while that he was on the man's list of suspected modernizers, but he'd been careful to limit his interventions to conversations with those best placed to achieve them – there was nothing on paper or tape to snare him. Still, the stare told him that the list might be shortening, or that *careful* hadn't been careful enough.

It would need more than suspicions, though, for Serov to dare to move – at least for as long as Zarubin was regarded as useful by the General Secretary. Even firm, undeniable proof of his links to the modernizers could be shrugged off – it was no secret that plenty of people in the Kremlin believed in these post-Stalin days that much more NKVD needed to be taken out of KGB. Still, there were *moves* and there were *incidents*, and no reason why a tragic, unexpected example of the latter couldn't be arranged. It was a strange phenomenon of high Soviet politics that an inordinate number of seemingly healthy men who stood in the way of other men succumbed unexpectedly to a heart attack, or stroke, or something sufficiently perplexing to earn an *unknown causes* on the coroner's report. Zarubin felt reasonably secure, but not in the least sanguine.

In the general shuffle following the meeting's conclusion, Serov picked up his papers and came around the table. He had found a smile from somewhere and pasted it almost convincingly to his face – a second cousin to the one he deployed at official receptions whenever a foreign diplomat's pretty wife wandered dangerously close to harm. There was nothing threatening in his body language, but as always Zarubin couldn't help but recall his reputation for taking over interrogations and showing his men how an enthusiast did it.

'Are you well, General?'

'As a young bull, Comrade Chairman, the odd bout of arthritis aside.'

'Ah. That'll be a souvenir from your Stettin days. Nothing like the miserable North German climate for tormenting the joints.'

'It's Poland, these days.'

'Is it? Well, the weather doesn't recognize maps, does it?'

With anyone else this might have felt like a pleasant conversation, of little weight or utility; but Serov didn't talk to his dog without there being a purpose behind it. He glanced around casually to ensure that none of the departing ears were deployed in their direction, and leaned closer.

'Speaking of Poles, that was a strange business, wasn't it?'

'Which business is that?'

'The traitor who turned out not to be, in my Third Directorate Section at Karlshorst.'

'I haven't heard anything about that.'

'Really? I'm astonished it hasn't done the rounds. Someone took it from me, investigated it very quickly and returned the exonerated item with all of its limbs intact.'

'Is that possible?'

'No, I would have said. But yes, as it happens. When I queried the matter I was referred to the Boss, who laughed it off – you know how he does, when he really doesn't want to discuss a thing further. I wondered who would have that sort of juice. And then I thought of you, Sergei Aleksandrovich.'

'Poles in Berlin aren't really my area of responsibility, Comrade Chairman.'

'That's what I thought. It's good to dismiss the possibility – I would hate for us not to be the very best of friends, always.'

The smile broadened (though the lizard eyes didn't crease even slightly), and then Serov was out of the committee room. Zarubin was almost startled. In his experience (and admittedly, he was alive still, so it was limited in that regard) it wasn't like the man to make a naked threat so publicly. It threw into the air any calculation of how exposed he felt himself to be, how quickly he might move to swat the threat, how close to ridiculous it might have been for him to have made the calculation in the first place.

By the time he returned to his office he was breaking the habit of an adult lifetime and twisting a problem in his head until he couldn't see either end of it. His secretary's presence there was as welcome as spit in a teacup.

Even Levin knew when to stifle his glibness. He cleared his throat. 'How did it go, Comrade General?'

'As badly as could be imagined. Serov more or less accused me of having a hand in the Wolinski business.'

'Oh.' Levin swallowed hard. 'Then I bring more bad news.'

'Excellent. Please don't spare me.'

'I received a first communication from … the subject, an hour ago.'

'That was remarkably prompt. Were we expecting anything?'

'Not yet, but Wolinski thought we needed to know this.'

'Because …?'

'Station Resident Korotkov has assembled a surveillance team for a street job. Bolkov's deputy told me that Wolinski's been included.'

'That's not too discouraging. It indicates that the investigation's conclusions have been swallowed at Karlshorst. Korotkov is moving on.'

'Possibly, yes. That isn't the bad news.'

'Tell me.'

'The team is to monitor a German national, one Otto Henry Fischer.'

'Christ. How …?' Zarubin sat heavily. There was only one possible *how*. If Fischer had earned an entire team on his back, Korotkov regarded him as big-game. Absent any obvious, other reason for it, this was KGB sensing that their toes were being stamped upon and looking to return the favour. How they came to that impression wasn't difficult to guess at. Levin had been given three tasks for his brief visit to Berlin and had been able to discharge only two of them, because his third contact had been absent without leave.

'Globnow is dead.'

Levin pulled a face. 'I hoped it was something else, but ...'

'They would have needed to squeeze very hard, and then ensure that he wouldn't warn me. Is it likely they wouldn't finish the job in the neatest fashion?'

Globnow had been Zarubin's longest-serving 'acquisition', brought into NKGB during the war and then extracted from its successor organization cleanly – a trustworthy, even-tempered man, entirely of his other, civilian life except when called back to duty. He hadn't deserved to lose it all at the end of a fist, or an over-prescribed psychotropic drug.

KGB had names now, and it couldn't be too long before histories were tapped and associations pinned. If Globnow hadn't said too much – and he probably hadn't, otherwise Serov wouldn't have needed to play at being friendly – then Fischer might not yet be compromised entirely. Even that hopeful possibility left a quandary, however. If Zarubin did the sensible thing and slowed or stopped his schedule to deflect KGB's attention, Serov would gain time to find other paths to his enemy's entrails; if, while under surveillance, Fischer was manoeuvred into place too precipitously, the nature and purpose of the thing might become apparent, giving the intended recipient of Zarubin's head-shot time to duck.

'Do we warn Fischer?' Levin was watching his superior closely, as if trying to read the swirl of options being tested.

'No, not … yet. If he gave a single backward glance – and he couldn't resist doing so - they'd know that *we* know, and Wolinski would be compromised also.'

'Then what do we – you – do?'

'We're caught in ice, and need a polynya.'

'A what?'

'Don't you read the *Polar Transactions*?'

'I'm a warm weather man.'

'Never mind. The only thing we can do is allow Fischer to proceed at his own pace. With Globnow gone we'll need a new contact point, but for the moment he can impress Brandt's office with what we've given him. Once he's in place there and trusted, time becomes less of an issue for us. We need only flick the switch when the moment best suits our purpose. You don't seem to agree.'

'I do, Comrade General. It just seems a pity. I found the man quite amenable.'

'As do I, Levin, but your empathy is almost certainly a variety of pity, which you need to guard against. Console yourself with the fact that he's a clever one, and very light on his feet. I fear he'll need to be both, with his scent in Serov's nostrils.'

24

'I have no idea what it is I'm suppose to be doing.'

It wasn't the best line with which to sell himself, but Fischer was keen to dampen expectations. The look it earned suggested that very few had been entertained.

Herr Othmar Brecker was a busy man. His eyebrows, restless hands and tendency to attach a sigh to almost every exhalation conveyed this with admirable economy. A more salutary rebuttal to the fictional spy's patient, calculating nature could hardly be imagined – and had been it been, no doubt Herr Brecker would have corrected it with another sigh, and raised his eyebrows to Heaven to beg the strength to endure such naivety.

Fischer accepted the unspoken admonishment gratefully. He was pleased that the low opinion he held of his talent for subversion was shared, and so obviously. He didn't like to disappoint.

'What you'll *do* is to convince Herr Brandt that your understanding of Kremlin politics is more perceptive and accurate than what's presently available to him. This will not be difficult. No-one in the West has a grip on how and why decisions are made at the highest level, what pressures inform them or what calculations are made in the process. Believe me, the CIA have been trying to part the veil for years, and failing badly. We see most of their reports – they're just about worthless. You've absorbed the materials that the General provided?'

'Yes, I think so. I've drafted this.' Fischer reached into the late Herr Grabner's briefcase and extracted a bound sheath of papers. 'It's a distillation.'

'How many pages?'

'Fourteen.'

Another sigh. 'Far too many. Herr Brandt believes that anything worth saying can be said in two pages, maximum.'

'Well it can't, obviously. But I've summarized – very broadly - at the beginning. In just over a page.'

Brecker sniffed and took the report between two fingers, with as much delicacy as if it had been used to absorb a little accident. 'If he doesn't care to read any of it before asking your opinions, will you be ready to offer something?'

'Of course.'

'Convincingly?'

'We'll know once he's asked the question. I'm told I have no problem being plausible.'

'By whom?'

'Zarubin, for one. It's his belief, apparently, that I could tell a lie and prove it.'

For a moment the other man seemed almost impressed. 'You know the General personally?'

'We're very old friends. In a way, we owe our respective lives to each other, though I doubt he's any more grateful for it than I.'

Not knowing what to make of this, Brecker offered a brief, hard look (it told Fischer that if he was attempting either to be opaque or amusing, he hadn't succeeded) and continued.

'It's very important that you don't attempt to be *jocular*. The Mayor is a serious man, and despises glibness.'

'I'll remember that.'

'And don't be ingratiating. Herr Brandt doesn't take to sycophants.'

'I'll use my tongue only to make words.'

Another hard look half-roused itself, but Herr Brecker was finding it difficult to keep his eyes on the half-ruined face. Not for the first time, Fischer appreciated its capacity to intimidate. He cleared his throat.

'When will I meet him?'

'He's speaking with the two deputy Mayors at the moment, so in about twenty minutes I should think.'

Fischer's stomach heaved. He had assumed that this morning's business was to be briefed by his fellow traitor for the eventual meeting, not be a pat on the back as he attached his ripcord to the fuselage. He had drafted his paper and now knew quite a bit more about Zarubin's opinion of Soviet politics than previously, but he had imagined that there would be time for further revision, to give him a little of the glibness he had been warned against. It would take one perceptive question, coming from a slightly unexpected angle, to throw him completely.

'Oh. Wonderful.'

The office door swung open and a young man stepped in. He and Brecker gave each other a shallow but solemn bow, like two archbishops acknowledging each other's eminence. Becker extended a hand towards Fischer.

'This is the gentleman I mentioned to the Governing Mayor: Herr Otto Fischer.'

Fischer received a lesser nod (archbishop to reformed prostitute, perhaps) and the offer of a handshake. 'Georg Walter. I'm sorry, but Herr Brandt's been called away unexpectedly.'

'Oh. Well ...' Relieved, Fischer picked up his report and offered it to Walter, who smiled and raised a hand. 'I'm sure it's extremely valuable, but Herr Brecker's recommendation is quite satisfactory. We look forward to working with you.'

When he'd gone, Brecker gave Fischer his first approving look of the morning. 'That went very well.'

I spent seven hours writing the bloody thing. 'What about references?'

'They have the fact of your appointment to the *Abgeordnetenhaus*, your degree certificate from Bern and the Knight's Cross award. Who else could they approach?'

It was a fair point. Presumably, Luftwaffe and Army Group North no longer maintained offices from which prospective employers might receive the necessary satisfaction: *This is to*

certify that Hauptmann Otto Henry Fischer invaded parts of
Belgium, Norway, Greece and the Soviet Union with industry,
seriousness and scrupulous attention to orders. His former
commanding officers have no complaints to make, other than to
regret his tendency to locate himself beneath plummeting
aircraft.

'So, I'm hired?'

'Start the day after tomorrow. We'll get you an office – or a
chair in one, at least – and a Mayor's pass. I'll make sure
Brandt sees the summary to this report. You might think of
preparing something on the likelihood of repercussions if the
Americans and British reinforce their bases in Berlin.'

'What the hell would I know about that?'

'What the hell would anyone?' Brecker smiled, a slightly
unpleasant effort. 'That's the beauty of prevalent ignorance –
no-one can gauge how close they are to the truth. Concentrate
your discussion on how much or how little agonizing will occur
in the Kremlin before they decide upon escalation.'

'So I'm so say there'll *be* escalation?'

The familiar frown returned. 'What's the point in saying
otherwise? You're only going to be valuable to Brandt for as
long as he believes he needs advising. When you write it, think
of what's likely to make him shit himself and then stir in a few
prunes – but not so many as to make it unconvincing,
obviously. In the meantime, I'll let the Allies know we have an
expert Kremlinologist in the Rathaus, if they'd like to consult.
They won't, but it will add to your reputation.'

'Kremlinologist?'

'A recent term, coined by the Americans.'

'Ah. Please don't say anything to BND.'

'I wasn't intending to – we don't want Federal Intelligence looking too closely at either of us. But why, if I may ask?'

'I have the wrong sort of history with Gehlen's people.'

'Should we worry about that?'

'Zarubin doesn't. It was a long time ago.'

That seemed to satisfy Brecker. He placed the unwanted report in his desk, checked his watch (one of the older-style Rolex coin-edges that didn't look to have been made for a giant's wrist) and sighed again.

'I have a meeting. Return at nine-thirty the day after tomorrow and I'll introduce you to a few people, Please be punctual.'

This seemed to constitute a farewell, so Fischer nodded and left the office without a further word. Whatever else he had to worry about, it wasn't accommodation. How many new men at the Rathaus were offered *two* offices in their first week? Only three days earlier he had brought a box of reading materials, pens and other stationery to the small room he had expected to share with Lamm and his colleagues, and it struck him that while he was in the building the honourable course would be to renounce his squatter's rights there.

Five minutes later he was wedged in among them, trying to extract his possessions. As usual, Herbert Lamm took the lead in responding to the revelation.

'Willy Brandt's office? Christ!' He turned to Dieter and Robert, who were gaping respectfully. 'Gentlemen, go home and tell your families that you've been in the presence of a prodigy. The man's been with us for just a few days, and already he's translated to Heaven!'

He looked solicitously at Fischer. 'Otto, I wonder what you had to offer? It can't be your wife – you don't have one. A soul you have no use for? The location of the Holy Grail?'

Dieter sniffed. 'If he owns a distillery ...'

'That's it! Our Governing Mayor likes a drink almost as much as he does the ladies. Or perhaps a vineyard?'

Fischer sighed. 'I studied the Soviet system at university – I'm wanted for a little advice, that's all.'

'*All*, he says! I could grovel from now until universal peace arrives, and His Eminence still wouldn't think to piss on my burning head. Admit it, Fischer – you have a ravishing sister, who at this moment is licking chocolate from the tip of Brandt's ...'

'He's looking to get some idea of what Khrushchev's up to at the moment. When I've been fully squeezed I expect I'll be wandering these corridors, looking for a home.'

Lamm looked serious suddenly. 'No, you won't. Listen, Otto, don't mess this up. We all know where Brandt's going, don't we? If you do well, you're likely to be offered a seat on the Bonn Express, and that train travels a long way.'

He reached into his drawer and brought out his half-bottle of Scotch (the level hadn't declined since he'd offered Fischer a welcoming drink almost two weeks earlier) and four small glasses. Every drop of the precious liquid was shared equitably between them.

'Gentlemen, to the luckiest bastard any of us have ever met - may he rise vertically, and fall onto the softest mattress!'

25

As a Pole, Wolinski knew something about walls pressing, but couldn't recall anything as bad as this. War, a cruel peace, the tortuous course of self justification that had allowed the brown uniform to be donned without the soul blistering – all had been Stations of a personal Cross, and every bit as painful as the overwrought depictions that adorned ten thousand Polish churches. None of it, though, had felt like a place from which escape was impossible.

It had left scars, obviously. Nothing worthwhile remained - no family or ties of belonging to ease the cruel passage of things from *then* to *now*; no hope of ever returning to Poland to resurrect a fragment of an older, better life. It had seemed as if a bedrock had been reached, the lowest level of expectation achieved, but that had turned out to be sheer optimism. *This* was a new place to be, and no door from it was visible.

The obvious question had occurred immediately – why was a Third Directorate operative being assigned to a First Directorate surveillance team? Section Chief Bolkov had explained that there were few people at Karlshorst whose command of German was so fluent that they could pass as natives, but that was shit – no-one speaking to Wolinski could miss the Polish inflections, the soft blurring of consonants. It had been a lie, delivered by someone who didn't care whether or not he was believed, but that hardly mattered to Wolinski. Nothing else that had happened in the past week had made any sense either.

The briefing had been cursory. The man was to be followed so closely that their breath would moisten his neck (though of course he was to think it a turn in the weather). His habits, friends, moods were to be minutely observed, photographed where possible and reported, and that was all – no snatch, no planting of incriminating 'evidence', no elimination. As a newcomer to First Directorate, Wolinski couldn't say how typical such instructions were, but a six-strong team seemed a heavy commitment for mere observation, give how many of KGB Berlin Station's resources were being devoted to the American reaction at the moment. Perhaps it was because this was a political crisis, and Otto Fischer was a politician, of sorts. Who was Wolinski, to say how such things went?

For almost half a day, this novel, inexplicable task had seemed almost a pleasant distraction from the personal drama of the previous days, because it was almost half a day before Wolinski caught a first sight of Fischer. The sickening shock of seeing him in the torn flesh had been difficult to conceal, but the other fellow (his name was Timochenko, like the old, useless general) had been watching the target closely, and didn't notice. Wolinski pulled out a notebook and recorded the time, place and activity, and this gave blood a chance to return to the face from which it had drained. They had followed him for almost an hour after that, from Rathaus Schöneberg to Stegiltz, via a cafe, grocery and wine merchant's. At any of these he might have made contact with someone; fortunately, Timochenko took it upon himself to be the tail on each occasion, and was able to confirm that only a waitress and the two proprietors had spoken with the subject. His partner had stayed at a safe distance all the while, having no intention of getting into range of even a casual glance.

Back at Karlshorst that evening, Wolinski reported the day's observations and a serious onset of the shits. It wouldn't buy much time, but this thing had to be thought through before panicked flight recommended itself too strenuously.

Hauptmann Fischer. A face, a visitation, from a distant, uglier past, now apparently absolved of everything except the curiosity of KGB. The questions swirled like powdered snow. What the hell did they want him for, and why had Wolinski been dragged into the chase? Who knew enough to make the connection, and what did it signify? Was the same bullet pointing at two targets?

The headache came swiftly, and hard. If whatever lay behind this couldn't be parsed, what decision wouldn't make things worse? If a manual existed for such a situation, it would urge a full, frank confession of what Wolinski knew about Fischer; but someone who had just been miraculously absolved of talking to the enemy didn't have room to be frank. In any case, drawing attention to that particular sliver of history might uncover other events, regarding which no degree of honesty could head off an execution.

Admitting to the truth was impossible; flight was effectively so. There was nowhere in the East that could offer a safe hiding place, while to defect would make the rest of what life remained a form of stasis, bereft of any good reason to continue it. KGB took care to put their major prizes in good apartments, with privileges an ordinary Soviet citizen could only dream about, and there wasn't one of them who hadn't become an alcoholic just as soon as his mouth could wrap around a bottle's neck. A defector's 'life' was existence in the purest biological sense.

What else, then? Would the information gathered by the operation require that Fischer be disappeared abruptly? That possibility hovered for a while. The man's death would tie off one exposure and keep the rest in their bag; but it would be the result of a decision in which Wolinski would have no say nor any means of provoking. Fischer alive, taken and interrogated, opened a fan of possibilities none of which could be gauged for their ability to wound. Fischer innocent and allowed to proceed unmolested was too convenient to be considered any sort of possibility. Wolinski had long since learned not to attach anything to wishful things.

The only feasible course occurred eventually, and it wore a crown of thorns. All that could be said in its favour was that it didn't rely upon the decisions of others, but its potential disadvantages couldn't be counted on a full complement of fingers and toes (nor measured accurately before Wolinski was in open ground with no cover). The first step was easy and easily the most dangerous, because it couldn't be reversed. Given the choice, Wolinski would have preferred to remain motionless for as long as it took to ensure that no other, better ideas were about to come to mind. The trouble was that neither fate, KGB nor Otto Fischer were likely to freeze in their orbits while inspiration wandered closer.

Is this my fault? For more than twelve years, Wolinski had shuffled as if every centimetre of ground had been warming ice over deep black water – twelve years of assuming nothing, missing nothing; of allowing no betraying sense of security to ease tensed shoulders. In all that time, no friendships had been entertained, no concessions made to the human need for a degree of belonging – all had been subsumed to the needs of the task, which was to survive until …

What? It had been going on for so long now that the purpose was almost the thing itself, a hermetic urge to live for the sake of carrying on in the same manner. Instinct had replaced rationality, and it was best not to dwell upon what was and was not rational.

And yet for all that Wolinski was here, halted, wondering how the trap hadn't been sighted earlier. From three directions – Karlshorst, Moscow and the borough of Steglitz – the past was pressing its claim for dues unsettled, and at least one of them couldn't be discharged for less than a life. There was no elbow-room, no time to find a way to retrace the shuffle - only a single path, stretching out to a point too dimly seen to make out whether it was ice still or free water.

26

'I have wonderful news, Comrade!'

Bolkov noticed the formal address, and there was a strained edge to Korotkov's brightness, as if that of a cancer victim whose remission diagnosis had come from his tobacconist. A provisional thought occurred.

Is even the Resident's office wired?

'*How* wonderful?'

'Comrade Serov is paying a visit to Karlshorst!'

That explained everything. Suddenly Bolkov, too, needed a lavatory. Serov didn't *visit* anywhere – he came down upon, crashed through, scoured or otherwise moved like a Mongol Horde across buttercup meadows. He much preferred not to step outside Moscow's Inner Ring these days, much less put himself into an aircraft, so when he did it was almost always bad news for some poor bastards.

Their Chairman had concurred that Otto Fischer might be associated in some manner with his enemies in the Kremlin; he had acknowledged that surveillance of the man was necessary; and he had agreed that putting Wolinski into the team might flush out any connection between the two. On paper at least, Korotkov and Bolkov had acted quickly, diligently and with particular regard to the threat to KGB autonomy. The trouble was that the paper sat on Serov's desk, and no-one really knew what was scribbled on it.

'When might we expect him?'

The brightness cracked a little more. Korotkov consulted his watch, which gave Bolkov the very worst news before his mouth began to move.

'He should be here soon. He left Moscow before breakfast.'

Serov and low blood-sugar levels was a combination not to be imagined. Bolkov thought quickly.

'We were going to host a Heroes' Day lunch next week. Can we bring it forward?'

'In just two hours?'

'We have at least five Generals on site – would they refuse the invitation?'

'It's the catering I'm worried about.'

Bolkov snorted. 'He's got peasant tastes. As long as the vodka flows and there's something to spoon onto black bread he'll be fine.'

Korotkov nodded. 'I can find a few cases of Odessagne – it might take the edge off whatever's biting him.'

'We'll need to think of plenty of toasts - the fair city of Vologda should be in there somewhere.'

'Why?'

'His family home.'

'The city or region? The name referred to both during the Empire.'

Bolkov chewed his lip. 'I don't know. Forget I mentioned it.'

They stared at each other, conspirators joined only by a common fear that what they couldn't grasp might turn and bite them. It was possible that Serov was coming to Berlin on entirely unconnected business, but it didn't seem the moment for optimism. Briefly, Bolkov entertained the logic that if they were deeply in shit it would have been a summons to Moscow rather than a visit, but when did logic have a place in their world? Who was to say how the Chairman like to play the end-game? Perhaps he planned to stone a brace of birds, then do a little shopping, take in a show at the *Komische Oper* and bang two or three German girls – it would make for a perfect day out of the office.

Korotkov had picked up his telephone. 'Yuri, please call around some lunch invitations. I want … Oh. Well, yes, of course. Don't keep him waiting.'

The phone went down as quickly as Korotkov's face. 'He's ...'

The door opened, and General Ivan Aleksandrovich Serov stepped into the office. He was smiling (which told them nothing), but as they struggled to accelerate out of their seats he waved them back with a hand. He was alone, when protocol demanded that dismissals and arrests required the presence of a clerk and at least two large, armed men.

'It's alright, gentlemen, this isn't a kicking.' The General took off his coat, threw in onto the arm of the office's only sofa and himself down next to it. By this time Korotkov had a bottle and three glasses on the table, and was pouring.

'I'm glad you're here, Bolkov – it saves me having to repeat myself. This business with our Pole and the German ...'

Korotkov and Bolkov glanced at each other. If it *was* a single business ...

' ... you kept it tight here, which was correct. We've now got to be shrewd, and by shrewd I mean not dumb. The situation in Moscow is coming to a resolution, and I don't want anything happening here that sends up a warning flare beforehand.'

'It was our intention to wait until we heard from you, Comrade ...'

'Good, then. You know that I've been compiling a list of suspects – men who might be working to alter KGB until it's something else entirely?'

'Yes, Comrade Chairman.'

'I've pared it down. That's to say, I still have six names, but five of them can now be discounted as being agreeable to the thing, not movers of it.'

'May I ask who they are?'

Bolkov hardly expected an answer (it not being his place to ask the question), but Serov rattled off the names without hesitation.

'Mikoyan, Podgorny, Kozlov, Brezhnev, Ignatov.'

Korotkov pulled a face. 'Apart from the first two, need we worry about them? They're hardly first-rankers.'

'The problem, Aleksandr Mikhailovich, is that most members of the Praesidium who would support our resistance to these manoeuvres were stained by their association with the so-called Anti-Party Group last year, and at present daren't lift a limp cock without the General Secretary's permission.'

'Speaking of …?'

'He continues to show me the greatest affection, which is as reassuring as when my dog wags its tail – they both love me, and would both eat me in a moment if the doors were locked and the larder emptied.'

'And the sixth name?'

'Mikoyan's friend, General Zarubin.'

'The traitor? Why he hasn't been shot already ...'

Serov held up a hand. 'Don't discount the power of *luck*. The gentleman has survived several moments that might have put him somewhere beyond memory. We have a system that recognizes loyalty or treachery, talent or stupidity in the most arbitrary manner, yet he's plotted a course that's carried him into the Kremlin. I don't underestimate him, but I will kill him.'

'He's been flushing out old NKVD men?'

'He's been whispering in the General Secretary's ear, and when Khrushchev goes looking for a second opinion, Mikoyan's always there to offer it. If it doesn't stop soon we may as well call ourselves Komsomol.'

'What will you do, Comrade?'

'Move carefully. Normally, I would wait for the man to make a mistake, but Zarubin tends to avoid them. However, I have an interesting piece of information that needs to be tested further.'

'May I ask what it is?'

'An American defector was asked to look at the alleged CIA report on Beria's chances of succeeding Stalin – the one that Zarubin brought back from the United States in '53. The man says that it's shit – that the Agency had no good information on Kremlin politics at that time, nor had attempted to make any advances to my predecessor. I think it may have come entirely from our friend's imagination. In effect, he forged his salvation.'

'Then the General Secretary owes him nothing.'

'A fact that I shall sharpen by suggesting that perhaps Zarubin came back with CIA's blessing.'

Bolkov couldn't stifle a laugh. 'The one would suggest the other, even if it's spurious.'

'That's the beauty of our profession – when nothing can be known for certain, anything can be the truth.'

Korotkov was nodding slowly. 'So you're convinced that Zarubin is responsible for both Wolinski and this German, Fischer?'

Serov shrugged. 'It may be that neither has even heard of the man. But given the absence of any information to the contrary, and the speed with which he appears to have arranged the Pole's exoneration, how likely is it that his was the anonymous voice that first made the accusation?'

'To what purpose?'

'To put a loyal pair of eyes into this Rezidentura, probably.'

'And Otto Fischer?'

'I don't know, but we've established that Zarubin and the fellow you snatched off the street ...'

'Globnow.'

'... were associates in MGB just after the War, and records tell us that at some point in the years before MVD and MGB were merged into KGB, the man died during a covert operation.'

'But ...'

'I know – curious, isn't it? So, the fact that this phantom mentioned Fischer's name before he died a second time is quite enough for me. As soon as I've settled with Zarubin, both Wolinski and Fischer are to be cured of their tendency to be a potential problem.'

'You wish them to be questioned first?'

'It might be useful, Aleksandr Mikhailovich. But thereafter they should follow follow their employer as quickly as pharaoh's servants.'

27

'Where are you, Otto?'

'Maleme.'

'That bloody airfield?'

'In every sense.'

It was probably unhealthy, but Fischer was beginning to embrace his sanguinary memoir for the comfort it brought, much as a child might a favourite stuffed animal. He had his instructions from Herr Brecker, and needed to think about – that is, to creatively imagine – the collective mind of the Soviet Politburo and how it functioned during a self-created crisis; but having re-read the material provided to him by Zarubin he felt that he had a better grip on the Periodic Table. It wasn't so much where to begin as to conceive what a beginning might be; so, lacking any inspiration, he had turned once more to the simpler matter of war and his blindfolded pirouette through it.

'Rolf was there too, wasn't he?'

Fischer half-turned to Holleman. 'We were in the same hole in the ground, for more than twelve hours. It was our formal introduction.'

'Well, at least you had a hole.'

'It was about five inches deep, and damp.'

'What, in Crete? In May?'

'I mean, once we'd pissed ourselves.'

'You should have had Max Schmelling punch a way out.'

'He was somewhere else on the perimeter that day. Anyway, he probably had his face pushed as firmly into the dirt as we did.'

'Still, you won.'

'Only because the enemy thought that they'd been beaten, and withdrew. If they'd stayed put we'd have been shot to pieces the following morning. As it was, I was certain I was living my last day.'

'How did it feel?'

'Unsatisfying. How about you? When your 'plane went down, I mean?'

Holleman considered the only section of the wall he had yet to paint. 'It happened too quickly to think much. I was struggling with the stick, and by the time I realised I was wasting parachute time I'd met Belgium. I may have managed an 'oh fuck' before it went dark, but it was only when I woke to just one leg that it occurred to me I'd missed a good death.'

'Good?'

'Oblivious, like a dog getting hit by a truck.'

'You wouldn't want time to consider life's ending?'

'No, because that would involve a degree of agony. What about Okhvat? You had more than enough time there, didn't you?'

'I can't recall a thing about it. I've been told that I screamed a lot, so I certainly *felt* the moment. My mind wasn't with me, though. When it returned I was already drugged to hell.'

'It was for the best, probably. Anyway, this staring at one's life as it ends is all crap. Butterflies don't do it, I expect, nor dogs - even without trucks to speed up things. Why should we be different?'

'You're probably right, Freddie. If I haven't been able to work out mine over six decades, I doubt that the last six minutes are going to help much. I should have been like you – found the right girl, had a family, thought about the practical things and left everything else to philosophers.'

Holleman sniffed. 'You found the right girl. It was just that ...' His eyes widened. 'Oh, shit, Otto, I'm sorry – about trucks, I mean.'

Fischer looked up. 'It didn't even occur to me. It hurts that she's gone, not how she went.'

Contrite still, Holleman watched his friend busily moving papers. It was his opinion that the past was in a very convenient place and best left there, but at the moment stirring old embers seemed preferable to the alternative, so he made no further objections. There was a spare pen on the desk that badly needed dismantling, and he had made a productive start on it when Fischer looked up once more.

'You never met her.'

'No. Your friend Earl told me she was very beautiful, and funny.'

'I told you that, too.'

'Yeah, but husbands are biased. Still, the evidence suggests that your taste was a lot better than hers.'

Fischer smiled. For a few moments he tried to return to Maleme, but war couldn't compete with Marie-Therese. He had a few hours only to prepare the paper that would stun Willy Brandt – or, more likely, his personal secretary - and some of those were drinking hours. Normally, he could sip wine and think at the same time, but sipping in the company of Freddie Holleman was not permitted (he always noticed, and topped up the slacker's glass so often that one had to choose between a ruined liver or carpet). He sighed, and pushed aside his *magnus opus*.

'What do members of the Politburo think about the *situation* at present?'

Holleman snorted. 'They're wondering what the Sweet, Holy Fuck Khrushchev has in his head.'

That seemed likely. The general (if uninformed) feeling was that the General Secretary led with his gut and consulted only afterwards. No doubt he could get away with it at present, having ridden out the Old Guard's attempt to unseat him; but Khrushchev was no Stalin and couldn't use the gentle hint of mass show trials and executions to keep his critics down. The trouble was, if Otto Fischer and Freddie Holleman sensed this then both Willy Brandt and Willy Brandt's pet hamster did too. Something more original would be required by Herr Brecker.

But then it occurred to Fischer that this was a game (if an ugly one), and that a statement couldn't be tested either way – it just had to sound credible. He and Freddie were former Lie Division men, whose primary task (other than drinking themselves into premature graves) had been to work military disasters into quasi-triumphs to feed to the German masses. By that measure, building a half-credible map of the Politburo's collective thoughts shouldn't be an impossible task. He picked up his pen.

'The ... rejectionist ... faction ... are ... not ... reconciled ... to ... their ... recent ... tactical ... defeat ... and ... will ... be ... ready ... to ... seize ... upon ... the ... General ... Secretary's ... perceived ... poor ... judgement ... should ... the ... Americans ... ignore ... his ... ultimatum.'

'Eh?'

'It's my expert opinion.'

'Oh.'

'Pass me the pile of stuff that Levin brought, will you?'

Zarubin had provided a few scraps of meat – dates and locations of unofficial meetings between Politburo members, sightings of important people in the wrong places and unexplained movements of expensive gifts between carpeted offices. It might all have been part of the usual course of business, but that hardly mattered. If any of it was capable of being checked and verified by Brandt's people then whatever Fischer wrote would have achieved at least a patina of credibility.

'Freddie, you were a communist once ...'

'Ssh.'

'Who in the Politburo would be most likely to face up to Khrushchev?'

'I was a policemen and Berlin city councillor – how many invitations to Moscow do you think I got?'

'I need a guess, that's all.'

'I'm five years out of all that!'

'Please.'

'Oh, for f … not Malenkov or Molotov. They're both finished now, even if they'd ever owned a single testicle between them - which they didn't. That hard bastard Kaganovich is always a possibility, but he's been around since Adam and Eve, and in any case he's probably too old guard even for the Old Guard.'

'Is that possible?'

'It's said that he was in the habit of scolding Stalin for being too soft and sentimental, so the chances are that anyone helping him on to the throne would be shot soon afterwards, just to keep things neat. If I had to bet my own money I'd put it on Mikoyan, but from what the newspapers say he's friendly with Khrushchev these days. Whether that means anything ...'

'It means that he stood for him and against the rebels last year, so they wouldn't trust him now.'

'How do you know?'

Fischer stared at Holleman. 'I don't, but who could say otherwise? I need someone else - surprising but not impossible - to burnish my genius.'

'Christ.' For almost five minutes, Holleman gave his patch of wall some further attention. Then he stood, limped to the window and stared out on to Lipaerstrasse while Fischer pored over Zarubin's material. There was a single sheet of paper, crammed with a familiar, spidery hand, that he hadn't noticed earlier. It took some time to read through it, but at the end it occurred that he'd become considerably better informed.

'What about Bulganin?'

'Mm?' Holleman turned from the outdoors, pondered it briefly and shook his head. 'He's one of the Invisibles. Take it as a rule, that anyone who survives more than two Soviet regimes is too sensible to stick up his head. He'll support whoever wins, for sure.'

'Alright. Aristov?'

'Who?'

'Averky Aristov.'

'Never heard of him.'

'Me neither, but he was elected to the Politburo in '52, got kicked out the following year when Stalin died, and then re-elected last year.'

'What's his background?'

Fischer consulted the paper once more. 'Metallurgy, Komsomol.'

Holleman snorted. 'If he's shone, it's been under a large rock.'

'Which makes him perfect. As a loyal Stalinist he was booted out, but, following the Anti-Party rebellion last year, Khrushchev rewarded his neutrality by bringing him back.

However, he's biding his time, and is thought to be positioning himself to take advantage of the present crisis if the General Secretary stumbles. It's known that he's very close to the Second Secretary, Alexei Kirichenko.'

'How do you …? Ah, you're talking shit again.'

'I am, Freddie, but it's the ripe stuff. Let's have him give a speech where he talks about closing the Missile Gap and making the current 5 Year Plan more than a stab in the dark.'

'And an anecdote about him having directed a stab or two at other men's backs?'

'Yes, that's good – a ruthless but efficient man, our leaders' worst nightmare.'

'I like this game. It reminds me of the old days.'

'I know. It's a shame the Silver Birch was RAF'd. We could have given this another hour and then spent the evening with *our* old guard.'

'The Liars.' Holleman's eyes misted slightly. 'Bless them. That van's still there.'

'What van?'

'The electrical engineers' van that was there yesterday. Across the road.'

'I didn't know it was there yesterday.'

'Well it was.'

'Perhaps it went away and returned. I told you that the old lady in the house opposite has died.'

'So they're re-wiring it?'

'Wiring it, more like. She'd lived there since before Lichterfelde had an electricity supply.'

'Either way, it would be a noisy job, wouldn't it - pulling apart walls and drilling?'

They looked at each other for a few moments. Fischer shook his head. 'I've only just started my traitor's career, and Gehlen's people aren't psychic. They're probably just lazy bastards taking their time getting the job going.'

'Are you *sure*, Otto?'

'No, Freddie, I'm not. It just seems unlikely.'

Holleman pulled a face but let it go, and Fischer returned to his great work of fiction.

'So … the … pertinent … question … is … how … secure … the … General … Secretary … regards … himself … to … be … at … present. If … he … feels … threatened … from … behind … he … may … not … have … the … leeway … to … ignore … American … 'brinkmanship' … and … will … almost … certainly … need … to … respond … forcefully … to … head … off … his … critics … in … the … Politburo. Unusual … troop … movements … are … to … be …'

'Praesidium.'

'What, Freddie?'

'Formally, it's Praesidium. 'Politburo' is slang'y.'

'I didn't know that.' Fischer corrected his text. 'It's useful having a Leninist in the house.'

'Kiss my ...'

Frau Benner pushed open the door with her foot and carried their tea into the room. Holleman offered her a bland smile while Fischer hurriedly cleared a space on his desk. She sniffed as she filled it with the tray.

'That van's still there.'

Behind her, Holleman nodded and jabbed a finger at the window.

'They're probably rewiring the house, Frau Benner.'

'No! Frau Kleist had electricity put in six years ago. They must be burglars.'

'The house was emptied two days ago.'

'Then they're kidnappers – or murderers!

'Right.' Fischer dropped his pen, stood and went to the front door. He was down the garden and through the gate before he realised that he was wearing his house slippers still (which were very comfortable but entirely unsuitable for the sort of desperate struggle in which a man might need to land a few kicks), but carried on regardless.

He pressed the former Frau Kleist's doorbell (he hadn't noticed it before, but it ended the debate about electricity), and stood back. A minute later he pressed again, with no better result.

Cupping a hand over his eyes he tried to peer into the hallway, but his least favourite form of window covering gloomed everything inside. After a further go at the doorbell he listened for a while, and, hearing only his own breathing, turned and retreated to his own home.

At the other side of the net curtain, a statue named Mikhail moved, half-slumped and replaced his pistol in its armpit sling. This was probably his twentieth surveillance assignment, but he had never before been nearly as close to the subject or needed to consider an extreme response. He was wearing a workman's overalls, but although he had studied German at Chernivtsi University and spoke the language fluently, his Ukrainian accent would have killed the illusion in a moment. As far as he knew, there were only two cardinal rules in his occupation: *Don't get caught*, and *If you do, put it right*. A termination without prior authorization was a risky step, but blowing an over-the-Line operation would be to invite a transfer back East, to some place where folk eat their own kids in thin years.

The target must have known that the house's owner was dead, so he suspected something – but not enough to go around the back and try the other door. It was the van, obviously. Had they been given more time to prepare the assignment KGB might have used one of their western agents to negotiate a leasing contract with the property's executors; if the operation wasn't being conducted across the line they would have used wireless vans, two or three in rotation, to keep the thing mobile and deter memories from jarring. Squatting in enemy territory was enough of a risk without inviting attention for the sake of it.

Mikhail was relieved that it hadn't been his partner Sergei passing through the hallway when the doorbell rang. The man was twitchy (a legacy of having remained in Stalingrad for the entire siege), and might have considered shooting the target a first rather than final option. At the least, the sound of the bell would have sent him into the air rather than immobility.

This was a strange job. He and Sergei had discussed it with one of the other teams, and though no-one had been stupid enough to express an actual opinion, neither could they recall having been part of such a large operation that hadn't been a quick abduction or a wet ending. *And* they had the Pole with them, the one who'd been sunk in chains and then resurfaced as if allegations of treachery could be made and dismissed without anything splattering. Until now, the worst Berlin assignment he could recall had been an ugly off-the-street snatch of a Soviet defector who'd imagined that he could betray his country and not spend the rest of his life in the American mid-west. He'd realised his mistake the moment he was in the van, and chose not to put himself through the ordeal of an interrogation (if a man decides to make enough trouble in a confined space in enemy territory, it's extraordinary how options contract). Putting that job against this, it was hard to choose a least favourite. At least a killing (however unplanned) wrapped up a problem. An open-ended surveillance offered all the fun of a difficult tooth extraction, without the grace of relief.

When he was certain that the target was gone, Mikhail backed slowly to the foot of the stairs and went up to the surveillance nest. Thick curtains over the room's only window, parted just a few inches, allowed a clear (and, through the binoculars tripod'd on a small table in the centre of the room, close) view of anyone entering or leaving the house opposite. At the rear of the room, a photographer's screen blocked any light that their tiny gas-stove might have leaked to the world, while a nod to domesticity was provided by the lucky Moscow Dynamo pennant, pinned to the screen, that one of the other team members brought with him on every operation (in contravention of strict protocols to maintain an evidence-sterile environment). There were no chairs, no mattresses, no other means by which a mind might be taken even momentarily off the job at hand, and once more, Mikhail couldn't help but feel that this sort of job was really the arse-end of the intelligencer's world.

Directly across the road, Fischer sat down at his desk and took up his pen once more. Holleman was on the telephone in the kitchen, making his daily report to Kristin, which meant that Frau Benner had finished her chores and gone home for the evening. A small, framed photograph of Herr Grabner's unfaithful young wife, hanging on the wall directly in front of him, invited some attention, and he was happy to oblige it. He knew little about how electricians worked, but unless they were a race apart they needed to be able to see what they were doing. It was dusk now, yet the house opposite was dark. He couldn't conceive any circumstance whereby the men would leave their van where it was and walk home. If they were having supper in a local cafe and returning to put in some overtime he would know soon enough. If they weren't, it might be that he had entirely miscalculated how much time remained to a man in his delicate position.

A part of him – less insistent than it should have been – regretted that possibility. More than that, he resented the likelihood that, if the worst came to pass, he probably wouldn't get the chance to ask politely who the hell it was that wanted Otto Fischer out of the world.

28

'Now, this is interesting.'

'What do you have there?'

'I should have thought you'd know, Levin. It was you who put it in front of me.'

'It was marked for your eyes only.'

'And you respected that?'

'Of course. If you want me to know what it is you'll tell me. If you don't, then knowing is dangerous - unless it's something denouncing me, in which case I wish now that I'd censored it heavily before pushing it under your nose.'

Zarubin had invited drollery, so could hardly object to it. He lifted the document.

'It's a summary of ongoing intelligence operations, by region – the quarterly report to the Security Committee.'

Levin frowned. 'You get that, usually.'

'Unofficially, yes. Our friend on the committee lets me have sight of his copy, though I always ensure it's back with him within the hour. This is different - see?'

For a few moments, Levin stared at the front sheet. He looked up. 'Oh.'

'That's just what I thought. The KGB stamp is an original, and *this* was inside.' Zarubin held up a small card. 'Sent to me personally, by Serov. With his compliments.'

'He's never done that.'

'Correct. I would guess also that he'd shoot anyone he caught doing it. Yet here it is.'

'Perhaps it's a peace offering.'

'A strange one, if it is. I'm not supposed to see this – I just make sure that I do.'

'Then why do you suppose he did it?'

'I *know* why he did it.' Zarubin flicked two pages, folded them over and handed the document to his secretary. 'Berlin operations, eighth item.'

Levin found it immediately. 'Fischer.'

'Not by name, but yes. A six-man team, continuous surveillance, Lichterfelde West. As far as I can recall from my own days in Berlin, the only thing that ever interested us in that part of the city was Camp Andrews, and to that vast job we never devoted more than one or two men – mainly to report on comings and goings.

'We knew already that they were watching him.'

'Yes, but Serov *wants* us to know. Is he that confident of winning?'

'Perhaps he ...'

'The question was rhetorical, Levin. He *is* that confident.'
Zarubin held up his card. 'My name's on the front, but there's also a courtesy-copy list on the reverse.'

Levin read it aloud. 'A.I Mikoyan, N.V. Podgorny, F.R. Kozlov, N.G. Ignatov. L.I. Brezhnev. These are your friends in the Praesidium.'

'Some of them, yes.'

'*All* of them.'

'With one important exception. The point is, two of those named are on the Security Committee and so would have received copies in any case. The list has no purpose or relevance, other than to inform me that Serov knows exactly what support I have, and where.'

'Should I be looking for another position?'

'If you don't mind wasting your time, by all means. If Serov can bring me down, he'll certainly ensure that any collateral problems are dealt with. You're my personal secretary, and therefore might know too much.'

Levin swallowed. 'He'd do something about *might*, would he?'

'Don't be obtuse. So, he's warning me that he's coming, and coming soon - which means he's very confident. Probably, he's drifted something in front of the General Secretary already, who almost certainly laughed it off and gave him one of those cryptic glances that can mean yes, no or I don't want to know about it. If so, he's either waiting to see who's still on his feet when the smoke clears, or he doesn't care one way or the other.'

'He might want *both* of you gone. Then he'll no longer owe anyone for his succession - apart from Marshal Zhukov.'

'Who was forced to retire last year, and now passes his days with his pet fish.'

Levin stared meaningfully, and nodded. 'So, he'd be sweeping the table clear, in effect.'

It was something Zarubin hadn't considered. No leader enjoyed being under obligations, and Khrushchev was more than usually sensitive to the fact that he had risen principally because he wasn't someone else. An at-a-stroke removal of his outstanding debts must have seemed an attractive proposition - particularly if, in cancelling each other, they left him spotless.

'How will he come for you?'

'Hm?

'Serov – how will he move against you?'

'That's a very good question, Levin. On the face of it, merely exposing my dabbling in Berlin should be enough. It isn't my place to set myself up in opposition to KGB, is it?'

'But …?'

'But it would make him look less than impressive. How had he allowed me to do what I've done? How could he not have seen it before now? If he's at all worried about efforts to unseat the old NKVD influences, he won't want to offer ammunition to his enemies.'

'An accident, then?'

'You're thinking a deft pin-prick, and me clutching my chest a few moments later? Yes, that's always a danger; but I doubt that Serov would want me gone without his hand being seen somewhere in the going. It might look too much like he feared me – he doesn't, of course, but his reputation as a ruthless bastard would lose its shine if the needle's hole were discovered. I think he's going to go with something else – a frame.'

'What?'

'It's an Americanism, referring to damning evidence, unexpectedly discovered.'

'A denunciation?'

'He'll need documentation also. We put Wolinski into prison with a mere allegation, but Serov knows he needs more than that to topple me. Unfortunately, he may *have* more than that.'

'May I ask …?'

'If you must. My CIA evidence of Beria's treacheries wasn't quite what it seemed.'

The expression on Levin's face sat somewhere between astonishment and admiration. 'You forged it?'

'CIA asked my opinion regarding the struggle to replace Stalin. I gave it, but then made it seem as though it had come from them – tweaked, as it were, to suggest that Beria had made secret representations to our enemy.'

'Holy Mother.'

Zarubin shrugged. 'At the time, no-one questioned its authenticity because it was just what was needed to bury the man – and everyone wanted him buried. Now, its true provenance would be a convenient stick to break over my head.'

'I really don't want to know this.'

'Then you shouldn't have asked. I suspect that Serov wouldn't be so confident it he hadn't discovered at least something of my deception.''

'So what can you do?'

'Don't look so worried, Levin - he isn't in the winner's enclosure yet. He knows he'll have to move with great subtlety, and it isn't his best talent. Last year's attempted coup has complicated things enormously.'

'How so?'

'The plotters had second thoughts about putting Khrushchev in the seat, but that doesn't mean they now regret having turned on Beria, because they know that the man would have buried them one by one, once he was secure. So, a revelation that he was *framed* won't cause any heartaches, even now. In fact, it might be a timely reminder of how closely everyone came to the execution cell. It isn't likely anyone will pat me on the back for it, but if I were Serov I'd want at least one more bullet in the chamber before I drew the pistol. I suspect he's thinking the same, otherwise why would he have teased me with *this* ...' Zarubin picked up the Security report and dropped it in his destroy bin, '... rather than move immediately?'

'Perhaps ...'

'What?'

Levin leaned forward and tapped the status report. 'Perhaps he's trying to provoke you into reacting.'

'That's my thought too. Obviously, I'm in a bad position to reciprocate immediately. I'm sure Serov has any number of dark secrets, but he has the monopoly on the resources that might find them. And he took care not to be involved in last year's farce, so I can't go with disloyalty.'

'What's left, then?'

'The threat of imbalance. Unlike Stalin, Khrushchev can't rule through fear. He beat off the plotters, but he needs their acquiescence still. If I'm gone, there'll be a tilt – the Old Guard will take heart and modernization of KGB become less likely. None of those who oppose them would step up and risk their own heads if Serov gets a clean shot in at mine - not even Mikoyan. So what I'm saying is ...'

'Your only hope is Khrushchev.'

'Who may or may not care. It's just that Serov can't know for sure, either way.'

'It's not the most hopeful prognosis.'

'No. Thank God for the uncertainty principle of Soviet Politics,'

'You'll just do nothing, then?'

'I didn't say that. Serov's search for the extra bullet lends us a little time, but not much. In the meantime, I need to take steps to protect that which is intended to deliver us. To make myself secure, I must jump into the pit.'

'Not ...'

'Unfortunately, yes. I hadn't thought it would be necessary, but please let our friend at Khodynka aerodrome know that I'm on my way. I doubt that it will be a fleeting visit, so if questions are asked I've been called away.'

'To where?'

'To ... Chelyabinsk Oblast.'

'*Why?*'

'Because it's far enough from here for communication to be difficult, should anyone attempt it.'

'I meant why would you go there? How would I explain it?'

'You wouldn't, Levin, because you're a clever man. You would merely shrug at the question, as any indolent, incompetent secretary would. Arrange to receive a couple of communications from me to support the fiction – something sternly exhorting you to prepare work for my return. It will cover you, to a degree.'

'And if someone sent by the General Secretary himself comes asking?'

'Tell him that the matter we discussed is in hand, and I'll be returning momentarily to bring it to completion.'

'And will you?'

'Levin, I promise you that if I don't, I won't care on way or the other.'

29

'So, who is Otto Fischer?'

Korotkov and Bolkov sat in the former's office, each holding a copy of the surveillance status report. It was not a substantial document (being necessarily provisional), but early surprises were preferable to the alternative. Their first reading had offered little to make their hearts race, however.

'When is the new House's first sitting?'

'On Thursday.'

'He's been to Schöneberg twice in the past three days.'

Korotkov considered that. 'It may not be significant. He's new, and wants people to think he's eager to start.'

'Do we know who he saw there?'

Since the moment he'd been appointed KGB's Berlin Resident, Korotkov had cultivated the friendship of Walter Ulbricht. One result of this was a gentlemen's-agreement access to two undercover *Stasi* agents, long-term employees of the Rathaus administration, who had access to the log-in books. They were used sparingly, and carefully.

'On the first occasion, no. The second time, he had an appointment with someone called Brecker, who works in the Mayor's office.'

Bolkov sat up. 'Is that usual?'

'It's hard to say. I doubt that it's common practice for new representatives to be invited to Brandt's office, but Fischer may know this Brecker personally. Or, his distinctive face and war record may make him something of a political asset to the Administration, particularly at a moment when they're pumping up their anti-Soviet chests. Again, we can't know whether it's significant.'

'We have nothing on Brecker?'

'No. But he works next door to Brandt's personal assistant, a man named Georg Walter, whom State Security attempted to recruit two years ago.'

'Attempted?'

'He told them precisely where to put their offer and then went straight to Brandt, apparently, to inform him of the approach.'

Bolkov suppressed a smile. 'I wonder what they dangled to tempt him.'

'Money, women, boys – the usual, I assume.'

'Not an apartment on Stalinallee?'

Korotkov snorted but then stifled it as he re-read something. 'It was determined that he lives alone, yes?'

'Fischer? He has a house-keeper, but she resides elsewhere.'

A man was observed standing at a window of his house at … 10.14 am, the day before yesterday – while Fischer was to the Rathaus, according to the other duty team.'

'A visitor?'

'There's no mention of a male leaving subsequently that day.'

'All the ground floor windows have lace curtains. They're certain it *was* a man?'

'They would have left the question open if there was any doubt. So, who is this person? A friend? Accomplice?'

'To what?'

'I don't know, but I need to. One of the teams will have to get in there and fix a wire.'

'It's risky.'

'It is, but we can't know whether Comrade Serov will move against Zarubin without us first having determined – *fully* determined - the situation at this end. Do you agree we should authorize it?'

Bolkov paused. As Station Resident, Korotkov had no need – or reason, even – to ask his agreement. This was to cover himself, obviously, and keep Bolkov's name firmly on what might turn out to be a charge sheet, if the operation was blown. Unfortunately, a credible objection didn't spring to mind.

'Yes, Comrade.'

'Good. Is there anything else?'

They both returned to the report. The one, obvious *thing* was Fischer's attempt to communicate with the presence in his neighbour's house. Clearly, he had noticed the vehicle. It was a bad error to have left it in sight, but nothing could be done now to reverse it. The van had been moved subsequently and Fischer hadn't returned; nor had anyone else come on to the property since. They could assume, therefore, that the teams hadn't been compromised, but only because their target *probably* couldn't call upon resources to investigate further. It was sloppy, unsatisfactory and just about all that could be done for the moment. KGB was not in a position to reinforce or alter the present dispositions without daring the Allies to notice what they were doing.

Bolkov shook his head. 'That van ...'

'I know. Someone's arse is going to be kicked when this is over.'

'Was it Wolinski ...?'

'No, I checked. The Pole is in Team Three – what happened wasn't deliberate, just moronic.'

They went back to the report. It was thin gruel, a summary of not very much, but then the operation had been ongoing for four days only. These things often took time to expose an atypical event because a definition of typical had first to be established, and people had different routines. It was entirely possible that the unfortunate, doomed Otto Fischer was guilty only of a lateral association with the mysterious Paul Globnow, in which case his death would be preceded by no useful revelations – merely a sequence of mundane, repetitive actions. Unfortunately, lacking definitive data that might determine this, they would have no more choice in the matter than Fischer himself. Serov had decreed that both Fischer and Wolinski should follow Zarubin to the afterlife, and no-one was going to question that.

Korotkov dropped his copy onto his desk and stared at the wall clock. If Serov had made up his mind, they were waiting only for word from Moscow that Zarubin was in, or about to be in, the net. When that word would come was, of course, the determining factor in how hard they continued to push this surveillance. Unfortunately, Serov would tell them when he told them, so the *push* would be as hard and as long as the proverbial piece of string. Korotkov hated having no initiative, particularly in his own garden. They were living through important times at the very centre of the world's turning, and this Fischer was a distraction at best.

Bolkov re-read a sentence for the twelfth time, and noticed it no more than previously. Once Wolinski was dead he had no idea how far the matter would splash back upon him. Serov had seemed friendly enough, but that perception was no more reliable than a cat's love, and Bolkov didn't doubt for a moment that Korotkov would happily conspire in any move to have him removed. Whether the allegation made against the Pole (and no-one at Karlshorst knew if it had been founded on evidence or spite) was in itself enough to stain him was a moot point. Third Directorate's work in the DDR had been effective, so much so that Bolkov might well turn out to be a victim of his own success. Eight years ago, there had been serious concerns about the morale and loyalties of Red Army personnel stationed here, but Third had weeded out the bad, worked upon the doubtful (hell, they'd even issued questionnaires to soldats to canvass their views, which was unprecedented) and instituted reward schemes for exceptional performance. Now, no-one worried about morale any more, or how Soviet Group of Forces in Germany might perform in a clash against the Allies, so the Wolinski incident might be enough to make Serov wonder: what is the *point* of Andrei Vasilyevich Bolkov these days?

He half-hoped that there was something to this Fischer business, so that his part in stamping on would be recognized. Then, the Wolinski thing might even be turned to his advantage, given how quickly he'd reported it to his Directorate Boss in Moscow. *That man Bolkov – he might look like the back of a shot-up tank but he's as sharp as the best of them. Let's bring him back to the Lubyanka and get him onto the sixth floor.*

'You're smiling, Comrade. Have you found something?'

'Um, no. I was thinking about the matter of interrogation.'

'Of …?'

'Fischer, and possibly Wolinski too.'

'You heard the Chairman. He wants them squeezed and dead quickly, once Zarubin's in the ground or disgraced.'

'I know, but I've been considering it. The man Globnow - he was former MGB, yes?'

'That's what Comrade Serov said.'

'Yet he managed to arrange his own apparent death, and then disappeared. That would be quite a feat, wouldn't it?'

It's certainly remarkable.'

'Impossible, I'd say, unless he had help.'

'Which would mean Zarubin.'

'Yes, and that begs two questions: why, and how many others are there besides Globnow?'

'Well we can't ask him now, can we?'

'Which is why I'm wondering if Fischer's interrogation would be more damaging than revealing.'

Korotkov returned to his wall-clock. Bolkov was right. Removing Zarubin and his two suspected accomplices here in Berlin might excise Serov's problem entirely, or only partially. *If* there were others, could they have something that might compromise the Chairman's position? The answer was unknowable, and would remain so until Fischer – and, possibly, Wolinski were questioned. But Bolkov's *why* put a question over the interrogations, in a way. If Zarubin had been assisting the discreet 'retirement' of agents, it couldn't be for compassion's sake. The prospect of some form of parallel intelligence network in Berlin - answerable not to the Chairman but to someone who could share his data directly with members of the Politburo – was unimaginable, much less tolerable. At the least, it could compromise the entire Berlin Rezidentura. How, they would be asked as they took a punch in the collective face (and God knew, it would be Serov doing the punching), could they not only allow it to happen but fail subsequently to even notice its existence?

Fuck. They were in a bind. Bringing in Fischer and Wolinski immediately and squeezing them would be the wisest move *only* if what they had to say wasn't too spectacular. Fortunately, then, it wasn't an option. Their arrest would wave a large warning flag in General Zarubin's direction, and, if he then escaped Serov's trap, bring the Chairman down upon them like an Assyrian with a grudge. They had to wait until Zarubin couldn't avoid the blow, but waiting might give Fischer an equal opportunity to slip away or further into a place where KGB couldn't follow. It was beginning to look as if the most prudent course – for Korotkov and Bolkov, at least – would be to arrange for a speeding car to slam into the man as he crossed a busy intersection, but despite the popularity of that tableau as a cinematic device it was extremely difficult to pull off convincingly. So again, Zarubin would be warned. Similarly, KGB had long over-employed the passing poisoned needle, and if Fischer merely dropped in the street from a suspected heart attack or stroke the General would assume the presence of a pin-prick without ever needing to see it.

The choice was hardly a choice at all, then. They couldn't yet seize and interrogate Fischer, they couldn't know what he'd spill once they did, and they couldn't knock him on the head with sufficient subtlety for it not to be noticed. It was to be a sitting-on-hands exercise, keeping company with a fond hope that the target was too dumb or oblivious to notice what was going on around him - and Korotkov suspected that Fischer was neither.

'I have another concern.'

'I'm sorry?'

Bolkov looked uncomfortable. 'We don't *know* that Fischer is an associate of Zarubin, so we're being prudent – firstly, in following his every move, and then dealing with him once the General is removed.'

'Prudence is good.'

'I agree, heartily. But assume for a moment that the man *is* in fact one of Zarubin's Berlin operatives.'

'Your point?'

'We shoved Wolinski into the surveillance operation to enable us to keep a single eye on two potential problems. We reasoned that, with luck, Wolinski might attempt to contact and warn Fischer, thus proving our suspicions correct. What we *can't* determine, however, is how Zarubin's Berlin network – if it *is* a network – functions in the absence of Globnow. Was he one of several potential contact points between the General and his foot-soldiers, or the only one? If the latter – did our removal of him force extemporary measures?'

'What are you thinking?'

'I'm suggesting that Zarubin may have made contact with Wolinski already, and used the opportunity - having no other recourse - to pass on instructions to Fischer.'

'Jesus.'

'Precisely. So, our subsequent placing of Wolinski in proximity to Fischer ...'

'May be doing the enemy's work for him.'

'Of course, it's only a possibility.'

That didn't loosen their bind even slightly. Korotkov was beginning to wish fervently that they'd reassigned Wolinski to duties at Wünsdorf, where about twenty thousand Red Army personnel could have done the necessary surveilling. He reminded himself that there remained a potentially optimistic side to this – that it was entirely possible that neither Fischer nor Wolinski were being worked by Zarubin. And then he reminded himself that it wasn't his business to hope for bests. An Intelligencer's universe couldn't allow for the random impact of particles, nor that the trajectory of a looming celestial body might not be of concern.

He scratched his chin. 'I'm having an unfamiliar feeling about this, Comrade.'

'Helplessness?' Bolkov wished he hadn't said it even as it was finding free air. Their mutual predicament was making him forget that Korotkov was not a friend, and therefore a potential enemy. It had been a question, but sounded too much like an admission.

It was a momentary anxiety, though. For the first time that Bolkov could recall, the Resident let his own shield fall away entirely.

'Something like that. We're waiting upon our Chairman, upon surveillance teams that contain at least one idiot and a potential traitor, and upon the dice landing favourably for us. I find it an uncomfortable place to be.'

It was a privilege, of sorts, to hear it. Korotkov hadn't been put in charge of KGB's most sensitive posting because of a lack of nerve. As loud and abrasive as he could be, he had as close to Serov's full confidence anyone might (Bolkov certainly didn't assume the same for himself), so his admitting to even a degree of anxiety was both startling and disconcerting. Had Bolkov not shared the feeling to a great extent, he might have felt almost honoured.

It was a moment, he supposed, for something bland and supportive, and even several hours later he was still wondering why he said what he did.

'Wouldn't it be a great relief if this Fischer could be made to just ... go away?'

For a few moments Korotkov stared at him, the fingers of one hand drumming on his desk, and Bolkov feared that he'd been too forthright. But then he realized that the eyes were working on something else.

'We …. no, it's impossible. Well, not impossible, but impracticable. And if not impracticable, practically suicidal. ' Korotkov gave his telephone an almost yearning look. 'Until Comrade Serov gives us the *go* order.'

'I suppose …'

'Yes?'

Bolkov swallowed. 'If some event were to necessitate an immediate decision on either Fischer or Wolinski, the Chairman could hardly criticize our response.'

'You know perfectly well that he could, and would.'

'But not if that event also, and unequivocally, clarified their threat to Berlin operations.'

'How could it do that?' Despite himself, Korotkov allowed a hopeful, rising pitch to betray him.

'At some point, we're going to dispose of Fischer.'

'Following his interrogation, yes.'

'And what if we don't mention that last part when we prepare our surveillance teams to make their move?'

'I don't follow you.'

'It's standard practice, isn't it, to forewarn a team that an operation may conclude with a kill order? What if we pass the word – now - that when the time comes, they should be ready to take him down at a moment's notice, and leave it at that?'

'Then ...' Slowly, Korotkov smiled.

'*If* Wolinski is one of Zarubin's people, Fischer will be warned immediately – *if* he's likewise. We can prevent that, of course, but we'll then have a definitive answer regarding both of them. In the same hour – or minute, if possible – we inform the Chairman of this entirely unanticipated development. Obviously, it will force him to move against Zarubin, but with Wolinski held incommunicado and Fischer thus kept unaware that he's been blown, Serov will have at least a brief time advantage. Whatever then happens, he can only conclude that we've acted correctly.'

Korotkov had been contemplating his desk, nodding as he listened. They would be going against their Chairman's express order to wait upon his Moscow business, and to interrogate the suspects before killing them; but he wouldn't need to know that. Even Serov allowed for fate and happenstance – what Intelligence Chief didn't? The risk was worth it, because if their fears were justified and Wolinski and Fischer were given time and room to further Zarubin's plans then the latter's removal might not be enough to prevent profound damage to KGB. The Berlin Resident could see that plainly, even if Serov himself was too focussed on his man.

He looked up at Bolkov. 'We'll do it.'

It was the right decision. His conscience was clear, even if his arse was twinging in anticipation of the kicking it might expect should anything not proceed smoothly. From the look on Bolkov's face he was thinking much the same thing. This was not usual business – in fact, Korotkov couldn't recall a situation quite like it. In other operations he had been obliged to make hard decisions quickly, or cast men loose, or commit to something without any sure prospect of success; yet even the worst of them had moved upon familiar rails, the common usages of the intelligencers' world. *This* had somehow mutated from a simple surveillance into a bare-footed dance on glass shards, the purpose of it lost somewhere beneath the music.

'Oh.'

Bolkov was looking at the report's final page, an appendix comprising a few lines of hand-scrawled data lifted from old MGB files. Korotkov hadn't bothered to read it.

'Have you found something?'

'He may be a former pimp.'

'What?'

'Fischer. He was in Stettin in the first months after the Surrender. No other connections or offences listed, but he was known to be consorting with a prostitute who also serviced Red Army personnel.'

'Who was the reporting officer?'

'There's no signature on file, apparently.'

Korotkov sniffed. 'I would give a month's salary if the man turned out to be no more than a pimp. I'd give it to *him,* in fact.'

'Technically, it's a criminal offence.' Bolkov sounded slightly hopeful, but Korotkov's cold stare dampened his mood.

'His imminent execution will rather square that account, don't you think?'

30

There was a bus service that might have taken Fischer from the end of his street directly to Rathaus Schöneberg, but he made his journey a little more tortuous. He walked from Lipaerstrasse to Lichterfelde-West S-bahn station, took the train but alighted one stop beyond Schöneberg, at Yorckstrasse-West, then retraced the route southwards to the Rathaus. He took the greatest care to make his many backward glances as casual as possible, yet didn't once see anyone who looked remotely interested in his progress.

He wasn't reassured. Since he had knocked on his former neighbour's door the hairs on his neck had refused to settle, and he trusted them implicitly. Every innocent explanation for the presence of that van was convincing, yet he couldn't convince himself. No aspect of his new career to date could have excited the least suspicion, yet he felt as twitchy as if a hundred eyes were upon him. He wondered if it was age, paranoia, cowardice or native common sense, and couldn't settle on any of them.

Despite the detour he arrived precisely on time for his appointment with Herr Brecker, but was asked to wait. He passed almost half an hour with *Der Spiegel* and its speculations on a coming East-West confrontation, refused several offers of coffee from an eager-to-please secretary and occasional caressed his report, as if its wilder stabs at a false reality might be calmed by the soothing motion. Eventually, Brecker emerged, tossed his head and marched back into his office without checking whether he was being followed.

The self-important act dropped the moment the door closed. Brecker turned and held up both hands.

'I'm sorry about that – Brandt's circumnavigation schedule's proving as easy to pin down as two butterflies fucking.'

'He's really going around the world? I thought that was just some nonsense for the newspapers.'

'No, it's happening. Canada, the US, Japan, the British Asian colonies, India – he'll be pulling heartstrings on behalf of plucky little West Berlin. And, of course, getting himself known as a world leader in-waiting. Is that it?'

'Yes.' Reluctantly, Fischer held out his report. Brecker took it and sat down.

'Do you mind?'

'No, please.'

Fischer sat also, and waited while the other man read the thing from front to back. Twice, he smiled slightly, the eyebrows rising as if some confection were almost too much to pass unchallenged, but he said nothing until it was finished.

'Excellent work. Was it the General's idea to push forward Aristov as a dark-horse challenger?'

'No, the fault's entirely mine.'

'This is very good. Utterly preposterous of course, but if asked, CIA and Gehlen's people will probably concur with its content, if only to deflect attention from the fact they haven't ever considered the possibility of Aristov. And it's good that you're emphasising Khrushchev's vulnerability – the last thing anyone in the West wants is to throw away what little they know of the present Leadership and start over.'

'So, this report will ...'

'Make the Mayor's bowel movements considerably easier. If it fully convinces him, he'll hold on to you like a love-struck calf.'

'I don't know if I can keep it going. Surely, someone's going to see through me eventually?'

Brecker looked surprised. 'Why? Most opinion on an enemy's mind and intentions is horribly wrong – look at the history of this century, for God's sake! If any decent intelligence had been available, would either war have started the way it did? All that's necessary is for you to be plausible – that, and obfuscating. The General will provide further information to allow you to refer to men and events about which they have little or no current understanding. With that, not only will your opinions be valued but considered a gold standard against which others are measured.'

'I'd still like to know what it's *for*.'

'The General doesn't confide his plans. All disinformation is good, though.'

Brecker looked down at the report once more as he said it, and Fischer took a strong impression that a matter had been swept off the desk abruptly. He changed the subject.

'So, you'll put this under Brandt's nose?'

'Almost as soon as I can get into his office. I don't want Georg Walter seeing it first and thinking he can deal with it himself.'

'He does that, does he?'

'He's an effective personal assistant, unfortunately. And, with everyone up to Adenauer himself clamouring for the Mayor's attention these days, very necessary. I'll tell him that this is remarkably important, and that Brandt should see it before he makes any more speeches about Berlin and the Ivans.'

Fischer had to remind himself that *this* was a pile of ordure, and that he wasn't really becoming an important person. Still, he couldn't ever recall having tried so weakly to leap so far. On the strength of two bad works of fiction he was about to be labelled a foremost authority. Perhaps he might supplement his representative's salary with a few media interviews in which, sucking on a pipe (a prop that invariably loaned gravitas to scoundrels), he would cast light into the more arcane corridors of Soviet Power, while anyone who tuned in from those corridors would stop, frown and wonder what the hell the idiot was talking about.

He only half-heard Brecker making his excuses (something about agreeing official statements with Singapore) and left the office, where he was stopped by the coffee-offering secretary (a serious, slightly flustered young woman). She held out a clip-board to him.

'Would you sign this, please?'

He'd obeyed before the question occurred. 'What is it?'

'The furniture requisition, for your office.'

'My …?'

'Second floor, south side. It's being emptied of shelves and lavatory supplies at the moment. Room 245 – it isn't very large, but you'll be able to seat two visitors at least.'

Dazed, Fischer accepted a key from her. He had never earned an (unshared) office in any of his previous employments, whether adequately or badly discharged, yet one was now being thrust at him before he had raised a single drop of perspiration in the cause of Berlin's governance. It was a profound lesson in the futility of effort. He even earned a smile from the young lady – who, presumably, had moved him from her nobody to someone schedule. He returned it, pocketed the key, and went to find his new kingdom.

He had tracked it down it (now cleared of disinfectants, mops, sponges and tissue but awaiting new furniture) before it occurred that he hadn't mentioned his raised neck-hairs to Brecker. He wondered why. He couldn't trust the man of course, but wasn't it his business to know if there was a possibility that the new man was being watched? He'd certainly have more ability to do something about it than the prey itself, yet the prey remained reluctant to put any more faith in the man than a fellow traitor deserved.

He had no reason to linger (he might have put his head around the door of Lamm and company's office to say good morning, but the revelation that he had one to himself might have tested their goodwill to destruction), so he departed the Rathaus and plotted a new course back to Lichterfelde, via a vast, circular three-bus route, north to Fehrbelliner-Platz, southwest to Dahlem Dorf and then east to the Botanical Gardens. Again, he saw no-one who evidenced any interest in him (other than a woman on the first bus, who glanced up at him momentarily and then did the familiar double-take of his damaged face before hurriedly returning to her book) And again, his neck-hairs told him to try harder.

Stepping off the final bus on Unter den Eichen, he might have walked directly home; instead, he made a comprehensive perambulation of every street between Hindenburgdamm in the east and Moltkestrasse to the west, and on the north-south axis between Hortensienstrasse and Augustastrasse, taking care to peer down every alley and parking bay he passed on the way.

It took him almost two hours, but he found the van in a service area behind a small parade of shops in Manteuffelstrasse. Two things made it seem out of place – firstly, the rear entrance it guarded was disused, the shop to the front having been empty for almost six months (he'd noticed over that time how the window had gradually filled with realtors' posters, testimony to the difficulty in re-leasing the tired, out-of-date premises); secondly, the telephone number on its side was a Reinickendorf exchange. It was quite feasible that an electrical engineers' company from the northern extremity of West Berlin had occasional work in Lichterfelde or Steglitz; but two, separate jobs in the space of a single week was stretching credibility. It was here for one reason – it had been noticed previously on Lipaerstrasse.

It took him five minutes to return to his house – a similar commute to that of whoever was watching it, he supposed. By the time he closed his front door he had decided to say nothing to Freddie Holleman (the eruption of a short but vicious brawl on the respectable, tree-lined street would do little for its reputation), nor to consciously adjust his routine over the coming days. A surveillance could mean several things, all bad but not all necessarily disastrous - it suggested interest in, but perhaps not full awareness of, Fischer's activities. A sudden swerve in any aspect of his habits might well confirm suspicions of …

What? That he was a Soviet spy? If so, it hardly seemed likely that Gehlen's crowd (he still couldn't think of them as BND) would watch from a distance when an interrogation could tell them so much more, unless they believed that they were laying a broader trap. Who else? Was it possible that *Stasi* had received word of Holleman's return to Berlin, and had sent a team over the Line to tie off unfinished business? That was even less likely – surely, he would have been cacked the moment a firm identification was made? To his knowledge, CIA were content to leave German nationals to Gehlen these days, and neither the British or French would dare to mount an independent operation in the American Zone. Which left …

KGB. Fischer smiled to himself. It would be a fine example of the beast eating itself, and hardly too ridiculous to conceive; but he couldn't think that they had so many spare resources that spies could routinely be spied upon by their own. In any case, what had he done to date that needed to be watched closely? He was a purveyor of fantasies to the office of the Mayor, a pretend authority on matters about which he was rehearsed by Moscow. If they were worried about his work, surely the simplest recourse would be to examine it directly, rather than peer through curtains at its author?

Ticking off all the possibilities wasn't helpful. Almost certainly, he *was* being observed, and there had to be a reason for it. Absent any inspiration, he had to assume that the exercise, whatever its purpose, was likely to conclude unpleasantly. From his own experience as a *kripo*, undercover operations rarely if ever just wound down and went away - budgets had to be justified and results demonstrated. It didn't matter that he might be entirely innocent of whatever was suspected; if this thing was being supervised by someone with sufficient ambition then a corpse would be a palpable result, even for a palpable error.

Options required information, and he had none. His only obvious recourse was to Zarubin, in the hope that the man would want to protect his investment. Unfortunately, assistance from that direction always came with thick, dockyard ropes attached, and Fischer was wound about too tightly as it was. Freddie Holleman's help would be unconditional, but extend to no more than half-dragging, half-carrying his friend to Zoo Station and the West. There was no-one else in, close to or familiar with the intelligencers' world who might begin to parse his present situation, his choices, his chances.

For the moment, then, he could only continue as before and hope that nothing he said or did tripped a wire. If all that Zarubin required of him was a supply of apparently informed opinions upon what the Ivans were thinking, he couldn't see how that wire might snap. If he was asked to do more, he would have to think again. If someone had made a decision about him already, he could reassure himself that there was nothing to be done, and that he probably wouldn't even feel the bullet pass between his shoulder blades.

31

Luci had been working on reception for four days only, and
was still in awe of the cool, sophisticated manner with which
her colleagues welcomed new arrivals, or gently indulged the
inconsequential gripes that guests seemed to assume were as
much a perquisite of their stay as a comfortable bed and a view
of the Tiergarten. Only an hour earlier she had watched, lost in
admiration, as Reino (who couldn't be much older than she)
allowed an irate Canadian gentleman to exhaust himself
berating the hotel management, his travel company and even
the German nation for what he insisted was the appalling
omission of a television from his room. While he was drawing
breath, Reino had explained that the Hotel am Steinplatz did
not place such devices in the bedrooms because it was felt that
they detracted from the establishment's *fin de siecle* charm (he
actually used the term); but that as a concession to modernity
there was a set in the lounge bar, should the gentleman wish to
avail himself of that pleasure. In the meantime, he would
instruct the bartender that the gentleman's first two drinks that
evening were not to be charged to his account, in the hope that
this would salve the trauma somewhat.

For a few moments a familiar struggle play across the
Canadian's face, the frustration of wanting to be angry after the
cause had been snatched away, and then Reino received the
gracious acknowledgment of a curt nod and a fine view of
shoulders, receding. He had turned to Luci and winked, leaned
closer, whispered *muschi* and then smoothly deployed his
dazzling smile at his next guest.

The obscenity had made her laugh. At home she wasn't allowed to use even mild epithets, so Reino's casual crudity added to her sense of having stepped out into a wider, more sophisticated world. When he went for his break she stood up to the dark, polished wood counter and mentally ran through his facial expressions, mannerisms and the various smiles that said welcome, oh dear and it has been the supreme pleasure of my life to encounter you, sir. The last had barely faded in her head when she was confronted by a handsome blond man in his mid-forties, beautifully dressed and groomed, wearing a very similar smile. She couldn't help but think of how Reino would regret not having dealt with the gentleman personally (he being very much more affected by good-looking men than ladies), but was pleased nonetheless to have the view to herself.

'Good morning, Sir - welcome to the Hotel am Steinplatz. How may I help you?'

It had been the first and easiest of the many stock phrases that she had needed to commit to memory, but the man beamed as gratefully as if she had offered him the Philosopher's Stone and a quick one behind the counter.

'Good morning! I have a reservation for three nights. My name is Krenze – Wolfgang Krenze.'

He handed over his identity papers as he spoke. The photograph bore no hint of a smile, but she decided that Krenze stern was just as pretty as Krenze amiable. Briefly, she noted the home address (a place in Bavaria she had never heard of) and felt her cheeks warm as she handed them back. As he tucked them into a breast pocket he gave her a look that hinted at some little pleasantry shared, and while she took it as a quite definite flirt the option of being offended didn't occur to her. She consulted her bookings and rooms schedules, found what she was looking for on each and tried to enter into the game.

'You've reserved a standard single room, but I can put you in one of our doubles with a northerly aspect. There won't be an additional charge.'

'Ah, that's very kind of you. I assume it isn't quite ready yet – may I leave my case here while I have lunch?'

She couldn't have refused – it was a small portmanteau, easily accommodated in the receptionists' den behind her. In any case, she didn't feel at all like denying him. In fact, has he asked her to be his lunch guest she would have begged someone to stand in for her and then begged five minutes from him while she refreshed her makeup. It couldn't happen of course, but the thought was pleasant enough for her smile to be entirely unrehearsed.

'I can put it back here. Please ask for me when you return and I'll fetch it. I'm Luci.'

'As in Lucille?'

She shook her head regretfully. 'Lucretia. My Father's parents were Italian.'

'Well, I much prefer Lucretia. For centuries, it's graced only the most beautiful women.'

Zarubin could feel her gaze warming his neck all the way across the lobby and out the front door. He was pleased that his little performance had yielded such pleasant results; otherwise, he hadn't the slightest interest in whether she (or any other woman - or man, for that matter) found him attractive or monstrous. Throughout his adult life he had assumed that his latent sexuality had taken lodgings in the placenta that his first breath had retired. He was quite capable of degrees of affection, but sexual longing was as much a stranger to him as a peal of bells was to a deaf man. Whether that was a curse or a blessing he couldn't say, not least because he had devoted such little thought to the question.

It was a pleasant day for December in Berlin, he had just proved to himself that he had it still (whatever 'it' was) and a nice, unhurried lunch loomed (it was the only truthful thing he'd said to sweet, young Lucretia), but the weight of his situation pressed too heavily for any of it to distract him. There was nowhere in this city that was safe for him, no stranger's glance that he could assume to be disinterested. All he had in his favour was that no-one would be looking for him here, plus the mild power of deflection that a few subtle props bestowed. He had his expensive Brook Brothers suit (the only fond memento of his American exile, he never wore it in Moscow), a hat to hide his strikingly blond hair (which, now he thought about it, he placed on his head) and a pair of plain glass spectacles (which, now he thought about them, he took from a jacket pocket and placed on his nose). Anyone who knew him would recognize him at a second glance, but he was hoping not to make himself so interesting as to encourage one.

He chose a small Bavarian restaurant just off Fasanenstrasse (principally to test his accent), and, over a cheap but excellent lunch (how could it not be, after five years of the Moscow Diet?), set himself to the problem of Otto Fischer. Had he the option, he would be in Steglitz already, knocking on the man's door, but the presence of a KGB surveillance team was a gentle discouragement. Probably, they had wired his telephone, so a call would be equally unwise. The only location at which he could be reasonably certain of accosting Fischer was Rathaus Schöneberg, but if the KGB operation had sufficient resources they might well be there, too. In any case, he knew that *Stasi* had people in there, one or more of whom, given cause or opportunity, might recognize him from his Karlshorst days. So, he couldn't wander around the building looking for Fischer – the man had to come to him. Risking Othmar Brecker was unthinkable; with Globnow gone, he was by far the most valuable of of small network of men in Berlin, and had to remain above suspicion. Which left the unaffiliated but amenable Herbert Lamm, innocent of anything but dislike of Willy Brandt and his works. A appointment with the gentleman shouldn't be too hard to arrange if Zarubin mentioned an old friend, recently elected to the *Abgeordnetenhaus*, and did Lamm know him by any chance?

Pleased by this resolution, Zarubin ordered a second glass of Silvaner and considered what Fischer should be told. He needed to know that he was under surveillance, and perhaps a little of the circumstances; but too much information would poison the broth. Fischer aware was good; Fischer running for the hills much less so. Doubtless, he would work out at least a small part of the truth for himself – the gap between his political experience and where he was going was too great to allow the story to be entirely credible; but it was only necessary to keep the fog thick enough to obscure the destination until he fell into it.

And then there was Friedrich Holleman. It had been five days since Levin encountered him at Fischer's home. Perhaps he was gone, back to Trier and oblivion. If not, he was a potential threat – not for what he knew, but for who he had pretended to be, back when he and Zarubin had worked together. Everyone else – KGB, K5 and VolksPolizei – had assumed him to be the hero Kurt Beckendorp; yet not only had Zarubin known the truth but used it to extract every last gram of the man's industry. Could that fact, discovered, be the extra bullet that Serov needed? Holleman in Berlin was both vulnerable and dangerous. He shouldn't have come here. He needed to go away, one way or the other.

An elegant plan, crafted carefully over several years, was beginning to fray at the edges. Zarubin wondered if Levin had been at all convinced by the nonchalance he'd attempted to project. Certainly, he hadn't convinced himself. He was attempting to trip the most dangerous man in the Soviet Union, the last brutal manifestation of the old regime still in a position to make the new one change course, and his only weapon was his agile mind. All the accumulated filth – the betrayals, execution orders, false promises and witch-hunts that had served as substitutes for a recognizable form of government – attested itself still in the Lubyanka's cellars, neatly ordered by reference to victim, date, accuser, momentary whim; all of it was accessible, but only to Serov and his lieutenants. No-one – not even Khrushchev – could afford to be sanguine about what the KGB Chairman knew or cared to reveal; no-one could be certain of surviving any revelation that he cared to make. He was the sort of enemy that a wise man would approach with armoured divisions behind him, not a handful of superannuated MGB operatives and a scheme that seemed more clever than it might turn out to be.

And Zarubin had only pushed the odds by coming to Berlin, the most sensitive province of Serov's intelligence empire, where KGB could not only call upon its own manpower but, from the rest of the Karlshorst complex alone, 83rd Motorized Rifle Regiment, 133rd Separate Guard Battalion and an MfS sonderkommando that surely would be only too happy to take time off from guarding the site perimeter to assassinate the Chairman's most persistent problem. That thought managed to sour the delightful Silvaner, and he left almost half of it in the glass when he paid his bill.

From a telephone kiosk he called the Rathaus and asked to speak to Representative Lamm. Fortunately, the gentleman was in his office, and agreed to see an acquaintance of Otto Fischer at short notice. 'Could you allow me an hour?' he asked -

which, given that the Rathaus lay four kilometres almost directly south, suited Zarubin perfectly.

He walked briskly, pausing only to examine his refection in a shop window on Landshuterstrasse. With all his props in place, he decided he looked exactly like Sergei Aleksandrovich Zarubin and no other. His nerves rarely needed massaging, but he had to remind himself that a successful disguise relied far more upon deportment than a bag of tricks.

When he reached the Rathaus he had to present himself at reception and ask for Lamm. This was the moment at which incurious eyes might light upon him and a memory stir, so he forced his shoulders back, spoke pleasantly but firmly and invited anyone to notice that he was a man entirely at his ease (he wasn't, naturally). As far as he could tell, no-one in the sparsely populated hallway paused in their busy passage to accept the challenge.

Lamm was prompt. The politician in him kept his curiosity in check, and he was as welcoming as if Zarubin had been a swing voter. Gratifyingly, his conversation at the desk extended only to a smile and hello; arm extended, he shepherded his guest to the main staircase and up to the second floor in less than a minute thereafter. A solitary frown intercepted them on the stairs, but Zarubin saw that it was entirely preoccupied before he had time to worry.

The arm halted him in an empty corridor. Lamm smiled apologetically.

'I share my office with half a football team, but there's a constituents' meeting room we can use.'

'Thank you. Is Herr Fischer ...'

'In the building, yes. I told him I had a surprise for him, that's all. He should be here soon. Would you like a coffee?'

'Perhaps when he arrives?' *So we can get you out of the way for a few minutes.*

The constituents' room was furnished with a selection of stand-chairs that had seen venerable service elsewhere, as if to encourage visitors to remain for the least time it took to vent their complaints. Zarubin resisted the temptation and stood by the window, which looked down on to Rudolph-Wilde Park. Lamm stood uncertainly, too polite to pry into the purpose of the visit but lacking any useful topic to fill the awkward pause adequately. He waved a hand towards the window.

'It's, um, a good retreat when small print becomes unbearable.'

'I'm sorry?'

'The park. A walk can loosen one's head.'

Zarubin examined the view as if to gauge its efficacy. 'Oh, yes. I imagine so.'

The door opened, and both men's relief lasted as long as it took to turn to the new arrival. Robert, Lamm's colleague and roommate, stepped in.

'He can't come.'

'Eh?'

'Otto, he can't come. He just telephoned, and asked me to give you the message.'

Zarubin, dropping any pretence of courtesy, glared at the unfortunate messenger. '*Why* can't he come?'

'He's been called into Willy Brandt's office – right away, he said.'

Lamm brightened perceptibly. 'Has he messed up already?'

'I don't know. I doubt it. Willy Brandt wants to speak to him, apparently. He was asked to clear his diary for the rest of the afternoon.'

32

Fischer's first instinct was to plunge his head into his copy of the latest report and try to memorize it, but the tone of the summons hadn't given an impression that he might take his time. He picked up the document, rolled it, straightened his tie, reminded himself that he wasn't an offending schoolboy and stepped out of his tiny office.

Perhaps it had been naivety, but even with Moscow's resources behind him he hadn't really expected to be dealing directly with the Governing Mayor. Brandt was the Coming Man, western Germany's *stupor mundi*, whose time was rationed like the last tin of pressed beef at Pitomnik. It hardly seemed possible that he would halt his headlong flight to greatness long enough to entertain, face to face, the ramblings of an amateur geopolitical seer.

During the brief time it required to tread carpet to the Mayor's office, Fischer told himself that he had a few minutes' grace at least. He could ask Brandt's secretary Georg Walter what it was precisely that was required of him; he might fashion something intelligible around this while he waited for Brandt's previous guest to finish his business; and almost certainly, he wouldn't be required to provide definitive answers on matters not covered by his two papers. *It isn't going to be an ordeal* he told himself, letting the echo soothe his nerves.

Georg Walter was standing in the outer office when he arrived. He smiled and waved a hand at a door.

'Ah, Herr Fischer. Please go straight in.'

Shit.

Having a very recent memory of his own storage cupboard, and a slightly fainter one of Lamm and company's generous one-man office, he was a little disorientated by the steppe-like expanse of the Governing Mayor's domain. Fortunately, its various vistas were broken up by plentiful leather furniture, expensive rugs and a rank of polished wood bookcases. In contrast, the Mayor's desk was modestly-proportioned, allowing two quite tall, steeply-leaning men to shake hands across its narrower side.

Willy Brandt didn't offer his hand, however. Fischer had to make do with the famous broad smile and the object itself directing him to a seat. He cleared his throat and advanced.

'Good afternoon, Herr Regierender Burgo ...'

'Oh, none of that, Herr Fischer – we're both servants of the People. May I call you Otto?'

'Yes, of course.'

'Then you must call me Willy. I've ordered coffee – or would you prefer tea?'

Fischer found it disheartening that the equally famous Common Touch was working on him, so much so that it was necessary to steel his cynic's soul.

I'm happy with either, thank you.'

'Good, good.' Brandt sat down and lifted a sheath of papers from his desk. 'Thank you for this. I hope you don't mind, but I sent a copy to Pullach to ask their opinion – your name wasn't mentioned, of course.'

The clarification managed to rein back Fischer's pulse from its threatened take-off. The last thing he wanted was for Gehlen's people to be reminded of a former pain in their collective arse and offered a reason to investigate his alleged qualifications.

'Of course not. What was their opinion?'

'Strangely, they didn't have one. They merely asked if they might retain it for their information, which I took to mean that they found it useful.'

'That's … gratifying.'

'Yes. So, Averky Aristov - I have to say, I didn't expect that conclusion.'

'It's a theory, and very provisional, obviously. I propose that he constitutes the least unlikely challenger to Khrushchev's position, and only then if the General Secretary loses the confidence of a majority in the Praesidium.'

'Why least unlikely?'

'The other possibilities are either too new to high office, too venerable, too risk-averse or too stained by their association with last year's attempted coup. Aristov has managed to make himself well-thought of by Khrushchev's allies, yet, as a former Stalinist appointee, he remains acceptable to the reactionaries.'

Brandt scratched his nose. 'From what little we know of the man, he doesn't seem overly ambitious.'

'He may not be - though of course, to become a member of the Praesidium indicates at least a degree of wanting to get ahead. He'd almost certainly be – and see himself as – an interim, collegiate leader around which the various factions would manoeuvre to place his eventual successor.'

'But in the meantime …?'

'*If* he replaced Khrushchev, it would be because the latter had failed to demonstrate sufficient backbone in dealing with the Americans – particularly since it appears to have been his idea alone to goad them with his demands regarding Berlin. Therefore, Aristov – or anyone else, for that matter – would be obliged to demonstrate absolute firmness, no matter how much they might regret the original cause for it.'

'Hmm.' Brandt studied his desk, and as he did so Fischer experienced a minor epiphany. He was quite *good* at this – at turning dross into something less than absurdity, and doing it with what seemed to be conviction. His Lie Division work had been a similar exercise of course, but back then he hadn't been required to stare his audience in the face to justify himself. It raised a terrible question: was he becoming an instinctive politician? And was he actually enjoying the experience?

The Mayor looked up. 'So you think it'll be a confrontation, whoever leads the Politburo?'

'I wouldn't say *definitely*, no. They're all aware that the Soviet Union has a military advantage only in conventional terms, and even that for just the first two weeks of any conflict. It's enough to get them to the Rhine, but they understand that the consequences could be extraordinarily bad. If Eisenhower decides his only option is to utilize his atomic bombers and missiles, the advantage passes to the West.' Fischer cleared his throat. 'Not to *us*, obviously – we'll be beneath it. But the

Kremlin greatly fears strikes into the territories of their Warsaw Pact allies, which could very well decouple them and leave a significant proportion of the Red Army too far west to maintain its supply lines.'

'I was going to ask about the Eastern Europeans.'

Christ. 'The Ivans can rely upon the Romanians – they fought well at Stalingrad, though on our side – but their forces aren't significant, nor are Bulgaria's. Hungary can't be trusted, not after '56. The Czech intelligence service is entirely loyal to Moscow, the Army less so. The Poles will mobilize, but to them the USSR is the enemy still, and no Soviet war plan relies on them for more than second echelon duties. Really, it's the East Germans alone who'll figure in the Kremlin's calculations. Once the bombs start dropping, no-one else can be trusted not to seek terms – and then, of course, the Red Army might be fighting on two fronts. All these things will be considered if it comes to brinkmanship.'

Fischer had no idea if a single word of what he'd said was anything other than nonsense, but he marvelled at how easily it had poured out. *This* was what an expert was – plausible, confident enough to give pause and sufficiently vague to deflect suspicion that he might in fact be a complete fraud.

He reminded himself that a degree of humility was necessary also. 'Naturally, BND could tell you much of this.'

Brandt nodded. 'I'm surprise you're not with them. After all, you were Luftwaffe Intelligence during the war. Pullach would seem to be a logical home for you.'

He couldn't keep *this* part of the deception going - it would take only a casual reference, an unguarded response to a question, and everything about Otto Fischer would be flipped.

'I was recruited by Gehlen, in 1946. To be frank, we parted on bad terms soon afterwards. The Org was going to ensnare a particular friend of mine, who at the time was a high ranking VolksPolizei officer. I assisted in his evading the trap. I should say that he's since defected, and given up what little he knew.'

The eyebrows rose considerably. 'Oh. So you'd prefer your name to continue not to be mentioned - in that direction, at least?'

'If that's acceptable.'

'Of course. It's the fate of modern Germany, that sides have to be taken. I assume there was nothing in this friend's past that will haunt us?'

'He was a fighter pilot, shot down over Belgium in 1940. After that, his tin leg kept him out of trouble. There are plenty of people at Pullach with far more difficult histories, who don't seem to cause Herr Gehlen any sleepless nights.'

Brandt squirmed slightly in his chair. 'A very good point. Otto, you've given a lot to think about. I'm going to Bonn tomorrow, to discuss the situation with the Federal Chancellor. In the meantime, please give some more thought to Khrushchev and his options. Will he consider another blockade of the city? What moves do you think we'll see, and what will they mean? That sort of thing.'

'Of course. Should I prepare something in writing?'

Brandt didn't answer immediately. He seemed preoccupied - which, under the circumstances, Fischer considered to be precisely the correct thing to seem. It didn't require any kind of expert to see that West Berlin would be the first casualty, should any confrontation between the Allies and Soviet Union ignite - it was, after all, both the cause and the prize. Unless the Americans and British were insane they wouldn't try to make a stand here. They couldn't reinforce their tiny garrisons to anything like the strength required to hold off the Red Army for more than a couple of hours, and stacking up martyrs wouldn't play well to their home constituencies. There would be an early decision to withdraw to the Federal Republic's borders (and perhaps even further, to avoid envelopment), and in the meantime the city would fall entirely under the DDR's control. At best, it might remain reasonably intact, to become the principal topic at the negotiating table; at worst, it would be the ground upon which a suspended conflict came to a resolution. Who would be comfortable being Mayor of something caught between two such titanic rocks?

The telephone rang, breaking Brandt's reverie. 'If you feel there's enough to make another report, by all means. Would you excuse me?'

Fischer couldn't find Othmar Brecker to report on his meeting, so he went back to his own office (which now seemed wretchedly enclosed) and wondered – as might an archer who hadn't seen the target or been marked by his judges - how he'd done. The purpose of it was as opaque as ever, but as far as he could tell he had fulfilled the letter of his assignment. Willy Brandt hadn't laughed him out of the room, nor even cast doubt upon what he had read – not openly, at least. If what he'd said about Pullach's reaction to the report was true, then the material provided by Zarubin had been strong enough to impress their dedicated Kremlin-watchers despite the fantastical use Fischer had made of it. Should he be proud of his success, or aghast that the nation's gatekeepers were gullible dolts?

He had given about ten minutes' thought to his next work of fiction when he recalled his surprise visitor. Lamm's coyness had irritated him, and he couldn't imagine anyone he might wish to see refusing to give a name. That had been almost two hours ago; no doubt the person was gone by now, but even someone pretending a sense of public duty shouldn't ignore a supplicant. He called Lamm's office. The line was engaged, so reluctantly he went to seek enlightenment.

'Don't worry, Otto! He was very happy to defer to the Man of the Age!'

'Who was he?'

'An old comrade from the war - Wolfgang Krenze.'

'Oh.' Fischer couldn't recollect the name, but that didn't mean they were strangers. Army and school days were very similar – you were thrown into proximity with a multitude of strangers, any of whom might have better reason to recall you than you they. Perhaps they had been in Fallschirmjäger training together; perhaps they had been introduced when Fischer joined 29th Motorized Artillery just before Smolensk; perhaps he had been one of the stretcher bearers who had carried him, screaming, from the field at Okhvat eight months later and had come to the Rathaus today to see if the view had improved since then. A name was just a noise; it was a face that dragged memories from the vault.

'Any distinguishing features?'

'Apart from his poor taste in friends? He's a remarkably good-looking man, a blond, the sort I always wanted to be instead of this comely creature (modestly, Lamm's hand swept across his chest), trapped in a fat bastard's body.'

Again, Fischer couldn't recall any famous beauties from his time in uniform, but then he hadn't been looking too hard. His mind dragged up a dim image of a fellow whose presence on evenings out in Belgium had always killed everyone else's chances of making it with the local girls; but he'd almost certainly been dark-haired, and even more almost certainly killed in Crete, in '41. And he had been Hans 'the Donkey', not Wolfgang.

'Did he say that he'd be coming back?'

'No. But he didn't said that he wasn't.'

With that helpful clarification, Fischer placed the mysterious Herr Krenze into his mental pending drawer, returned to his office for a copy of the Imported Soft Fruits Pricing Regulations (1958, ii) - upon which he and the other 132 representatives would be voting the following day - and departed the Rathaus. It was only three-thirty, but deceiving people was surprisingly heavy work and he felt the siren pull of a glass of wine even more than usual. For once, he wasn't dreading an evening in the company of Freddie Holleman. If the conversation could be directed away from the present situation, its inconsequentialities would further loosen the knots.

It was strange, but now that he was assuming himself to be followed he no longer bothered with evasive manoeuvres. He caught a bus directly from the Rathaus to the stand outside Lichterfelde S-bahn station, and, ten minutes later, stepped through his garden gate. Between there and the front door, a slight movement disturbed his right-side lateral vision, and he turned to take in the genteel prospect of his friend, pissing into the peony beds.

'Freddie …?'

Holleman tried to look over his shoulder without spoiling his aim. 'Sorry, Otto. Frau What'shername's cleaning the bathroom, and I've blocked the downstairs' *kackstuhl* with furniture from the sitting-room. I'm painting it tomorrow.'

'Couldn't you wait? What about the neighbours?'

'No, I couldn't. And they can't see anything from the road, can they? Not that it wouldn't be a treat if they could.'

It was almost dark now, so Holleman was probably right; but large men emptying themselves in front gardens wasn't what residents of Lipaerstrasse were used to, and Fischer had no wish to be labelled a social problem.

'Well, shake it off and come inside.'

'We need to talk about your escape plan.'

'Tomorrow - we'll think of a plan tomorrow. Let me tell you about my remarkable day, and then we'll get hammered.'

At a bedroom window across the road, Sergei took a fourth photograph as the larger of the two subjects – the one with a limp, the severity of which suggested a partial amputation – passed in front of a lit window. Despite the anxiety attacks that sometimes made his difficult moments even more difficult, Sergei had an extremely steady hand with a camera, and the f 1.5 Helios could suck in light where it hardly existed. He was fairly certain that his first shot would turn out to be uselessly blurred, but the rest would be sharp enough. If the man *could* be identified, he would be.

They had been told of the pending kill-order only four hours earlier, before he and Mikhail began their day's shift. He wondered if the new fellow would now need to be included in it. Taking down two men simultaneously - without advertising the fact - was not an easy task. Each team had a Mosin-Nagant sniper's rifle, but unless the target presented himself (or themselves) conveniently, the job would almost certainly need to be done close-up, with suppressed pistols. One man could be taken by surprise quite easily; an extra pair of eyes often caught an approach, and reacted. That would mean noise, and this street contained a high proportion of retired gentlefolk who were likely to be at home throughout the day. Sergei wasn't worried about being caught; by the time the police arrived the black team would be well across the Line and safe. They hadn't yet been given the story, though. Karlshorst might want this to be an object lesson, which was the straightforward, uncomplicated option. Or, if they decided that the situation was sensitive, it might need to look like a burglary gone badly, or a suicide (a suicide pact, if the second fellow's luck was out), or even nothing at all – in which case the removals team would need a street-full of oblivious residents to be minding there own businesses, not whatever was going on at number 87. Whichever was the case, doubling the body count more than doubled the obstacles to a clean job.

Still, it would be over soon. None of them was enjoying this assignment - it was too far from home, too exposed, too liable to be interrupted by everyone from real estate dealers to the local butcher, come to find out why the old lady's account hadn't been settled recently. All of that added to the usual boredom of surveillance. Sergei could recall the best of them – a two-day job opposite a secretarial college in Weissensee. The view had been delightful (particularly during lunch hours), the mark – a German employee at the Rezidentura, known to be passing low-level stuff to the Americans – both regular and careless in his habits. Even so, the minute-hand on clocks had seemed to freeze. No-one enjoyed this kind of work, not even the ones who did it best.

33

Be prepared to terminate the mission abruptly.

The order might have been alluding to a hurried extraction of
evidence of their presence in Lipaerstrasse, but Wolinski didn't
think so. They were being put on notice - that Otto Fischer had
a very short time remaining in this world, and that the teams
had better be sure that their head-shot skills were up to scratch.

It ended the conundrum, the unpleasant gift of initiative.
Wolinski no longer need dwell upon what might or needed to
be done, because Karlshorst had removed the choice. Fischer
was going to die, and soon, apparently.

It had been Timochenko, summoned to the presence of
Korotkov himself, who had returned with the news. At least
they now knew how big a thing this was. Everyone's
assumption had been that the operation came directly out of
Seventh Directorate (Surveillance), but if the Resident himself
was involved, briefing ground troops directly – and, according
to Timochenko, looking shaky about it - the instructions much
have originated from a higher plane, which meant Moscow.

What had Fischer been doing, to earn such august attention?
Wolinski had no close ear to that ground, but a quick-kill order
was usually intended to cauterize a wound and prevent
significant harm to KGB interests. And yet they had been
surveilling the man as if he were a stranger, an outlier whose
relevance needed to be gauged before any judgement could be
made. On the back of that alone, the order didn't make sense.
There had to be something else.

And there was the other thing. Since Timochenko's return he had been casting strange, sideways looks. It was nothing obvious enough to be pinned - more the sort of half-questioning glance that wanted to know whether a fart had come from his own arse or his neighbour's. Most people wouldn't have noticed it, but Wolinski's antenna was acutely sensitive to anything either side of normal. It might be that he'd only just heard of his partner's arrest, imprisonment and subsequent exoneration, but that didn't seem likely. If there was one thing that a tight, over-populated clutch of intelligencers couldn't help but indulge, it was the gossip-reflex.

The two of them would be on-shift again in three hours. Would the kill-order come through then? If it did, no doubt Timochenko would take the lead. That was only logical. Unlike Wolinski, the man had a great deal of experience of this kind of work and was just about the best marksman at Karlshorst, a steady hand with a clear, untroubled mind behind it. Fischer would be a target on a range, and he'd want the first, only shot at it. The second fellow – the limper who enjoyed pissing out of doors – might be tossed to Wolinski as a treat. Timochenko would think of it that way, no doubt.

Everything was settled. If it was to fall to them, they would be told whether discretion or a mess was required. They would discuss it, briefly – the approach, the kill, the extraction – and then carry out the order with as much care and as little thought as it required. After that, the report and debriefing, the brief stand-down to unwind any tight heads, and then a new assignment – hopefully, in Wolinski's case, to something involving a desk and mountainous quantities of paperwork.

That would be very pleasant. Tracking down and reporting misbehaviour among Red Army personnel had seemed tawdry, back when it had filled the professional horizon. Now, it would be a feather pillow, a holiday almost. But Wolinski suspected that things wouldn't be returning to that degree of normality. *This* was a test, obviously, but for what couldn't yet be located in the mist. All that could be done was to find a wall against which a back could press, to account for at least one direction from which the thrust might come.

How that might be done was a question that had kept company with Wolinski for years, flitting in and out of view. Now, it was dead centre, hovering, blocking the path – if it *was*, or ever had been, a path. There was no time left, no space for turnings; a decade and more of lies and pretences had achieved no more than to push their conceiver towards what was more likely to be a funnel's neck.

34

Like any good secretary, Levin, having some spare time in the absence of his demanding boss, decided to attend to the administrative accretions that the scheduling of more important work made inevitable. He completed requisition orders and statistical surveys, re-checked his typing (of Zarubin's more important correspondence), re-re-checked typing from the pool (of everything else) and made a start on winnowing out redundant material from his extensive archives, where materials too important, useful or sensitive to be misplaced in the Kremlin library found a home.

On the latter task he circled for a while, extracting data that hardly registered in memory anymore, needed for the preparation of briefings to the Council of Ministers on matters that had gone away, resolved themselves or ossified in the geological deliberations of sub-committees assembled for the purpose of perpetuating themselves. Eventually, he seized the hot iron and turned to a section of his filing system in which circulars from the Department of Works were dumped. He had chosen it as his special place, because although all departments received this paperwork, no-one who didn't work for the Department of Works could have a conceivably sane reason for reading it. It was where he put certain things – things that couldn't be left in a locked drawer, or in the apartment he shared with two junior lawyers from the Procurator General's Office, nor even in a station locker whose key number had been carefully filed off (an option he had considered briefly, until his nerves shredded at the prospect of random, master-key inspections).

At the moment, the thick wad of senseless information contained a single radioactive element, encased in a thin loose-leaf folder. It comprised two sheets of paper stapled together, upon which were scribbled notes and a short list of telephone numbers, none of which had a name or country-code attached. The keenest, most suspicious eye could find nothing there to warrant a probing question (much less an investigation), but the sum of it represented the most courageous thing that Levin had ever attempted.

And stupid, of course. What more apt label was there, for someone who tells ninety-five percent of the truth to one of the most intelligent men in the Soviet Union? Since the moment he had drawn General Zarubin's attention to the curious history – *most* of the curious history - of the Pole Wolinski, Levin had occupied a state between abject fear and shame. He owed a huge debt to the man for pulling him from the Lubyanka's administrative sub-stratas (where his over-active mouth had earned him almost daily reprimands and threats of transfers to industrial concerns east of the Urals – hell, to east of the Stanovoys), and into the almost monastic calm of the Kremlin Palace. He owed him more for his new accommodation and salary, for the forbearance, for being treated as a person rather than a cog or an arse to be kicked on bad days, for no longer being the butt of 'jokes' about twisted legs. All of that was now in the scales, weighing against his treachery.

He had withheld an important detail, and made up a little story to disguise the fact. Had he mentioned everything at the start, Wolinski might yet have been a sound, usable choice; but Zarubin would have sniffed at the business like an explosives dog. Having done so, he might even have found further advantage to be milked from the situation, but Levin had made a promise in order to extract the information, and once he'd committed himself there had been no feasible way to re-tell the story. So, he was being both inadvertently honourable *and* treacherous, and it was an uncomfortable place to be.

If Fischer were either to be successful in his task or snatched by a KGB team, Levin's sin of omission wouldn't matter; if Wolinski simply carried on as before, working for Karlshorst but passing information as and when the General required, it wouldn't matter. Only if two unstable substances were brought into proximity - and one of them reacted badly - would there be consequences. Unfortunately, Levin had not the slightest ability to influence that convergence. He was obliged to wait, to see how it played out. That might not have been too difficult a vigil were the General not in Berlin, getting close both to danger and revelation.

He wished now that he been able to resist the bargain – or, that he hadn't been quite so ingenious in trying to meet it. He might have thought of something else, some other way to get what he needed; but when he delved into the story his cleverness had taken command and common sense had been told to sit in the corner. He had ignored a great truth - that histories should always be feared. They wore large skirts, and no-one could know all of what lay beneath them.

35

Though he occasionally played football after a fashion, Bolkov was not a fit man; yet on a miserably cold December afternoon he jogged more than half the considerable distance between the Dram Theatre on Ehrenfelltrasse and the Rezidentura. A voice in his ear had interrupted his enjoyment (or, rather, endurance) of a performance of some indifferent but safe Russian composer's latest symphony, but his mild annoyance had shaded to more-than-mild panic when he got the full message in the foyer. Korotkov had asked him to come to his office as soon as possible. And he had said please.

It was one that senior KGB personnel tended not to use, except when ordering at a bar. Korotkov had never deployed it within Bolkov's hearing – at least, not to lower-rung men. So, when the messenger told him that the Resident had stressed the word, Bolkov had to fear the very worst (though he couldn't quite imagine what that might be). He moved quickly, and only slowed in order to recover some degree of composure as he approached the Rezidentura's main entrance. An infarction in the reception area would almost certainly be regarded as a bad career choice.

He was sent straight into Korotkov's office. The Resident was on the telephone, but he waved his visitor to a seat and continued shouting. It was something about extraction, and Bolkov didn't assume for a moment that teeth were involved. When the receiver went down, Korotkov pushed a sheet of paper across the desk. It was a facsimile, sent from the Lubyanka.

The porcupine's location presently unknown. Assume all things now coming to a resolution. Move immediately and decisively. Serov.

Porcupine was the Chairman's designation for General Zarubin, so the rest of the message hardly needed parsing. Mingled with his prudent revulsion for the word *decisive*, Bolkov felt almost relieved. All initiative – and responsibility for what came of it - was now removed; it had become a matter merely of throwing a switch and allowing the mechanism to complete its run. So what was worrying Korotkov?

'I'm worried.'

'The order's clear, Comrade Resident.'

'I know. But what if ...'

'Fischer and Wolinski aren't all of it? If our moving against them will leave some part of Zarub ... Porcupine's Berlin network intact?'

'Yes.'

Bolkov shrugged. 'I'm sure the Chairman has considered that possibility. The risks of not moving *decisively* must be paramount in his mind.'

Korotkov nodded, without putting much conviction into it. Serov's orders had to be obeyed promptly, and his memory of them being, in fact, *his* orders would remain clear – for a time. But if, eventually, some surviving shard of Zarubin's old Berlin operation pushed its head above the surface to embarrass the decision, would he continue to shoulder responsibility? Or would a Station Resident's career seem a necessary and convenient price to cover that stark fuck-up?'

Because he couldn't quite see how any wrong move might rebound upon him, Bolkov was almost enjoying the other man's discomfort. 'I don't believe we have any alternative, Comrade. We've talked about that exposure before now, without finding a path around it. The thing's out of our hands.'

The nod was firmer this time. 'You're right. If Fischer and Wolinski aren't dealt with now, them being innocent of anything won't matter any less than their absolute guilt. As for any others ...'

He stood up abruptly. 'As it happens, the timing's perfect. Wolinski's on the kill-detail, so Timochenko will deal with Fischer and his loose-bladdered friend, and then ...'

'The friend too?'

'What choice do we have? Anyway, it might turn out to be the correct move.'

'Why do you say that?'

'We have no record of anyone matching the man's description - so, assuming that he's a German, I passed the photograph to MfS to see what they might have. Marcus Wolfe called me this morning. He can't be sure from the image, but our mention of a limp interested him. They misplaced a high ranking VolksPolizei officer five years ago – a one-legged gentleman of somewhat coarse manners. If it's him, they'd be pleased to welcome him home, in whatever condition.'

'If he's a defector, he might be another part of Zarubin's network.'

'That's my thinking. At least, we can dress it that way for the Chairman. Walk with me to the radio room, would you? I have a call to make – to Lichterfelde.'

36

Zarubin was a patient man. He had survived and prospered for so long because he made a point of not rushing things - be they reactions to events, decisions or leaps into fog. It was an easier quality to sustain, of course, when circumstances didn't require a degree of judicious panic. During his time in the United States, patience had been necessary more as a social tool, to prevent him from doing violence to people who believed that a missed breakfast constituted hardship, and a willingness to continue until lunchtime some sort of endurance. In Stettin, it had prevented him from moving against his uncle before a sufficient length of rope had been fashioned to do the job properly. At other times, it had allowed him to side-step the fates of men who rushed to seize a prize before it had been checked adequately for thorns, or pressure-plates. At the moment, its utility was more doubtful. He was deep in enemy territory without any recourse to assistance, a clock was ticking loudly and he could almost feel the busy fingers beneath him, tying his shoelaces together.

His one vulnerable flank was currently under KGB's keen eye - a wide-angled, acutely-focussed organ. He couldn't wander into its field, couldn't drag the object out of it without betraying both him and it, couldn't lift a receiver and make the easy call. He wasn't able to move safely in any direction, yet to wait upon events would be to invite a shot at a stationary target. He enjoyed conundrums, usually, but not this one.

Following his failure to speak to Fischer at the Rathaus he had returned to his hotel, eaten an unsatisfactory meal in its restaurant and retired early. The bed was soft and yielding, and he slept well despite his several frustrations. When he woke, he ordered breakfast in his room and took his time with it, sipping coffee while his attention wandered between the complementary *Berliner Morgenpost* and a fine view over the southern stretches of the Tiergarten. It was pleasant, comfortable, a honeyed trap. Here, he would be tempted to bide his time, to let things play out while he looked for an opening. But in Moscow, Serov might be moving, making a play to topple his most irritating rival. It didn't do to be out of the office for long at such times.

Even now, he couldn't bring himself to countenance the most obvious option – to access his existing telegraph line to Othmar Brecker and use him as a conduit to Fischer. It had taken years of painstaking work to put him where he was – a trusted, senior member of the present city government whose value could hardly be overstated. If Fischer failed in his present task and fell, Zarubin would have to re-draw his strategy from scratch; if Brecker was exposed, all games were over.

What options remained? A 'chance' meeting in the street, at some location where KGB hopefully wouldn't be watching? An innocent party paid to deliver a note to Fischer, in the equally forlorn hope that he or she wouldn't be intercepted and squeezed? A suicidal carrier-pigeon with an up-to-date street-map of south Berlin? In his pleasant hotel room he played with mad ideas, and closed upon nothing practical.

Eventually, the only viable course became too insistent to ignore. If Sergei Aleksandrovich Zarubin couldn't intercept and speak with Otto Fischer safely, then he had to become someone other than himself. He dressed and went down to reception, waited until Luci had finished with a guest (whose shower was too cold, or hot, or wet, or didn't have a sufficient view of the Tiergarten with its curtain drawn) and then asked her recommendation for a good, local hairdresser. Surprised, she gave his perfectly-groomed head a doubtful glance and extracted a courtesy card from one of the holders on her counter.

'*Udo Friseur*, Charlottenburg. It's quite expensive, though.'

'Then I expect he'll make a good job of it. Thank you, Lucretia.'

She flushed sufficiently to warrant a second smile as he pocketed the card, put on his hat and pointed himself at the dangerous outdoors. Fortunately, *Udo Friseur* was barely ten minutes' brisk walk from the hotel. It occupied a central portion of a low, smart block of shops, and though Zarubin was momentarily nonplussed to see display windows filled with images of young men affecting the exuberant style of the Memphis hip-swiveller, the remainder of its décor seemed reassuringly staid.

Inside, he was told that he might need to wait a while before Monsieur Udo was available. The gentleman was prompt, however, and within five minutes Zarubin was in the chair, swathed and looking up at the proprietor's expectant face.

'Shave it off, please.'

Aghast, Monsieur Udo stepped back. 'But ... you have *beautiful* hair.'

'I'm tired of it. It makes me look too young.'

'You don't think that's a good thing?'

'Not at all. And the eyebrows ...'

'Not those too?'

'No. I'd like them dyed, please – dark enough to be visible.'

With great reluctance, Monsieur commenced the shearing, wincing every time a large clump of blond waste-matter fell to the floor. When it was half-done, Zarubin regretted his decision terribly; when it was finished he was pleased to hardly recognize himself. The eyebrows were a master-stroke. Usually near-invisible, they gave his face an open, guileless expression (which was more than a little ironic), but with a little help from his forehead the new pair made him look permanently preoccupied, even cross. He overtipped his host, thanked him sincerely, and, out on the street once more, dropped his hat into the first waste bin he passed. There was no point in disguising a disguise.

Two or three brief self-examinations in shop windows reassured him that he was a new man – a middle-ranking bank official who didn't enjoy his job, or any sort of lawyer (the suit didn't allow him to pass for anything more modest). When he returned to the hotel, Luci was dealing with a new arrival. She glanced at him without interest, and it was only when he asked her colleague for his room key that she turned, mouth open, to take in the modified Zarubin. He wasn't a great student of human attraction and hardly needed to be; had he returned drunk with his trouser-fly open and a prostitute on each arm she could hardly have been more horrified. He gave her another smile (which no longer excited the merest response in her cheeks) and went upstairs.

His bed had been made, the room tidied and fresh flowers placed in the table vase. With the dollars in his wallet he could afford to remain here another two or three weeks, gradually re-westernizing himself. He looked at his watch and pushed away the thought. It had to be today. Even with a satisfactory disguise, every hour he remained in Berlin was another gift to

Serov - another chance for him to put a worm in the General Secretary's ear. Faithless men didn't ever change their skins, it would say; innovations for innovation's sake was always a mistake, it would suggest; and on the matter of what damage Serov could do to the reputation of any man in the Praesidium - were he given sufficient cause - it need not utter a single word. Zarubin needed to stamp on the worm before it got anywhere near the ear.

His small bag was packed within two minutes. He stripped, showered and dressed, putting on the shirt that the hotel laundry had pressed immaculately (they might have made a fortune from a small franchise in the Kremlin Palace) and left a large tip in the ash tray next to the bed. Down in the lobby, he checked out (relieved not to be confronted by Luci) and asked if a taxi for Tempelhof might be arranged. When it arrived he gave the driver new directions, and, on the forty-minute drive to Lichterfelde, surreptitiously checked the magazine in his Makarov.

He paid off his ride at Friedhof Lichterfelde and walked northwards up Moltkestrasse until he came to a second-hand shop. There, he found an overpriced but serviceably nondescript overcoat that was long enough to conceal most of his New York tailoring. Once donned, his transformation into a grey teutonic swan was complete. Contemplating his reflection in the shop's tailor's mirror, his eyes tried to focus through, rather than at, it. All over Berlin, creatures similar to himself passed as discreetly as fog, their only anatomically distinct feature the hand that offered a ticket to an inspector, or dropped coins onto a kiosk counter and snatched up a newspaper. Unless KGB training had modified drastically since he has plied the trade in this city, the twitchiest operative wouldn't give him more than a get-out-of-the-way glance.

Don't relax. By way of penance he practised a slight stoop as he retraced his steps to the Friedhof, watching the procession of paving stones approach and disappear. Once among the gravestones he transferred the pistol from his briefcase to a coat pocket and found a bench near a small brick chapel whose flanks were guarded by low, thick hedges. His hotel copy of the *Morgenpost* provided ample cover as he marked time, waiting for the winter light to fade (though in almost two hours he heard footsteps on the shale path pass by him only once). When a distant clock chimed four he folded the newspaper and stood. His briefcase, pushed well beneath the bench, remained where it was. Whether things went well or not, he would have no further use for a razor, spare shirt or change of underwear.

Lipaerstrasse was as he'd expected – a street of pleasant, substantial houses interrupted by an occasional small business premises. He walked past number 87, continued for about two hundred metres, turned and retraced his steps as if he had recalled some errand. His examination of the terrain was necessarily casual, but nothing more was required. The houses flanking Fischer's residence had lit windows already. One of only three across the road that offered a useful field of view was likewise illuminated, while another was dark but with a Volkswagen parked in the driveway. The third had a property dealer's sign nailed to the front fence and drawn curtains over each of its darkened windows except one – an upstairs bedroom, looking almost directly onto number 87, that showed a gap of some five centimetres.

He counted paces back down to the corner of Augustastrasse, turned left and then left again onto Hindenburgdamm, where he recounted as he walked northwards. He stopped outside a motor repair shop. For a moment his hopes drained, but next to the premises was a fenced-off alleyway with a gate. Without drawing attention by glancing around, he walked straight to it, twisted the handle and stepped through.

His luck was sublime. The alley petered out into waste ground, heavily hemmed in by trees and shrubs. He forced his way through those facing the back of the motor shop and emerged into an area dug out for vegetables. Directly ahead of him, forming a boundary to the allotment, was a head-high garden fence, which, unless he had miscounted, belonged to Lipaerstrasse 87.

It was almost dark now. He climbed the fence with the grace (though not quite the volume) of a disoriented boar, and dropped to the other side. The ground there was flat, but the impact made both of his ankles complain about every one of their forty-six years. A line of drying clothes on a washing-line hid him from the lit kitchen window, allowing him to limp to the side of the house unobserved. As he caught his breath and allowed his eyes gradually to accustom themselves to the narrow pathway's gloom, his foot noticed something not quite right. Bending, his hand outstretched, he made contact with what felt very much like a shoulder, a diagnosis that was confirmed when the hand found the wet head above it.

Something cold and horribly familiar pressed against the back of his neck. He straightened slowly, his arms half-raised at the required crucifixion angle.

'Please don't move' the muzzle said, very politely.

'Why are you here?'

For someone who was hosting a member of the Soviet General Staff, a corpse and its probable murderer (not to mention a defector from East Berlin's VolksPolizei force), Otto Fischer seemed reasonably relaxed; but then, the man had always displayed a knack of not wearing his thoughts too prominently.

Zarubin smiled (but kept his arms very still). 'To present you with our employee of the month award.'

'You may as well sit.'

'Thank you. May I remove my coat?'

'As long as you leave the pistol where it is.'

'Of course.' Carefully, Zarubin shrugged his new purchase off his shoulders and let it slip from his arms onto the floor. He lowered himself into a deep leather chair, further stunting any chance of flight. He turned slightly, to the pleasant, scowling face of Friedrich Holleman.

'Hello, Inspecteur. How is life in Trier?'

The scowl deepened. 'The better for being far from clever fuckers.'

'Yes, it must be. And you are Wolinski, I think?'

The muzzle remained unnervingly steady. 'You know I am, General. You chose me, remember?'

Surprised, Zarubin tried to keep the smile in place. 'Why would you say that?'

'Because it was arranged that you would.'

Before this intriguing suggestion could be explored, Fischer extended a foot, used it to drag the overcoat towards him, stooped and picked it up. He extracted the Makarov from the pocket and ejected its magazine, which he waved towards Zarubin. 'I assume the new look wasn't entirely a sartorial decision?'

'My hair? No. A disguise, hopefully reversible. It's better that no-one thinks I'm in Berlin.'

'He's playing games with KGB. With the Chairman, in fact.'

Zarubin turned to Wolinski once more. 'Where *do* you get your information?'

Holleman snorted. 'He hates it when someone knows more than he does.'

'It's a good question, though.' Fischer looked at Wolinski. 'As is why you happen to be here, now.'

'I'm here because they put me into the surveillance team. I would have preferred to choose my own time and place, but that wasn't possible.'

'Because ...'

'The options narrowed, then they disappeared. The kill order came through a few minutes before my partner knocked on your door.'

'I haven't thanked you for that.'

'His name was Timochenko. He was very good, apparently. I don't think you'd have had much of a chance.'

Zarubin had definitely felt a head shot in the darkened side-passage. It had to have been done very coolly. He cleared his throat.

'You must regret having had no choice.'

Wolinski stared at him. 'Almost, yes. One thing made it a little easier.'

'What?'

'He was Russian.'

Fischer, too sensitive to how the walls were closing in on the here and now, interrupted. 'How long do we have?'

'Less than an hour, probably. We were to make our own way back across the Line, but it was decided that your bodies weren't to be discovered – I suppose because it would have given Chairman Serov a little more time to move against *him* (the muzzle waved slightly) before he could be warned. People will be here soon, to clean up.'

'Right.' Fischer turned to his latest guest. 'You'd prefer to come with us, I take it?'

Zarubin nodded. The danger was real and pressing, yet he wanted nothing more than to huddle with Wolinski and extract every microgram of what he didn't know. He couldn't recall ever having been this eager for enlightenment. 'Where are we going?'

'Somewhere safe, for the moment at least. But we need to arrange something first.' Fischer glanced at Holleman. 'You should call him now.'

The big man nodded and limped across to the telephone. He dialled one digit too many for a local call and one too few for a Federal exchange.

'Kommissar Albrecht Müller, please. Yes, I'll wait.' Holleman rested the receiver on his shoulder and for a few moments examined the ceiling that he wouldn't now - or ever - have an opportunity to paint.

'Hello, Albi? It's me again. No … hang on, will you …. shut up, you cock! I have a tip, that's all. Something's going to kick off tomorrow morning, on the S-Bahn network. The *wessie* workers are sick of being harassed by your BahnPolizei goons, so they're calling a flash, three-hour strike. Yeah, at eight o'clock. What does it matter? I just do. If you put out the word it'll shine your shoes with Upstairs, won't it? Because you've done me a couple of favours, that's why. Yeah. How's the wife? The girls? Ah, good. No, I won't call again, ever. I promise.'

'He'll do it?'

Holleman nodded. 'If he thinks it's genuine, he's obliged to. It won't get him into trouble?'

'No. There'll definitely be a stoppage. I'll see to it.'

Zarubin looked hopefully at Fischer. 'You have a plan, Major?'

'A sort of a plan. The best we could think of.'

Holleman offered his ex-boss a rare smile. 'We thought of it last night, when we were *very* pissed. And it won't help you much.'

Fischer pulled back a curtain slightly and peered out onto Lipaerstrasse. The nearest street lamp was about fifty metres away, but its glow penetrated the gloom sufficiently to reveal an absence of watchers.

'We have to go. I'll just put together a few things. Do the same, Freddie.'

'Alright. Are you sure the place still has a roof?'

'I think so. Are you sure it has a high perimeter wall?'

'It did, in 1911.'

'We'll hope for the best, then. You'll take these two there directly – a taxi shouldn't be any risk. I'll follow on after I've spoken to our friend.'

'By taxi?'

'Of course not.'

'What, then?'

Fischer laughed. 'I thought you were a policeman, Freddie. Haven't you detected our garage?'

He was almost at the door when a worming thought became too persistent to resist further. He turned to Wolinski.

'You haven't said *why* you're doing this.'

The Pole unscrewed the suppressor from its pistol and placed both on the table, severing them from their incongruous relationship with the staidly-tailored, two-piece tweed suit.

'Many reasons; among them, to apologize.'

'For what.'

She looked up from the weapon and smiled, and to Fischer it felt like a burden of years had lifted.

'I hated you for a long time. That was wrong of me.'

38

Being a Union official, Paul Heinkel sometimes received unexpected visitors in the evenings – colleagues whose grievances were so pressing that they couldn't wait until the next workday to discuss them, or who didn't understand that a man could set aside his duties to his comrades in the same way that an accountant could his calculating machine, or a plumber his spanner. He always tried to be gracious about these interruptions, and sometimes he almost succeeded.

This evening, the knock on the door was almost welcome. Traudl was learning to play the violin (her teacher having previously praised her skills with the recorder), and applied herself with the same grim determination that had almost shattered Paul's nerves the previous year. This time it was worse, of course, because although one could certainly play the wrong notes on a recorder, it was difficult to make any one of them sound bad in itself. With a violin, bad was very easy indeed. In fact, a good note sounded so rarely that it arrived almost as the balm of Heaven.

The unexpected visitor was doubly welcome for not being a supplicant. The poor man's face was difficult to look upon, but he seemed a pleasant sort, and had done Paul a great favour in helping him expel the detestable Macke family from that part of Berlin. It was also a considerable honour to be able to welcome – genuinely, welcome – a member of the City's Government to his very modest home. He almost regretted that it was very dark outside on Körnerstrasse. Several adept gossipers lived hereabouts, and might have made a great deal of it.

He invited Herr Fischer into the hallway, took his coat and asked Traudl to pause her sawing for long enough to come and say hello to the great man. She did so, holding out her hand for it to be shook and staring up shamelessly at the war wounds.

'Hello, I'm Otto.'

'I'm Traudl Heinkel, like the aeroplane. Would you like to come in?'

Fischer refused a coffee but sat down when the lady of the house offered the sofa. Paul waited – not a little relieved - while she placed her violin in its case and took it to her bedroom before nudging the conversation.

'Is there something I can help you with, Herr Fischer?'

'Actually, I came with news.'

'Nothing bad, I hope?'

'It might be. A colleague's had word that the BahnPolizei are going to come down on DR's western employees. They think that some of them are selling stuff under the counter to their eastern colleagues.'

'They are. It's been going on for years. Everyone knows, but no-one complains about it.'

'Well, they've decided to do something about it. They're going to make a few examples – stop-and-searches, followed by dismissals or demotions, probably'

'How does your colleague know this?'

'You'll understand that I can't say - but it's definitely happening, and tomorrow morning. The exercise commences early, at eight o'clock.'

Paul's lips tightened. 'It isn't the first time they've had a go, but usually it's about politics. They put up anti-capitalist posters yet claim that we're the ones causing trouble. Right. I'll let the Union know.'

'What will they do?'

'The only thing that's open to them – withdraw our labour. We'll turn up for work so they can't say we're absentees, but if they think they're getting anything more than that ...'

'You can arrange that at short notice?'

Paul laughed. 'It's one of the few benefits of being an island – we can get word 'round to everyone in a couple of hours. It'll be solid – so solid that a few of our *ossie* mates might join in. I'll make sure that they all know who to thank for this.'

'That isn't necessary. I don't like the City being disrupted, but this behaviour's too arrogant.'

'Well, *I* can thank you, at least.' Paul stood and held out his hand. Fischer took it and cleared his throat.

'Before you do, may I ask your advice? It's a rather urgent matter.'

39

'Mother of God! You're certain?'

Korotkov looked sourly at Bolkov. 'It's not the sort of thing that could be misinterpreted. The cleaners found Timochenko dead and Wolinski, Fischer and his crippled friend gone.'

'So we were right about them.'

'Practise *not* saying that, if you could.'

'Of course! I meant ...'

'Never mind. Obviously, if they go to ground we're finished. We can't realistically search for them in a half-city of some four millions. We have to hope that they've planned an early escape, or even - if we're *very* lucky - that they panic.'

'They might have false papers.'

'Obviously. But Fischer isn't going to to be able to hide that face, however good the paperwork. We have a chance, if they move soon. So, we cover the roads and railways. If they use either, they'll have to pass through two checkpoints – the Berlin boundary and DDR-Federal border. If they choose the swift, borderless option, we have a few good people at Tempelhof. Organizing 'plane tickets and a scheduled flight takes time – it would give us a chance to arrange something. Crossing a field from the terminal building to an aircraft allows a lovely long shot.'

'If they decide to wait it out …'

'Then we have a very painful interview with the Chairman to look forward to.'

'What could we have done differently?'

'It was our – well, *your* – idea to put Wolinski into the surveillance operation. In retrospect, not the best move.'

There it was – the end of an uncomfortable truce. Korotkov was going to save his own hide, whatever shit fell.

'I didn't twist your arm to agree to it, I recall.'

'No, you didn't. I wish that Wolinski had been better vetted.'

'So do I. She's been with us since before KGB *was* KGB, so who brought her in and when is probably to be determined by a coin.'

Both men examined their options for a while. The best that could be hoped for now was that Serov was in a position to move against General Zarubin – in fact, that he had done so already, thereby making the fates of Fischer, Wolinski and whoever else the man had in Berlin a lesser matter. Even if part of his network survived, it was likely to be compromised - perhaps effectively neutralized - by the beheading, the component parts sinking into whatever dark place might best hide them. In that happy event, the Chairman might not feel obliged to regard the Lipaerstrasse debacle as a matter worth revisiting, particularly if it could be put right by a couple of belated executions on a runway, or at a checkpoint somewhere in the DDR. With a favourable wind and …

'He's not going to forget about this, is he?'

Bolkov's put it so plaintively that Korotkov almost wanted to reassure him, but the question had been horribly rhetorical.

'I doubt it. We could argue that any operation has its risks – Christ knows, Serov's had enough failures himself – but it's not the sort of thing he'll want to hear.'

'Could we infer that Timochenko was incompetent?'

'Yes, if we want Serov to come straight back at us with *why didn't you know that already?* In any case, the poor bastard's record was exemplary. He was an excellent killer, who was only brought down by a surprise shot to the temple.'

'That was Wolinski, yes?'

'It was a Soviet seven-millimetre bullet, so we may assume so. The bitch must have expected and objected to her imminent execution.'

'You can't trust your victims these days.'

Korotkov looked sharply at Bolkov, but the quip had been delivered with a more-than-straight face. In fact, misery was plastered all over it. As Berlin Resident, Korotkov had accumulated enough merits in-post to have a chance of surviving this disaster, but a mere Station Directorate chief – particularly one whose role had been growing less important in recent years – had no cushion beneath his arse. Unless his immediate boss Yudkin was prepared to argue his case in Moscow (and he probably wasn't, not to Serov), Bolkov might be looking at an imminent transfer to the VIP subway protection sub-Directorate – or, God help him, KGB's Finance Department.

'Well, we must try hard to prevent her leaving Berlin.'

Bolkov was chewing the inside of his cheek. 'Do you think she – they – might go over to the Americans, or British?'

'It's traditional, isn't it? But in this case I doubt it. They have little to offer. CIA in particular likes to get its money's worth, so they'd run the risk of being squeezed for what little they have and then dumped with the price of a train ticket, which would leave them more vulnerable than before.'

'That's a pity. Having them snapped up and evacuated might solve our problem with Serov.'

Korotkov considered that possible ending. Even to wish for it was treasonable, obviously, but defection had its attractions. Wolinski and Fischer would be gone, and unable either to hurt or be a further burden upon KGB's Berlin operations. After they were safely elsewhere it shouldn't be too hard to wrap up – to find three recent corpses, put them in a car and have it crash and burn as it sped towards the Federal border. The Chairman would eviscerate them if it ever came out – which it might, should a rogue CIA or SIS man come their way and offer it during his de-briefing. Would Serov care by then, though, if Zarubin was safely in several shallow graves?

Recognizing the first stirrings of a migraine, he stopped that line of thought in its tracks. 'We seem to have come full circle. It's only days since we were thinking of ways to anticipate a kill-order.'

Bolkov nodded gloomily. 'I was only speculating. Perhaps we've over-thought the situation from the beginning.'

'A shrewd, if belated, judgment. For what remains of this nightmare, we'll follow procedures precisely. I'll alert all checkpoints and put marksmen on standby, should we get word from Tempelhof.'

'And the Chairman?'

'If he's trying to track down the General and finish him off, we probably have a little time before he washes the blood off his hands, files the paperwork and remembers us.'

40

What had been the Salomon Freischule, and, more latterly, the Augsburgerstrasse Grundschule, was a low, red-brick building with hardly an intact window on its southern fascade. Its perimeter wall, once a three-metre high obstacle to young Berliners absconding before the end of classes, was now a much-reduced, wildly uneven remnant, allowing passers-by an unhindered view of the rest. As upon every other night, no illumination shone from its abandoned interior. However, in an interior, windowless room, the old Direktorin's office, three people huddled around the sparse heat and light given out by a portable gas-stove.

'God, it's cold.' General Zarubin shivered down a little further into his new-old overcoat, and wished heartily that the tasteless, fur-collared alternative he'd briefly considered and rejected had been given a second chance.

'Don't be a homo. You were on the Eastern Front.' Friedrich Holleman had no coat but was pretending an indifference to the cold. His voice, tremulous as a Rhinemaiden's, gave him away somewhat.

'I was in an *office* on the Eastern Front. And the office got warmer as it went west.'

The third huddler said nothing. Her bare legs were tucked beneath her body, her arms folded tightly across her chest, and her chin, pressed to her chest, made a poor job of blocking the cruel draught. By now she had given up any hope of the Russian offering his coat, and was trying not to think about it.

The hope kindled momentarily as he turned to her.

'How did you know?'

'Know what?'

'About my business with Serov?'

She released a hand to rub some warmth into her forehead. 'It's the wrong question. Or a question requiring the wrong answer.'

'I don't enjoy being teased.'

'My knowing is incidental.'

'Not to *me* it isn't.'

Holleman shifted slightly, farted even more slightly and groaned. 'Just tell him. He won't shut up until you do.'

'If you think so. I know because your man Levin told me.'

'When he spoke to you in Berlin? Why would he do that? He'd know that if I found out I'd throw him to the ...'

'Because he thought that I could help, as you did. You chose me as your insider at Karlshorst because of an item of information you managed to dig up - specifically, that I was at or near a dacha outside Pushkino on 3 February 1955?'

'I ... yes.'

'Actually, no. Levin was able to give you that scrap because I offered it to him - almost four months ago.'

Aghast, Zarubin entirely forgot about the cold that was gnawing at his extremities. 'What don't I know?'

'More than you think, I expect.'

'What do you want?'

'To wait, until Fischer comes. I'll speak more when he does.'

Holleman smirked as he adjusted his metal leg. Zarubin glared at him. 'Do *you* know?'

'She hasn't told me a thing. But I still know more than you. I know *her*, for a start.'

'How?'

'We met a long time ago, in very different circumstances.'

Zarubin was about to explore this further when the half-unhinged door creaked and a heavily-laden Fischer entered.

'I brought what blankets we had. And this.'

This was a large tin; he placed it on the floor and shrugged apologetically. 'It's as sweet as hell, but I can't think of anything else that occupies such little space for its calorific value.'

'What is it?'

'Fruit cake – *königskuchen*. Frau Benner bakes one for me every week. I usually throw it to the birds.'

'You bloody genius!' Without waiting for anyone else to express polite interest, Holleman ripped off the lid, tore a large piece of cake and aimed it at his mouth. It had almost reached it when he thought of something.

'Did you bring water?'

'No. The Commission report says that the plumbing in the staff lavatory is working still. The building's been used occasionally as a warehouse by the Roads Department, so they kept it connected.'

Wrapped in blankets and working through a dense iron ration, no-one spoke for a while. Zarubin watched the other three carefully, trying to come to terms with being the least-informed person in the room. Eventually, Fischer noticed his discomfort, and, swallowing a piece of cake with every indication of disgust, cleared his throat.

'Why have you come to Berlin?'

'To warn you that you were being watched.'

Both Fischer and Holleman laughed. 'Thank you. That was thoughtful.'

'Obviously, had I known what *she* was going to do I wouldn't have bothered.'

'I can't believe that. You couldn't stand not knowing.'

That was true, and Zarubin didn't try to argue. He needed information quickly, and then to get out, back to Moscow, as soon as the engines of the Antonov AN-8 presently sitting on the concrete at Schönefeld could be warmed up. It was clear already that both Wolinski and Fischer were off the board, or at least not in position; what might be done about that – and about

Levin, once he got his hands around the man's throat – was still unclear.

He turned to the Pole. 'You were going to tell me more.'

Her eyes were on the small portion of *königskuchen* she had taken from the tin. A raisin, apparently more fascinating than it had any right to be, was slowly extracted from the rest, examined carefully, and transferred to her mouth. She looked up and frowned at the wall opposite.

'What do you know about me?'

'That your name isn't Wolinski. That your recruitment records are missing. That you were at Pushkino on that very important night three years ago, and though I don't know why, the fact of it remains extremely significant.'

'Because …?'

'Because the legendary Vasily Blokhin, hero and monster,, died there that night. Overwhelmed by his crimes and almost certainly only half-sane by then, he placed his gun in his mouth and put an end to bad dreams.'

'I doubt that he was ever *nearly* sane.'

'A moot point. But you admit that you *were* there?'

'Yes.'

'Your purpose?'

'Not yet. My name isn't Wolinski, as these gentleman ...' she gestured towards Fischer and Holleman, both of whom were listening intently '... can confirm. The precise date, location and circumstances of my joining KGB – I should say NKVD, back then - are missing because I arranged to have them misplaced. It was remarkably easy. Before I joined Third Directorate I was in Administration, where incompetence is enshrined as holy tradition. It was there that I had access to resources to chase one of two … objectives.'

'Will you name it?'

She shifted lightly, lifted a finger and pointed it at Fischer. 'To find *him*.'

'Why?'

'To put something right. He knows what it is.'

Fischer shook his head. 'There was no debt.'

Zarubin climbed to his knees and leaned over the stove to warm his hands. 'Why would you think that KGB had information on him?'

I didn't, but having joined them it didn't seem sensible not to test the possibilities. If the Soviets had captured him during the war there might be an interrogation, a paper recording his transfer East, a notification of death in combat. What I found was … unusual. It pushed me to look harder.'

'What did you find?'

'You. First in Stettin, then in Berlin – using him, betraying him, putting him into a place he couldn't be reached. At first I thought, this is a man with a grudge; but you kept him alive, which seemed either whimsical or sadistic.'

'I thought I'd been careful with the paperwork.'

'Not careful enough, and when you defected to the Americans you lost control of what was, and wasn't, known. Fischer's time in Sachsenhausen was particularly well-documented. He was a difficult prisoner.'

'So Karlshorst found a history. I hadn't expected that.'

'If they did, it was some other way. As each piece of evidence surfaced I used and removed it. There's a hole in KGB files where Otto Fischer should be.'

Globnow, then. It was final proof, if it were needed, that he had been grabbed. Zarubin knew the man wouldn't have given them anything, had he been in a state to resist. It was another crime to lay at Serov's door.

'Why did you do it?'

She was addressing Fischer, her expression considerably warmer than the one she'd deployed at Zarubin, yet he seemed uncomfortable with the attention.

'It was no trouble for me.'

'It must have been. You set free two labour camp inmates, two Poles, and what were you – a captain? There must have been repercussions.'

'Actually, the commanding officer agreed to it when I made the suggestion.'

'I still don't see *why*. I just want to know.'

She still doesn't remember the boy. It had been a half-hour's frantic coupling on a Baltic beach, four decades ago – why should she? And yet a small, aching part of him had wished that she had seen through the mutilations, to recall something more memorable than it must have been for her. Absent an adept torturer, he knew that he would never, ever volunteer the revelation.

'I can't resist attractive women. I did it to flatter my ego, and because I *could* do it.'

It wasn't nearly an adequate explanation, but she said nothing more. She was puzzled still, trying to bridge the gap between a casual good deed and a life-saving act of altruism. Had she remained in the labour camp she may not have lived to see the end of the war – or been used terribly by the liberating Soviet troops, as so many forced workers had at the 'liberation'. She had been given a chance at a life beyond Peenemünde, and grasped at it like a flung rope. He felt almost proud of her.

Zarubin was checking his watch every other minute, as close to twitching as Fischer had ever seen him. Even a clever man misfires occasionally, but to have his plans atomized without sight of the reasons for it must have been a punch to the gut. For someone who had been on the sharp end of his other schemes, it was an enjoyable spectacle.

The General waited long enough to be certain that she wasn't going to speak again, and then coughed gently.

'You went to Levin. Why?'

'To have you become interested in me.'

'For Fischer's sake?'

'No. He was – forgive me – an incidental interest. What I wanted from you, and why I joined KGB, are the same thing.'

'Which is?'

'To hurt those who've hurt me.'

Zarubin settled back against the wall. He looked slightly more relaxed for having heard something he could at least understand.

'When the surrender came I had no idea to do anything but find my brother. He'd gone West – the last I heard was from a French friend who'd been in the camp, who wrote to tell me that she'd met him in Paris. I found her there at the end of '45, but but by then he'd fallen sick and died at the Saint-Antoine. After that, I turned around and went home. I knew already that my parents were dead, but I had an uncle, Tadeusz, who was living still. I stayed with him for almost two years, until he completed his researches and gave me something to fight for.'

'What was that?'

He and my father had a sibling, Frédéric. He was the real thinker in the family, a philosopher at Lwow University, but he'd gone into hiding at the start of the war, and all contact with him ended in early 1940. My uncle Tadeusz had been in the book trade before the war, but after the Germans invaded he became something else. He collected information to keep people, lost people, from passing into oblivion.'

'Your uncle is the Archivist? The Archivist of Toruń?'

She smiled sadly. 'He died, two years ago. And he hated that name, though it was meant to honour him. An archivist records the past, the lives of fled souls; what he did was to try to find the living, no matter how hopeless the search. He once told me he did it because he wanted to piss on the graves of Hitler and

Stalin, by collecting those who, against every effort of two gigantic machines, had survived them. Of course, the one he was seeking above all others was his own brother.'

'Did he find him?'

'He found his death, probably in a padded cell, in May 1940.'

'Katyn?'

'He wasn't even a soldier. You could make a wretched case for executing an enemy's military officers in cold blood, against every international convention. But, just like the Nazis, Stalin wanted to end Poland's future as a state. Her intelligentsia were considered just as dangerous as her armed forces, so Uncle Frédéric - who had flat feet, bad lungs and a horror of any form of violence - was dragged from a prison to a death cell, where someone put a bullet into the back of his head.'

Zarubin studied the floor between his feet. Revenge was an excellent motive when it didn't splash, but he was beginning to conceive how little grip he'd had on his own strategy, and it hurt. He could see where this was going, and he suspected it had already begun to drag him with it. He looked up at her. She was waiting expectantly, knowing what he was going to ask.

'Pushkino, 3 February, 1955.'

'Yes.'

'It was you.'

'It was.'

'The report's conclusion was suicide.'

'Of course it was. Naturally, the investigators assumed it was Serov's doing, so they gave him what they thought he wanted. I expect he didn't care. By that time it was far more convenient to have the man out of the world.'

'It must have been … satisfying.'

'No, just necessary. I'd never killed anyone before.'

'And this evening?'

'Timochenko? The second – and last. I hope.'

'So. The famous, hideous Vasily Blokhin?'

'I can't be certain that he pulled the trigger at my uncle's execution, but they say he killed – personally, killed - over seven thousand men in the course of just twenty-three days, and all in that damned cell. That was close enough for me.'

'He was a strong man. How did you overcome him?'

'I didn't need to. He was drunk, almost incoherent, and probably half-mad by then. I knocked on his door and he let me in. They hadn't even given him a guard to watch his front gate.'

'He was the greatest still-living embarrassment to Khrushchev's new order. I think it was only the shame of their own former collusions that stopped them burying him. So you just shot him? In the mouth?'

'No. First, I told him why I was there. He didn't seem disturbed by it - he even offered me a drink, but then said no, he didn't want my arm to shake. I think it was an attempt at humour. We talked for a while, and then I realised that I had something.'

'Something?'

'Something that might be traded.'

'For what?'

'For more of what I wanted. And a way out, when it was done.'

'You wanted more than Blokhin?'

'I wanted everyone, but I knew that was impossible. Beria conceived the thing, but he was already dead. In my dreams I wanted Stalin roasted slowly on a spit, but that's what it was – a dream. In any case, he was gone too. But the organizer – the man entrusted with the plan – was not only alive still but raised up for his part in toppling Beria. I wanted Serov.'

Zarubin snorted. 'In a hundred years, you couldn't ever get near him. And if you did, he'd snap you in half.'

'Of course I couldn't. Of course he would. I didn't say I need to pull the trigger myself.'

41

Holleman held out the cake tin to Zarubin, as if he could still have an appetite. He ignored it.

'How did you know?'

'About you and Serov? I didn't, though there were clues. I work in Third Directorate, where most files on suspect Soviet military personnel begin their lives. *You* have a very large one, as you might imagine. It was added to last year, soon after the move to oust Khrushchev failed. We were told to look at any of your past associates who'd since sinned – to find someone who might, with encouragement, provide a bullet. The order was signed by Serov.'

'Were you successful?'

'You know we weren't. You don't make acquaintances, much less confidants.'

'No. I've always worried about other people's mouths.'

'Your story was very unusual, though – a defector, re-defecting, who wasn't immediately put out of his indecisiveness, and who then found an office in the Kremlin. A man doesn't get to cheat the system so blatantly without raising grudges. And Serov doesn't take an interest in someone without there being cause for it.'

'Still, it was supposition only.'

'It was, until I found your secretary Levin, and put a case.'

'A case?'

'That if you *were* in opposition to Serov in some way, and a person might be able to assist with certain information, might you be interested?'

'And he said yes?'

'He did.'

'And why didn't he inform me of it? Why the pretense of having dug up your history on his own initiative?'

'Because you would have wanted everything immediately. And then I would have had nothing to bargain with. I made it a condition, that he didn't tell you. Perhaps I should have thought of something else. Your method of snaring me – the allegation and exoneration – was stupid. It lit me up, when I should have been invisible.'

'If I'd known you *wanted* to help I wouldn't have done it. You said a bargain - bargain for what?'

'I want to get out, cleanly. If I gave you what you needed to beat Serov, you'd make sure that I was erased.'

'Why didn't you just run before now, go straight to the Americans?'

'If I had, you might not have got the better of Serov. And I want that very much.'

Zarubin gave his shoes more attention. Fischer was blown, so at least half of his carefully-wrought plans were sinking slowly into a latrine. He didn't trust his powers of persuasion to decisively move Khrushchev towards him and away from Serov, while the latter might already have a sufficient weight of evidence to do the job to his advantage. Given the nature of the enemy, this wasn't going to be a drawn out campaign, a chess-marathon of clever, subtle moves. It would be a single, carotid-severing slash, given or received, and in Zarubin's case at least, definitely fatal. It wasn't as though he had the luxury of choices.

He nodded slowly, reluctantly. 'There's a very comfortable hotel, less than a kilometre from here. You'll stay there tomorrow while I buy you a change of clothes, some hair-dye and a 'plane ticket. I assume you have a convincing passport?'

'A French one, yes.'

'Then the following morning we'll get you to Tempelhof and on to a Paris flight. After that it's up to you. If what you give me is sound, then I promise that no-one will ever come after you. Once things have worked themselves out – I mean, if I'm not dead - you can get a *poste restante* address to me via *this* number. I'll arrange to have some money sent to you. It won't be enough to live the sweet-life, just a discreet one. Is that enough?'

'Thank you.'

Zarubin turned to Fischer. 'I could arrange a ticket for you also, but frankly I don't want to. In any case, they'll be looking for your remarkable face. It would be a death-sentence, for both – all three – of you, if you travelled together.'

'Freddie and I have a way out of Berlin. But thank you for almost caring.'

Holleman looked up from his knees. 'We have?'

'I'll tell you later.' Fischer was watching her, trying not to let relief take the heat out of his nerve-endings. They were all in the furnace still, but he trusted Zarubin enough – *just* enough – to take him at his word. A man whose self-regard shaded into outright vanity was as careful of his reputation as the shine on his shoes, and an outright commitment put money on it. He might regret the necessity of the bargain, but he was likely to keep it. In any case, the uncharacteristic emotion his face was betraying suggested that he considered it a bargain in every sense. He was watching her as if she might explode.

'Well, then. What do you have?'

'When Blokhin saw my gun he asked if Serov had sent me. I told him no, that this was a personal thing, but he didn't hear a word of it. He called him a coward, a faithless shit – that he'd dropped his old comrade as completely as if they'd been enemies, but wasn't that what turncoats and traitors did? I wasn't interested in what he meant by it, but there was no shutting him up. He said that Serov and he had been in the same room when news of Stalin's death broke. They'd both gone to see Beria immediately, and urged him to deal with Khrushchev before the man got his pieces on the board. The old monster had been nervous, though, lost without his old boss to cover for him, and told them that he'd wait and see how things moved before he made a decision. When they left him, Serov had turned to Blokhin and said that they'd just witnessed Lavrenty Beria put a gun to his own head, and that they should make their own arrangements before they were made for them. So, they went to Khrushchev.'

'And told him that Beria was coming for him?'

'Yes. That was what made Khrushchev go to Zhukov and persuade him that no-one was safe as long as Beria was in post. With the Army behind him, KGB couldn't - didn't - do anything when he denounced their boss in front of the Politburo.'

Zarubin nodded slowly. 'That's … useful, but not conclusive. If I go to Khrushchev with this he'll just confront Serov, listen to the outraged denial and we'll be back where we were, except that Serov will have a motive to smash me immediately with whatever he's got.'

She glanced at Fischer and then back to the General. 'You're not quite as clever as they say, are you? I told you that Blokhin's death was determined to be suicide by the KGB investigators. That means Serov's name was on the thing, whether it appeared in ink or not. The report went into the record – it's still available, and filed where it should be. If you go to Khrushchev with what I've told you, Blokhin's suicide becomes suspect, doesn't it?'

'Suspect, yes, but not ...'

'Yet it couldn't have been suicide, not according to the evidence. Blokhin was shot in the mouth at close range – close enough for it to have been his own hand.'

Zarubin frowned. 'What are you saying? Are there fingerprints …?'

'Yes – Blokhin's, on his own gun, which I put in his hand after I'd blown off half of his head.'

'But ...'

'The bullet that was pulled out of the wall was seven-point-six-three millimetre, standard Soviet issue, which is why the investigators assumed the 'suicide' to have been arranged by their boss, and proceeded accordingly.'

Zarubin's shoulders dropped slightly as he relaxed. 'Oh, my God ...'

Holleman's gaze passed between them. 'I don't get it.'

The Russian laughed. 'You wouldn't. Blokhin's a legend we don't discuss much – the greatest identified mass-murderer in human history, a man who liked to work as a machine does. He didn't pause, didn't wipe his brow, didn't ask for a moment to steady his hand. He would put a bullet into someone's head, go next door to do the same to another one, and by the time he returned the next poor bastard had been stood over the drain. He had an assistant who would take the emptied gun from his hand, put in a fresh magazine and pass it straight back so as not to disturb the rhythm. He executed – literally – hundreds at a time when the circumstances demanded it, and until his forced retirement never seemed to reflect upon what he'd done. In a savage way, he perfected his own means of production; but to do that, he needed to keep the machine oiled.'

Fischer had been listening, putting the pieces into the only possible order. He cleared his throat.

'Ordnance?'

'Yes! Until the purges in '37 he used what he was given, but no-one could have anticipated his efficiency. Every Soviet-made pistol is of simple construction, to permit field-repairs when necessary. Unfortunately it's often necessary. They overheat, jam, even backfire when muzzle tolerances aren't sufficiently close. The universal-issue Tokarev TT-30 was one he complained of with particular vehemence. So, he put in a requisition, and it was met almost instantly.'

'What?'

'The Walther Model 2 – a bagful of them, and enough ammunition to start or end a war. He was a great admirer of German craftsmanship, and between assignments famously carried his collection in a large leather shoulder bag – a shade of leather that precisely matched that of the butcher's apron, hat and long gloves he wore as he did his business. And the Walther Model 2 ...'

'Fires six-point-three-five ammunition.'

She coughed to regain their attention, and took back the story. 'The investigators saw it immediately, of course. I'd put a Walther into his hand, having made the selection from about five he kept in his desk drawer. But what could they do? The bullet was admitted into evidence because it was *there*, and even terrible, secret events are recorded precisely. The contradiction was striking, and irrelevant – they assumed Serov had wanted an embarrassment dealt with, so the report went in unaltered, and was probably never read. And now, that same contradiction confirms that it *was* an execution.'

Zarubin stood, and brushed down his second-hand coat. 'No one will believe Serov for a second if he denies it, because no-one will mistake the motive.' He shrugged. 'Perhaps he won't even *be* asked. Why would he?'

He turned to her. 'You know that he won't be execute? We don't do that any more, not our senior people – the purges are too fresh in mind for that. Besides, he knows a great deal too much, and no one can be certain of sweeping up all the evidence before it explodes.'

'I don't care. I'll take what I can.'

'Well, humiliation can be hurt more than any bullet. Alright. We should go to the hotel now – it's nearly light.'

They were almost at the door when Fischer spoke. 'We're not done yet.'

'Major?'

'It's not *major* - it's Fischer, or nothing. We won't be seeing each other again, so you need to explain things.'

'Things such as ...'

'Two lost years – years in which I waded through local politics. The lost evenings, the constant complaints and bickerings, the rank ingratitude, the remarkably evasive Herr Globnow and my recent, glittering career as a political analyst. Why?'

'Because, of course, I needed a man in Willy Brandt's office. It would have been a tremendous coup, something to rub deeply into Serov's face when it's him and his *Stasi* friends who are expected to do that sort of thing.'

'But you *have* a man in Brandt's office – Othmar Brecker.'

'A very valuable man – one who's going all the way to Bonn. He's far too precious to throw away.'

'Throw away?'

'To *sacrifice*, Ma ... Fischer. It's not the mere fact of your presence in Brandt's office that would have checkmated Serov, but your exposure as a Soviet spy – one, moreover, giving advice on the Kremlin to the most powerful German in Berlin. Brandt would have fallen like a rotten tree, and I would have risen like Christ.'

Zarubin paused, and examined Fischer's face. 'Oh, don't sulk! The most they would have given you is five or six years in a comfortable prison - but of course, the first time we took one of theirs I would have put you to the top of the exchange list. You would have come to Moscow, to find an apartment with your name on the door within walking distance of mine. With a supply of good French wine and my expense account at the only decent Italian restaurant within the ring road, we could have seen out the Cold War very comfortably.'

He turned to the door once more, but paused. 'Now, are you *sure* you have a way out of Berlin? You know I'll worry until you're safe in the Federal Republic.'

'I doubt I can be safe there. But yes, we'll out of Berlin and the DDR ...' he checked his watch – a Luftwaffe Titus Geneve D, the only surviving memento from his repairs business, a reminder not of his war service but the delicious few years in which he'd bothered no-one and almost no-one had bothered him - 'by midday today.'

'Ah. Good, then.'

He was through the door in a moment, but she lingered on this side of it, looking at Fischer. And the longer the look endured, pinning him, the more he realised that this was an awful moment in which they both understood perfectly well that the grenade was in his court. What could he say, that wouldn't mark him down as a dolt, a born-again virgin, a pitifully old, wrecked artefact?

It came to him suddenly, so excruciatingly unoriginal that he almost punctuated it with a groan.

'Will I see you after this?'

She smiled, as if it just might be the correct answer. 'Well, that depends.'

'Upon what?'

She reached beyond the door, grasped something and dragged it back – a Russian General, very keen to be in Russia.

'… on how he makes it up to you, for the terrible inconvenience he's caused.'

Fischer was expecting the only Russian-language retort he knew, but Zarubin opened his mouth, closed it again and turned his eyes to the Heavens to witness his anguish. When they came down he patted his chest with both hands, withdrew a small notepad and a biró, and with a finger of the pen-hand made the turn-around gesture to her. Fischer found their unconscious intimacy intensely troubling.

'This …. is a number and password for an account at the bank of Landolt & Cie, in Neuchâtel. You'll need to go in person, of course, but no difficulty will be made about your face or anything else. Just try to dress respectably, and don't blow your nose on a sleeve. And please – no more than five thousand dollars? I may very well need the remainder quite urgently, if her information isn't convincing enough.'

'There!' She turned and gave Zarubin a solemn nod. 'You've saved some money.'

'Have I?'

'My exile's pension. It may not be necessary now.' She turned to Fischer, and for once he saw something less than absolute certainty in her gaze.

'How much *after* were you thinking of?'

42

'No more politics, then.'

'No, Freddie. I was a representative for longer than Goebbels was Chancellor, so I'm content.'

'He was that for what, a day?

'I'm not sure it was a *full* day. I could be wrong.'

'How are we going to do this?'

Fischer and Holleman were walking north and west in the first hint of daylight, and though no destination was yet clear the largest obstacle to further progress in that direction was Zoo Bahnhof. The bigger man felt a small stab of disappointment. He'd expected something more clever from his friend.

'You're going to get on the seven-thirty express service to Frankfurt.'

'Express! Fuck off!'

'Well, it will be, once you're over the border. You came here with false papers, naturally?'

'Agilmar Tuft, native of Kaiserslautern, where I practice chiropody.'

'Agilmar?'

'Yeah. It sounds beefy, like I should be wielding a sword.'

'The only thing that identifies you is your limp – and mouth, of course. Try to say very little, and be respectfully timorous at Potsdam-Griebnitzsee and the national border. No-one's going to make you.'

Holleman paused in mid-limp and frowned. 'What about *you*, though?'

'The drains.'

'No, you cock! Border guards have been patrolling them for years – I mean, the few they haven't blocked off with wire or concrete. Or both.'

'I know, I was being winsome. What did we do last night, before we left?'

Holleman thought for a while. 'Tried to raise some goodwill?'

'We did. And it happens that we raised a deal of it. I asked Paul Heinkel if there was anywhere on a train that wouldn't be inspected at the borders – anywhere, even if I had to hang upside-down with the gravel scouring my arse. He just laughed, and told me not to visit the cinema so often. He said that there are certain chambers on every train that sometimes are sealed off, with a metal band franked by a DR stamp. It guarantees that they've been inspected and contain no *ossies* fleeing to the west.'

'Chambers?'

'Toilets, Specifically, broken toilets.'

'That's a joke, right?'

'Think about it. Most of the border-crossings are manned by guards who share a large, draught-plagued hut on the platform. They're overworked, hardly paid and get it in the ear constantly from Deutsche Reichsbahn for making the East German leg of these journeys a creeping national humiliation. They examine only what they're told to, and if the official DR seal is unbroken, well, what's the incentive to go poking through turds?

'You're certain?'

'Usually, I'd be mildly optimistic, but not today. At eight o'clock, every western s-bahn employee is going to withdraw his labour, and the BahnPolizei, whom you warned about it, are going to wade in. If they've any sense, they'll have organized reinforcements first. And where would they come from?'

'Potsdam.'

'Which will therefore be undermanned when we arrive, so the turds will be as safe as they're ever going to be. At the Federal border, the guards will see the DR seal, know that it's been inspected already at Potsdam – because they'll call them to confirm it, and because they know that trains never, ever slow to a boarding pace between the two checkpoints – and then they'll wave on the *wessies* with their customary bonhomie/'

'Heinkel thinks it can be done?'

'It *has* been done – twice, in the past four years. Understandably, they keep it for special circumstances. Which I am, apparently. He 'phoned two men last evening to arrange it. I'm to drop on to the lines at Fasanenstrasse – there's an embankment there - and walk until I find the outermost hut marked 13. They'll dress me like them, bring me in to the rear of the train and put me in the first shitter.'

'What if you're spotted?'

'Then I'd be very unlucky. BahnPolizei check everything very carefully at the eastern terminus, because it's their job – their *sole* job - to look for *ossies* fleeing west. When the train gets to Zoo Bahnhof, why would they be alert? It's just *wessies* boarding there. Heinkel told me that the guards usually jump out at Zoo for coffees and pastries, then they get sharp again as the train pulls into Potsdam. His mates will be getting me into the toilet while things are fairly slack.'

'They're authorized to seal it?'

'No, but Heinkel had a fake seal made, and he has a small supply of the authorized metal bands, both of which he should have passed to his mates already. He's at Zoo now, putting a line-item in the incident book for when it's examined, later this morning.'

'Oh.' Holleman frowned, but made no further objection. They walked on, and in less than five minutes the bulk of the Kaiser-Wilhelm Memorial Church loomed. Fischer reached out and halted his friend with a hand.

'We'd better separate here. Get some breakfast, don't be conspicuous. I'll see you in a few hours, if things go well.'

'Otto ...' The big man's eyes watered, and he struggled to speak. 'Are you sure? *Will* I see you again?'

'I can't say, Freddie. Germany isn't safe for me, because if Zarubin takes on KGB and loses, I'll be part of the clean-up – even if I'm as far west as Trier. That's if the lavatory masterplan works, of course. If it doesn't, we needn't worry about the longer term.'

'Christ.' Holleman opened his arms and for several seconds wrapped Fischer in a death-embrace. He released him abruptly, turned and walked away. Goodbye was bad luck to old soldiers, even those whose memories didn't dwell upon war and the things it had done to them.

He was almost lost in the gloom when he stopped and turned once more.

'Otto, please remember ...'

'What is it, Freddie?'

'Don't flush.'

43

He couldn't recall when, if ever, he'd been this sore. Almost every joint in his body had put in a transfer request; his muscles, more used to ill-treatment, merely refused to work properly when he asked for yet one more final push. Only his hair had no complaint to make, though he couldn't speak for when the hat came off.

It was there for the cold, not the pale, weak sunshine that had raised his spirits after several days of oppressive greyness. He had welcomed the gloom at first, thinking that in such weather he might as well be putting his back into something strenuous; but that had lasted as long as his back was the only part of him to complain. After that, he had learned the very hardest way that digging was the sort of exercise that used a body harshly without imparting any benefits of fitness or wellbeing.

Still, looking down the newly-terraced slope, he felt he had cause for pride. It wasn't a small job for three men yet he'd done it alone, and had his mind not been weighed by the prospect of the deer- and rabbit-fence he needed to build before he started planting he might have felt a little smug about ... and the frames, he reminded himself. Vines couldn't grow without frames.

Twice already that morning, he had almost called a halt and gone up to the (only half-ruinous) house for a hot drink and several blessed minutes in front of the fire, but he doubted that he'd be able to resume his flagellation after that sort of indulgence. The third time, he just dropped the spade and let his body make the decision. It wasn't a close vote.

When he reached the top of the slope and stepped onto the area he'd laid to gravel the previous week he paused, as he nearly always did, to take in the view. To the southwest, the village of Penas was hidden by a wooded ridge, but to the north he had a clear view of the southern suburbs of Braga, and sometimes, on clearer days, he imagined that he could make out the towers of her cathedral. Between he and they, innumerable folds of land held their own little worlds, each yet to be explored by him. At the moment the view was heavily misted, and hardly any sounds (other than those made by the local wildlife) reached this high; yet his aching shoulders almost vibrated with the sense of things hovering closely, waiting to be found. He wasn't a young man, but sometimes – usually when he'd had a glass of wine - he felt as if he might be at the start, rather than the conclusion, of a journey.

The thought returned, the one he'd been surprised by several times in recent weeks – a thought that had no place in his head yet seemed to be making itself a comfortable bed there. As far as he knew there were no psychiatrists in this deeply rural area, so he couldn't ask whether he might be allowing what was unfamiliar to skew his judgement towards a pleasant form of delirium.

Am I a lucky man?

'You've won the lottery!'

He should have heard the bicycle wheels crunching on the gravel, but he'd found that distractions took him easily these days. Salvador, the postman who served the villages hereabouts, was holding out a single letter.

'I've what?'

'Won the Monte lottery!'

'But … I didn't enter it.'

'Your wife bought a ticket, three days ago,'

'She's not my ...' He was pleased with the progress he'd made with the Portuguese language, but hadn't yet thought to research the word for *sin* - nor, for that matter, social attitudes towards loose living in a region where wives put on mourning whenever their husbands worked away from home. He decided to postpone the revelation.

'How much?'

'Nearly four thousand escudos! That's about … twelve dollars, US. You can collect it from the Post Office.'

'The church roof needs mending, doesn't it? Tell them it's a donation.'

Salvador tapped the side of his nose. 'Greasing local opinion? Very shrewd. How is your digging going?'

'Very well. I now have an old man's back.'

'Viniculture's a hard life, at first. What are you putting in?'

'Tinta Roriz.'

'Ah, very wise – both hardy and hard to ruin. We had an Englishmen up near Braga, came in the late '30s with a fat wallet and an idea to make a fine wine. The idiot put in nothing but Tinta Cão, thinking he could talk it into producing heavily. Six years later he went home, penniless.'

'I'm not going to *make* wine. We'll sell our grapes to the cooperative at Guimaraes. And we won't bank on it – that's why we're putting in plums and apples on the other slope. And, if that isn't enough, potatoes and cabbages will grow anywhere.'

'Ha! You and your lady have a strategy! I passed her on the Penas road, by the way. She should be here soon, if the brute doesn't get stubborn.'

'Brute?'

'Your goat.'

'We don't have a goat.'

'Yes, you do.'

'She went for bread, and coffee!'

'That'll be what's tied to its back, so it's earning its keep already. Are all German women so clever?'

'She's Polish. Her name is Zofia.'

'Ah, yes, German women – and beautiful, too! We used to watch the newsreels, when that other fellow was in charge, the one with the moustache. They all look to be such healthy girls.'

Salvador's own, more luxuriant moustache hardly hid his leer. Blond hair being an unusual sight in northern Portugal, the man with the badly mutilated face had already noticed its effect upon the local population – though not as much, he imagined, as had the woman they assumed to be his wife. She didn't seem to mind; perhaps at her age the attention of village roués was not to be entirely despised. And perhaps the theory was one he would be wiser not share with her.

'I've sometimes wondered why a couple of Germans would want to live here.' Salvador waved a hand that took in the various, glorious panoramas, which he regarded with something approaching contempt.

'I've been thinking about Portugal for a long time. From what I read it seemed so ... different from what I knew.'

'Well it would, wouldn't it? For my part, I've always wanted to see Germany, though I expect it's too late for me now. It's ...'

Fischer waited, knowing that he could be neither offended nor flattered by an opinion on something about which his own feelings had never quite solidified. Inevitably, his transplantation had amplified a sense of apartness that had been with him for years, unwanted though not bothersome, a mouse that lived quietly in the shoe he never chose to wear. He was, incontrovertibly, a German, yet what made him so had been solely a matter of geography, not constituency. He was a Usedomer by birth, Stettiner by adoption, Berliner of necessity; yet for all that, identity had been elusive, a consequence of whatever he had been attached to at a fortunate moment (and God knew, there had been few enough of those). Untethered, he was Otto the half-lopped-off limb, the smudge on the canvas, the inadvertent participant, the one who found the door before others cared to look for it. To anyone seeking to put a perspective on any the sum of all that, he would heartily recommend alternative employment, or at least the comfort of strong drink ...

I don't need to be anyone, any more. He turned to the postman, who was carefully filling his pipe with what he called his 'special mixture' (a blend which, did it not so obviously deter flies and mosquitos, Fischer would have assumed to comprise mostly dung).

'I'm sorry, I was thinking about our new goat. What were you saying?'

'Mm? Oh, Germany - that I'd like to visit, if I ever had the chance. It has such an *interesting* history.'

Author's Note

In the last days of December 1958, KGB Chairman I.A. Serov was removed from his post and appointed Director of Soviet Military Intelligence (GRU), a 'sideways' move that was widely seen as a distinct demotion. When asked the reason for it, Khrushchev joked that Western diplomats were seeing 'too many policemen' around the Kremlin. Serov's successor, A.N. Shelepin, was of course a policemen also, and Khrushchev was never to offer a more convincing explanation. Serov was removed from his GRU directorship following the Cuban Missile Crisis, and, after Khrushchev's ousting, stripped of his Communist Party membership. He died in 1990.

In a strange irony, one of Shelepin's first act as KGB Chairman was to write to Khrushchev, urging the destruction of all KGB files on the Katyn massacre (which offered a rich seam of damning data on Serov's part therein). The General Secretary refused to permit this. Despite a reputation as a Stalinist hard-liner, Shelepin subsequently introduced a graduate-hiring programme for KGB, and demoted or dismissed many NKVD-era officers, a policy which is generally recognized to have improved markedly the organization's efficiency

Almost from the moment he took up his post, Shelepin clashed with KGB's Berlin Resident, A.M Korotkov, whom he disliked both for his connections with Serov and as a potential rival within KGB. For more than two years he harangued the Resident on administrative matters, the relationship between Berlin's KGB Rezidentura and *Stasi*, and on how the various KGB Directorates in Karlshorst reported to Moscow (the latter was not within Korotkov's remit or ability to alter). Finally, in

June 1961, following yet another stormy meeting with Shelepin, Korotkov met his old boss Serov at the Dynamo Stadium in Petrovka for a game of tennis. During the match, and like so many other Soviet officials who represented an inconvenience, Korotkov died of a heart attack. Whether ill-health, Shelepin or Serov were responsible cannot be determined.

V.M. Blokhin, the executioner of almost every senior politician and officer sentenced to death during Stalin's purges, and, in 1940, the most prolific killer during the Katyn operation, was forced into retirement immediately following Stalin's death, despite Beria offering a glowing character reference on his behalf. His own death, on 3 February 1955, was recorded officially as suicide. By then, he was known to be experiencing severe mental problems and had an alcohol addiction. The details of his equipment and methods as offered in the text are a matter of historical record. No doubt there have been more prolific murderers in the bloody story of the human race, but none that have been identified by name.

Willy Brandt went on to become Chancellor of Germany, of course. His subsequent policy of pragmatic engagement with the Soviet bloc – *Ostpolitik* – was eventually much valued by Moscow and detested by the East German regime (who regarded Brandt as a cynical manipulator of public opinion, both in the West and East). He resigned from the Chancellorship in 1974, following the revelation that one of his close aides was a *Stasi* spy. Ironically, KGB regarded his fall as a near-disaster, not least for the loss of his calming voice in international relations.

Printed by Amazon Italia Logistica S.r.l.
Torrazza Piemonte (TO), Italy

16748013R10192